FOREIGN DECEIT

DAVID WOLF BOOK 1

JEFF CARSON

CROSS ATLANTIC PUBLISHING

DAVID WOLF SERIES IN ORDER

Gut Decision (A David Wolf Short Story) – Sign up for the new release newsletter at http://www.jeffcarson.co/p/newsletter.html and receive a complimentary copy.

Foreign Deceit (David Wolf Book 1)
The Silversmith (David Wolf Book 2)
Alive and Killing (David Wolf Book 3)
Deadly Conditions (David Wolf Book 4)
Cold Lake (David Wolf Book 5)
Smoked Out (David Wolf Book 6)
To the Bone (David Wolf Book 7)
Dire (David Wolf Book 8)
Signature (David Wolf Book 9)
Dark Mountain (David Wolf Book 10)
Rain (David Wolf Book 11)
Drifted (David Wolf Book 12)
Divided Sky (David Wolf Book 13)
In the Ground (David Wolf Book 14)

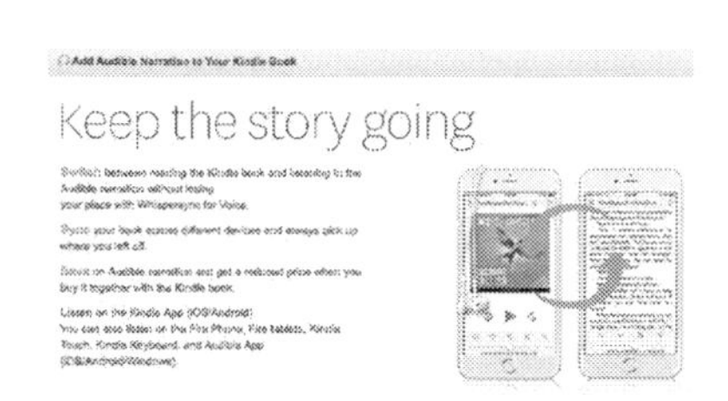

Click Here to Instantly Add Audible Narration starring Sean Patrick Hopkins and keep the story going wherever you are!

CHAPTER 1

"I DON'T KNOW where the hell she is." The woman's tone suggested a mother would be the last person to know where her teenage child was. "Julie don't spend much time here. I assume she's off with Jerry doing something." She waved a dismissive hand to the forest behind the two sheriff's deputies standing in front of her.

Sergeant David Wolf shifted his weight and the wood of the front porch deck creaked underneath his boot. Wide spaces yawned between cracked and warped boards, which were jam-packed with tubular spider webs. They must have been well fed by the cloud of flies that swarmed the stinking place.

The siding of the house was brown, though Wolf suspected at one time it had been white.

"Jerry's parents reported him missing this morning, Vicky," Wolf said. "Been missing for two days. That's why we're here. We know they've been spending a lot of time together lately. We understand they're dating."

Vicky Mulroy stared with half-closed eyes.

Deputy Tom Rachette huffed, seeming to come to the same realization as Wolf that she was completely stoned. "Do your daughter and Jerry Wheatman often go to a specific place, ma'am?" Rachette puffed his chest and hooked his thumb conspicuously near his pistol, trying to wake her up to the fact that two deputies of the Sluice County Sheriff's Department were on her doorstep.

Vicky seemed to snap out of her daze and smiled apprais-ingly at Rachette, revealing brown teeth and black windows where teeth used to be. "I ain't seen Julie in at least three days." She paused and squinted at Rachette's name badge. "I don't think I've ever seen you before, Deputy ... Ra-shette." She flour-ished her hand.

Wolf sighed. Rachette hated that pronunciation. The young deputy preferred his last name to rhyme with the sharp hand-held chopping tool, not, as Rachette had once put it, some la-de-da French lord's namesake. Wolf had seen this exchange between Rachette and other people before, usually ending in Rachette losing his temper.

Wolf put a hand on Rachette's shoulder before he could speak and stared expectantly at Vicky.

Her smile faded and she turned to Wolf. She studied him up and down with hunger in her eyes and not a hint of shame about it. "You still lookin' good," she said.

Wolf didn't blink. He may have been looking good to her, but Vicky Mulroy looked like shit.

Wolf knew she must be thirty-eight years old, give or take a year or two, because they'd been in the same classes throughout school. But she looked older than her years.

During the raid of her house a year ago, he had been shocked at the sight of her and just what the drugs had done to her once pretty face. Now she looked even worse. Her body was bone thin. Pocked with open sores, her sunken face now looked like someone had flung a meat chili at her and she hadn't yet bothered to wipe it off. Her dark-brown hair was stringy, slick with grease and sweat, clinging to her forehead. Her eyelids drooped like they were made of lead, and it was taking all her strength to keep her pale-blue, bloodshot eyes open.

Then there was the smell. Wolf moved over, hoping to side-step the cat-urine stench of crystal meth mixed with the musky scent of humans who had given up on hygiene billowing out the door.

Rachette turned his head and put his sleeve to his mouth, apparently taking the same onslaught to his senses.

"Jerry Wheatman's parents are pretty worried. Aren't you worried that Julie hasn't been home for days?" Wolf asked.

Vickie's eyes darkened. "I guess that's why she stays over there so much. Those Wheatmans sure are a nice, loving bunch of people. That family of fairies turned my girl vegetarian, you know. Pansies."

"How about Bill?" Wolf asked with growing impatience. "Has he seen Julie lately?"

"I don't know."

"Is he working at the station right now?" Wolf, just like everyone in town, knew that Bill Mulroy was a lifelong employee of the Mackery gas station at the end of Main Street.

"Far as I know," she said.

Wolf suspected they weren't going to get anything more from this lead other than sick to their stomach. "Please let us know immediately if you see or hear from either one of them. It may be normal for Julie to be gone for days, but Jerry's folks are pretty spooked. And ..." Wolf paused. He wanted to tell her to shape up and quit smoking the meth. That he was going to come arrest her and Bill if they kept it up. That she wasn't being a good mother to her daughter. That she needed to pull her head out of her ass, and how he remembered her as the cute girl he'd kissed in sixth grade. But Wolf had been intimately close to people on drugs and had witnessed the effect of drugs on them.

And speeches never worked. So, instead, he said, "Take care, Vicky."

She eyed Wolf up and down once more, her eyes turning dark again. "Sure thing, honey. Say hi to Sarah for me, okay?"

Wolf blinked.

Vicky Mulroy read his expression and looked satisfied. Then she laughed and turned back into the darkness, the screen door slapping shut.

Rachette wasted no time getting off the porch, leaping down all three of the rotted steps. As Rachette landed on the gravel, he sucked in a breath and coughed. "Good Lord, something's dead in that house."

"Just a steady diet of meth and alcohol," Wolf said, walking down the steps after him, "and all the fun stuff that brings."

An uncomfortable silence enveloped them as they walked back to the road. It was no secret—both men were thinking about Vicky's mention of Wolf's ex-wife.

It was common knowledge around town, as juicy tidbits about people's personal lives often were in such a small population, that Sarah Wolf was a pill-popper, and that she had recently completed yet another attempt at kicking the habit. In fact, Sarah Wolf would be back today from her stay at the Whispering Pines rehab facility in Vail.

Since Vicky Mulroy had been aware of this fact, her words were laden with meaning. Wolf was trying to figure out what that meaning was. *Say hi to Sarah for me.* Was that to say that this meth-head, Vicky, had a recent relationship of some sort with his ex-wife?

Wolf was pretty sure his Sarah hadn't ventured into trying any harder drugs than Oxycontin. Wolf had seen the distant look in Sarah's eyes, dilated pupils, lethargy, aggressive language and slurred speech. But he hadn't seen any sign of her doing any of the hard stuff—the smoke, snort, or injection kind of stuff.

Maybe Vicky was just trying to say, *Worry about the drug addicts in your own life and get off my case.* Wolf hoped that's what she meant. Suddenly, he was keener to see Sarah than ever. He needed to look in her eyes. He hoped it would be different this time around. Maybe the fourth time was the charm.

"Well, looks like we've got two missing kids now." Rachette looked back at the tiny run-down shack in the pines. "Do you think Jerry and Julie just ran away? I know I would if I lived there."

They reached the Ford Explorer and got in. Wolf buckled his seatbelt and stared out of the dusty windshield toward the couple of hundred square foot building where Vicky Mulroy and her husband confined themselves in a hazy vat of noxious chemicals for most of the day.

The shame was that the piece of land their house stood on was a perfect place to raise a family. It was hugged on all sides by virgin forest. There was an open grass field to the south. Just a few miles from town, but in the boonies—far enough so you could feel like you were really roughing it.

But this place was too rough, Wolf thought. Too rough for sixteen-year-old Julie, that's for sure. Too rough for a kid of any age.

"I don't know, but it definitely looks like Jerry and Julie are together, wherever they are," Wolf said.

It was common knowledge around town that Jerry Wheatman and Julie Mulroy were sweethearts as of the past year or so. They were attached at the hip, figuratively, and probably literally, being as they were sixteen years old. Had Jerry and Julie come up with a plan to up and leave? To run away to a better place?

For Julie Mulroy, that theory would make perfect sense. How could anyone live in this godforsaken place and not either fall into a life of drugs or make serious, actionable plans to leave? Word was around town that the coming-of-age daughter was kind of a rebel, but didn't do drugs. If that was true, how could she bring herself to stay here?

Jerry Wheatman's life was a different story altogether. Like Julie, he wasn't known around town as someone who experimented with drugs, but the similarity ended there. He wasn't considered rebellious in any way. He came from a loving family environment. He came from a stable home, with stable parents, who had stable jobs, which earned stable incomes.

Wolf knew the Wheatmans well, and he thought Jerry wasn't the type of kid who would run away. Jerry Wheatman was more the type of kid who would simply ask his parents to let Julie live with them. He would probably explain her hard situation, and they would take pity on her and open their home to a teenage girl in need.

No. Wheatman and Julie weren't on the run. Running away would have been a big deal for Jerry, Wolf thought. Not a realistic decision he would have made. All indications from the Wheatman family had been that everything was perfectly fine. There were no fights at home with either of his sisters or with his mother and father. In fact, his parents reported that Jerry had been in a very happy mood as of late.

Was that *very happy mood* of Jerry Wheatman's an indication of his blossoming love with Julie Mulroy? Maybe Wolf was wrong. Perhaps Wheatman's reported good mood was a state of giddy anticipation, knowing he and his young love were about to run away together. Or maybe the happy situation Jerry's parents had described at home was all a lie.

"What do you think?" Rachette asked, breaking Wolf from his thoughts. "Do we go talk to Bill Mulroy? See what he has to say?"

Wolf looked at his watch. 9:34 a.m. Bill Mulroy would be

manning the cash register at the Mackery gas station. "I think he might know something. Maybe Julie confides in her dad more than her mom. Let's go."

Wolf fired up the Explorer and headed down the forested road toward town.

CHAPTER 2

Wolf and Rachette rode without talking. They were just as comfortable in silence as in idle conversation, and it was one of the many reasons why Wolf liked having the young second-year deputy in the car with him.

The warm sun streamed in through the windshield, and the windows were cracked open to let the chilled late-summer breeze in the cab, carrying the citrus-sweet scent of pinesap.

Wolf eyed the clouds swelling behind the southwest peaks. They would billow high and mash into large thunderstorms within a few hours. Late summer was the time of year when the monsoonal flow brought moisture from Mexico, up through Arizona and New Mexico, and finally into the Colorado Rocky Mountains, unleashing huge torrents of rain all along the way.

After the dry and smoky fire season, Rocky Points, and the rugged land surrounding it, was turning verdant once again. They had dodged a bullet this year, getting through the dry months without seeing any major fires nearby, and Wolf now welcomed the danger of the town going down with floods versus up in flames. Wolf knew that the day the gray and brittle beetle-kill pines that blanketed the valley caught fire, it would be hell unleashed.

They passed aspens with pockets of gold among the green leaves, a sign that autumn was near at 8,500 feet, despite the steamy weather they were having.

The radio crackled. "Calling all available deputies." It was the voice of Tammy Granger, receptionist, dispatcher, and wearer of a thousand other hats at the sheriff's office building in downtown Rocky Points. "We just got a call from a hiker. She's seen a body on the lower Pine Cliffs Trail at the base of one of the cliffs. She says the victim wasn't moving. The hiker will stay in the trailhead parking lot until we get there."

Wolf and Rachette eyed each other. Wolf flipped the lights, gunned the engine, and picked up the radio. "Wolf here. We're on our way. We're in town now—we'll be there in a few minutes." Wolf hung the radio back on the dash, knowing the other deputies would be lining up to chime in their positions and ETAs.

Wolf also knew Tammy would be alerting the fire department, and Summit County Search and Rescue, telling them to stand by in case they needed the helicopter. Those actions were standard procedure, the responsibility for which fell on her, and Wolf had learned over the years that Tammy neither needed nor welcomed being reminded of her duties.

"All right, everyone." The radio almost vibrated off its clip. "I need all on-duty deputies on their way to the Pine Cliffs trailhead, right now," Sergeant Derek Connell said.

Rachette shook his head and pleaded silently to the ceiling of the cab.

"Tammy," Connell continued, sounding like he now had half the radio in his mouth, "you need to contact RPFD—that's your job. Also, call Summit and get them pre-flighting the chopper. We may need an air extraction."

The radio fell silent. There was no response from Tammy. Rachette smiled wide, and Wolf couldn't help curling his lips. He pictured saliva dotting Tammy's desk as she hurled expletives at the radio.

"Tammy. Do you copy?" Connell asked.

"Sure thing," she said.

After a few seconds of desolate radio silence, it crackled back to life as four more deputies gave their positions and ETAs.

Deputy Wilson, one of two rookies in the department, clicked on. "Deputy Wilson here. On my way. I'm near the trail now."

"Don't let that woman leave, and wait for me to ask the questions," Connell said.

"... Sir," Wilson said, apparently pushing the radio button with poor timing or in a bad reception area.

The radio went silent for a few seconds, and Wolf let out his breath, hoping Connell's on-air tyranny was over. It wasn't.

"Do you copy, Officer Wilson?" Connell asked in a drill-sergeant tone.

"Yes, sir. Understood."

And with that, the radio fell silent.

"Holy shit," Rachette said looking out the window. Although Deputy Rachette often uttered that particular expletive in the course of a normal workday, he rarely did so with such gusto.

Wolf knew what Rachette was thinking. He knew what every single person on the radio was thinking. In one week's time, a council of Rocky Points and Sluice County political officials was going to convene to carry out the task of selecting a new sheriff of the tiny sliver-like county located in the central Rocky Mountains of Colorado. While other counties chose their sheriffs through a vote of the citizenry, Sluice County was different. Sheriffs were appointed into office, not voted in, and since that was the way it had always been and the way it currently was, everyone listening to Sergeant Derek Connell's radio rage knew there was a very good chance they were listening to the next sheriff of Sluice County. A tyrant with a badge who would be a nightmare in the highest office.

Luckily for the rest of the department, another qualified candidate stood in Connell's way: Deputy Sergeant David Wolf. Wolf, who was considered by all who had to work in the same county as Sergeant Derek Connell as better suited for the position, did not kid himself—Wolf wanted the job. There was no indifference about his future. Wolf hoped he himself would be the council's appointee, and no one else. Wolf's father had been sheriff many years ago, and since the day of his father's death in the line of duty, Wolf had had the goal of becoming sheriff embedded within.

The current sheriff, Harold "Hal" Burton, knew this. Burton was on his way out and had mentally checked out a year ago, and for that year he'd effectively given over the reins to Wolf. It was clear to the deputies in the department, and to the residents of the town of Rocky Points, that Wolf was being groomed to be the next sheriff of Sluice County.

But Wolf wasn't the kind of man to get overly confident about anything. His years as an army ranger had taught him that with harsh lessons. So, assuming he was guaranteed for the council appointment never crossed his mind. Assuming he was the best candidate? Well, that was just the truth. But that still didn't mean he was a lock.

Until recently, Sergeant Derek Connell had seemed resigned to that truth, taking it as fact that Wolf would be Sheriff Burton's successor. In fact, on many occasions, Wolf thought he'd read relief in Connell's demeanor when Wolf had taken on more and more responsibility over the last year.

So why was Connell flexing his muscles of authority so hard

now? It was like he'd been putting on an act for someone for the past two weeks. For whom? For the other deputies? Were the members of the county council listening right now on police scanners? Was Connell now suddenly interested in becoming sheriff? After a full year of showing no initiative?

Whatever was happening, Wolf didn't like it.

They drove down Main Street with the lights flashing and no siren. What little traffic had existed on a summer Monday morning in a small ski-resort town had since died out, so Wolf didn't bother blasting the town with noise.

They drove to the north, past the Mackery gas station, and out of the town proper. After a mile or so of puddled cattle-fields, they took a right onto the rutted dirt road that led up into the surrounding mountains, and to the trailhead for Pine Cliffs Recreation Area.

Rachette had been looking at Wolf with a worried expression for most of the drive, apparently sensing Wolf's thoughts. "That guy can't become—"

The truck lurched and bounced with a deafening roar as they made their way up the rock-strewn road through the forest.

"Yeah, I know. Let's just concentrate on what we've got going on right now. When we get to the trailhead, let me handle Connell. Just don't talk to him."

Rachette held his hands up. "Sounds like a good idea to me. In fact, that's a major goal of mine every single day: Don't talk to Sergeant Connell."

...

Ten minutes later, Wolf slowed the SUV as they passed the road sign for the trailhead lot. At one time, it had read *Pine*

Cliffs Trail and Recreation Area, but the writing had since been obscured by rusted bullet holes, and one had to infer its meaning.

The lot was a small clearing in the dense forest off the side of the road, empty except for Deputy Wilson's department-issue SUV parked next to a newer-model Nissan truck.

Wilson was shuffling his feet and anxiously wiping his face, but visibly relaxed after realizing it was Wolf and Rachette, and not Connell, who would be joining him on scene first. The woman watched them approach with red, wide eyes.

Wolf slowed almost to a stop, and then turned into the lot, rocking the Explorer back and forth as it passed through a deep puddle. Wolf recalled that it had been two days since the last rain. By the looks of the darkening sky, the puddle would be growing much larger in a few hours.

Despite all the recent rain, the lot was dusty and Wolf and Rachette got out of the SUV and stepped into a swirling cloud they'd kicked up.

Wolf resisted a sneeze and grabbed his buffalo felt Stetson from the back seat, but waited to put it on. He walked to the woman and held out a hand. "Hello, ma'am. I'm Sergeant Wolf."

The woman looked to be in her early sixties. Short in stature, thin, and fit looking. Her gray hair was cut short and tucked underneath a red nylon hat with an oversized bill that shaded her face.

"Hi," she said. "I'm Jennifer. Jennifer Branson. I was just telling the officer ... uh—"

"Deputy Wilson, ma'am," Wilson said.

"Yes, Deputy Wilson, about the form I saw at the base of the cliff."

The form. That was an interesting way to put it, Wolf thought.

"I know you've already called this in on the phone, Ms. Branson, and now you've told your story to Deputy Wilson. But I need to hear what you've seen. If you could start from the beginning, please?"

"Yes, of course." She turned and pointed to the trailhead sign at the edge of the parking lot. "I went on the lower Pine Cliffs Trail, there. About three miles up ... at least, I think it was about that far. I'm sorry, I've never been on this trail before today. I'm from Denver, and I've been up here on vacation for the past week. Staying in town."

"About three miles up?" Wolf asked, pulling her back to the important details.

"Yes. About three. I–I think. I was looking up at the big cliffs on the left there, and then I saw a form at the base of one of them. It was, well, it was like a person lying there." She whispered the last part and her eyes became unfocused.

Wolf placed his hat on his head, and then gently placed his hand on her shoulder. "I know this must be difficult, ma'am. Can you tell us any more? Was the person moving?"

She shook her head. "He wasn't moving."

"He?"

"It looked like a boy."

"Did you notice what he was wearing?"

"It was a boy." There was more conviction in her voice now. "And I could tell he was dead." She looked up at Wolf with shining eyes. "He was wearing a blue vest and a yellow shirt underneath it. And jeans, I think. I remember the vest and shirt. I'm not sure about the jeans."

Jerry Wheatman. His parents had described his outfit as such when they'd visited headquarters earlier that morning.

"I just stared up at him," she continued. "He couldn't have been more than fifty yards away. I don't think I breathed that whole time. I just stared. I couldn't believe what I was seeing.

Then I realized I was looking at a dead body, and I just freaked out." She shook her head again and looked at Wolf and Rachette with wild eyes. "I just freaked."

Wolf nodded. "It's hard to see such a thing, ma'am."

He didn't want to press her too much about the condition of Jerry Wheatman. She saw what she thought she saw, but they weren't going to rely on the fifty-yard diagnosis of a witness to tell them Jerry Wheatman was dead. Wheatman could be clinging to life by a thread at the base of that cliff, waiting for rescue, and the Sluice County deputies would treat the situation accordingly.

But Wolf silently suspected otherwise. The kid had been missing for two days. Now he was lying at the base of a cliff with the clothes he was reported as wearing when he'd gone missing. *Short sleeves and a vest.* It hadn't rained in the past two days, but it had still been frosty cold the past few nights. They were now sitting at 9,200 feet, give or take a few hundred feet at Jerry's location. If he were badly hurt, clinging to life, with massive external and internal trauma from a fall, the exposure would have been almost impossible to survive.

They turned to look at the road as a cacophony of sirens and revving engines came into view. The lead SUV kicked up a huge plume of dust that obscured the other three flashing roofs behind it. One by one, the department vehicles shut off their sirens as they neared, keeping their strobes twinkling.

The front vehicle, however, kept the piercing whine of the siren going up to the last. Only after it had barreled into the lot, almost scraping the bumper off and shooting muddy water out twenty feet to the side as it plowed through the puddle, did it fall silent. *Connell.*

"Thank you, Ms. Branson," Wolf said, turning back to the woman, ignoring the stampede. "I know you're experiencing a lot more than you bargained for this morning. But we're going to need to take your official statement as well."

She nodded. "I should have stayed in Denver this week."

Wolf looked toward the trail signs denoting the upper and lower routes of the Pine Cliffs Trail. The lower route was an eleven-mile loop circling the mountain. The upper route was much shorter, going straight up the mountain, offering three hundred and sixty-degree views of the valley and town below and the surrounding majestic peaks.

The upper trail was a straight up-and-down path rather than a loop, and wasn't for the faint of heart. The entire mountain was a bulge of granite, and the freezing and thawing of the rock over millions of years had carved off huge chunks, leaving numerous sheer cliffs on one side of the trail. Those with any fear of heights stayed on the Lower Loop, which didn't necessarily keep them out of danger. Wolf recalled that two years ago a school bus-sized boulder had dislodged and tumbled down the mountain, crossing and blocking the lower trail below. Thankfully, it had happened in the middle of the night and no one had been hurt.

Wolf turned back to the onslaught of vehicles just as a huge cloud of dust overtook them.

The first truck slid next to Wolf's SUV and Connell jumped out, rocking the vehicle, feet touching the ground just as the wheels skidded to a halt. He rounded the back bumper and materialized through the brown cloud like a wrestler emerging from the tunnel on the way to the ring.

Connell's heavily muscled arms swayed, outstretched from his sides due to the massive bulk of his chest. His huge legs wobbled then flexed into solid trunks as he stepped, threatening to split his uniform pants with each step.

Wolf knew Connell spent a borderline psychotic amount of time in the gym for moments like these. Connell lived for the look of awe and fear that bent people's faces as he approached. He lived to intimidate.

Connell approached with such speed that he looked like he might tackle the woman.

Jennifer Branson, along with Deputy Wilson, stepped back as Connell stopped on a dime in front of her and outstretched his hand. He loomed over her with intense glacial blue eyes. His small mouth was pursed with a serious expression.

"Ma'am, my name is Sergeant Deputy Connell of the Sluice County Sheriff's Office. Please tell me what you saw."

Wolf stepped away and motioned for Rachette to follow, and then made his way to the other deputies now milling outside their vehicles.

"All right, everybody. We have a victim at approximately three miles along the Lower Loop, near the base of one of the cliffs. His description matches our missing person wearing a blue vest and yellow shirt." Wolf motioned to Deputies Hilton and Walters. "You two get going now, double time. We'll be on your tail."

The two deputies grabbed their first-aid bags out of the truck and bolted to the trailhead.

"Hey, what the hell is going on?" Connell's voice boomed, his back now to the woman.

Hilton and Walters hesitated and looked back.

"Get going!" Wolf said. "Now!"

The two deputies exchanged a glance, turned, and left in a blur.

Wolf ignored Connell's huff of protest and turned back to the men. "Right, we'll need an official statement from Ms. Branson here." Wolf looked at Connell. "Sergeant Connell." Then Wolf turned back to the wide-eyed group of deputies. Wolf could feel Connell's icicle glare behind him, but he didn't care. His patience was running short with Connell's alpha-deputy demeanor, and time was running short.

"Baine, Wilson, Rachette, stick with me," Wolf continued. "I need someone else with Sergeant Connell to secure the parking lot, which is now the rescue staging area. I want everyone else on the Lower Loop." Wolf pointed at the cave-black sky in the southwest. "As you can see, we need to move fast. Let's go!"

Five deputies broke off and ran to the trailhead, then took a right following the Lower Pine Cliffs Loop arrow. As expected, no one volunteered to stay behind with Connell.

"Yates!" Wolf called. Deputy Yates stopped short of the trail sign and turned around like a man just picked out of a crowd to be executed. "You're staying here."

Wolf could sense Connell's presence next to him expanding with boiling hatred. Wolf turned to face him. "We'll keep in touch. Who else is en route?"

Connell didn't answer. Instead, he stepped so close that his SCSD baseball cap slipped underneath the bill of Wolf's Stetson.

Wolf didn't move or blink. Despite the muscles and aggressive body language, Wolf knew Connell for what he really was. Connell, along with all the other bullies he'd encountered in his life, was a coward.

Connell's cool gaze fractured for just a second, then he raised his lips.

Wolf assumed Connell was trying to smile nonchalantly, but it was more a snarl, like a rabid dog baring its teeth. Wolf had seen the same look from Connell many times. It was classic Connell—trying to look composed as he seethed with hate and lusted for violence.

Only Connell never acted on his impulses with Wolf. Not since the seventh grade, when Wolf had put Connell in his place. Ever since that day, Connell had kept his hatred for Wolf corked tightly, never again acting on it. Wolf wondered whether that cork was going to blow. If it did, Wolf was smart enough not to look forward to that day. Connell had spent a few thousand hours in the gym since seventh grade. Then again, Wolf had killed a lot of men since then. Many men, much more dangerous than Connell. And Wolf knew his relaxed glare at the moment told Connell exactly that.

Enough time had been wasted. Wolf backed away and turned to Rachette and Baine. "Get the cameras. We'll need casting material. Bring it all." He turned toward the trail and began walking when a heavy hand thumped down on his shoulder. Wolf turned quickly, certain he would see Connell's hurtling fist.

"We'll both go up top together," Connell said with a strained smile. "Wilson, please get an official statement from this woman, and Baine, Rachette, you're coming with us."

Connell swept past Wolf and took a left at the sign, following the Upper Loop. He lunged up the rocky trail with the ease of a large game animal. After thirty feet, he wheeled around. "You guys coming or what?"

Wolf looked at Wilson and Yates, who were exchanging relieved looks. "Talk to you soon. Keep anyone else that shows up right here, unless I say otherwise. I want this trailhead closed off."

"Yes, sir," said Yates.

"Yes, sir," said Wilson.

They both looked like they'd just won the lottery.

"Lighten up, you two," Wolf said.

Yates and Wilson exchanged puzzled looks.

Wolf shook his head and started for the trail.

CHAPTER 3

For a few minutes, they trudged up the trail, Connell setting a calf-cramping pace in the lead, leaving Wolf, Rachette, and Baine well behind. It was obvious that Connell had the destination in mind—the top—and he was treating the hike like a race he was going to win at any cost.

The first quarter mile of the trail was steep, switching back and forth through the ponderosa pine trees, and Wolf's lungs pumped hard to wring the oxygen out of the Rocky Mountain air. He'd grown up in the mountains, no more than a few miles away, and he was used to the depleted oxygen. But his lungs stung, and the back of his throat tasted like rust. Wolf's relaxed attitude toward vigorous exercise for the past few months was catching up to him.

During the six years of his life as an army ranger, Wolf had been in the kind of physical shape only achieved by the likes of top professional athletes or an Olympian. Army ranger school was designed to kill the spirit of men, and Wolf had endured it. And then, when it came to serving his country, to killing men and protecting his brethren, he did so in a way that stood out in his battalion. Exertion like this wouldn't have even registered in his conscious mind back then.

Today, Wolf still had a strong physique, as he'd had fifteen years ago, though it was a faint shadow of what it had once been. Once a bulky six-foot-three man pushing two hundred and thirty pounds of muscle, with the typical delta-shaped upper body of a ranger, now he was more thin and wiry, hovering around two hundred pounds. Now, rather than spending any time in the gym, he was hardened by spending more time outdoors than in, and by using his hands to fix, and haul, and bait, and shoot things.

They reached a flattened part of the trail after the initial climb, and Wolf's legs ached as he walked the flat ground. Rachette and Baine were close behind, panting through clenched teeth. They continued to an opening in the trees, where the trail cut through a small field of grass and wildflowers.

Sergeant Connell stood grinning. "What's the matter, guys? You need to hit the gym a little more with Uncle D and spend a little less time at the Sunnyside."

The Sunnyside Café was the best breakfast joint on Main Street, and Wolf thought the amount of time he spent there, at least three mornings a week, was just perfect. As far as spending more time at the gym went? Maybe Connell was right.

Wolf stopped and turned. The field to the west meandered down a few yards and ended abruptly against the backdrop of a forested valley floor. It was like looking at the edge of an infinity pool. The grass just ended, and then there was nothing. It was the first of many cliffs, and Wolf knew he was looking at a sheer drop of at least twenty feet.

"I already checked," Connell said. "He's not at the bottom of that one and not at the bottom of the next three, which you can see from up there. He must have fallen off the top." He whistled. "Sure is a long drop from there. Shit." There was more amusement than sympathy in Connell's voice.

Wolf turned back toward the way they'd come and then back toward the cliff.

"Fine, take a look for yourself if you don't believe me," Connell said.

"I'll take your word for it," Wolf said, looking down at the ground of the trail.

"Seriously, you guys gotta get in the gym more," Connell said. "Your face is pasty white, Rachette. What have you—"

"Check this out." Wolf pointed at a line of deep shoe prints in semi-dry, flat mud. He felt one of the prints.

Rachette and Baine came over, and Connell put his hands on his hips and stayed put.

"It rained two days ago, right?" Wolf asked.

Rachette and Baine nodded.

"A couple of inches dropped in a few hours. At least, that's how it was in town."

"I'd say this trail got about the same amount," said Rachette, seeing Wolf's line of logic.

"What?" Connell walked over, bent down next to Wolf and hocked spit on one of the footprints. "Whatcha got, Columbo?"

Wolf glared at Connell and stood. "There are three sets of footprints here. Made after the rainstorm, which was two days ago, which puts the placement of these footprints right at the time Jerry Wheatman went missing. Which means we're probably looking at Jerry Wheatman's tracks."

"And two people he was with," Rachette said quietly.

"What? How do you know that? Those could be anyone's shoe prints. Could have been that Wheatman went up by himself and decided to see if he could fly. Then two other completely unrelated people come up for a hike, don't see a thing, then just head back down." Connell shook his head and started walking up the trail. "Good try. I'm heading up."

"Then where's Wheatman's car?" Wolf asked.

Connell stopped and frowned. "What?"

"Wheatman's car would still be sitting in the parking lot down there if he'd come up by himself. Rachette, Baine, take casts of all three of these. If you come across any prints pointing the other way, cast those, too. Catch up to us."

Wolf started after Connell, and Connell turned and set an even faster pace up into the trees.

CHAPTER 4

ANOTHER TWENTY-FIVE MINUTES into the hike, Wolf came around a bend to find Connell sucking greedily on his water bottle at the base of a rocky incline.

Wolf found it an odd place for Connell to stop, considering it was just below the top of the hike. Apparently Connell had abandoned his race to the top.

Connell held out his water bottle to Wolf.

Wolf frowned at him and shook his head with a small laugh. "No thanks. I've got my own. What's going on? The top's right there. Why'd you stop?"

Connell shrugged as he took another long gulp. He finished and let out a long burp, pointing to the top. "After you, *Sheriff*."

Wolf gave Connell a long look and started up the incline. It was steeper than any part of the hike so far, and Wolf gripped the warm granite outcrops to keep his balance.

"You're not sheriff yet, you know," Connell called from below.

Wolf sighed and turned to Connell. "I know that, Connell. Believe me, I know that. Now should we keep going?"

Connell didn't say anything at first, just stared at Wolf.

Finally, he smirked and repeated his earlier reply. "After you, Sheriff."

Wolf eyed him, and then scrambled up the rest of the trail, wondering what the hell that had been about, suddenly more aware of his surroundings.

As Wolf summited the final incline, a wind bore into him, threatening to peel the Stetson off his head. He took it off and relished the short-lived breeze as it wicked the sweat off his closely cropped hair. He closed his eyes and let the warming sun and cooling breeze comfort him for a few seconds after the grueling exertion of the hike.

The breeze stopped, and the air went quiet and still.

Connell was still standing at the base of the incline below, still drinking from his water bottle. He was either sulking or contemplating something pretty hard. Wolf couldn't tell which.

Wolf took a deep breath and looked at the high plateau he was now on, which marked the end of the line for the trail. Ahead was a flat slab of rock, and to the left was a gradual rise into a dense pine forest, then the top of the mountain a hundred or so feet above that. And to the right was a sight that sent Wolf's blood pressure up. A forty-foot drop straight down to a thin trail below.

Wolf scanned his watch: 10:45. The hike had taken forty-five minutes. Their pace had been brisk, and the men below would be even faster. But the route was circuitous, and Wolf estimated they wouldn't be in view below for at least another fifteen minutes.

Wolf surveyed the area. The rock outcrop he stood on was large and expanded out in front of him. At some point in the past few thousand years, a mammoth chunk of rock had cleaved off and tumbled down to his right, leaving a near vertical cliff face and a field of boulders below. Wolf knew it was steep. The rock-climbing route up the face was given a grade of 5.11, considered difficult to all but the most skilled climbers.

However one got to the top, whether climbing or hiking, the top offered a magnificent view to those who braved it. Bright flecks of light shimmered off the metal corrugated roofs and windows of tiny buildings on the distant valley floor like diamonds in the sun. The town of Rocky Points, Colorado: Sluice County's biggest and most populated town, which wasn't to say Rocky Points was a metropolis, by any means. Rather than suburbs of a city, surrounding the town below were seas of green meadows and darker green carpets of pine trees as far as the eye could see. Some of the rolling mountains jutted into the sky so high that there were no trees on them. Those that weren't swallowed in storms at the moment gleamed with red, gray, and brown streaks of rock with the occasional white vein of snow that survived the summer.

Two of these treeless peaks were jagged with rock spires looming over the town below. Underneath the peaks, a maze of grass- and flower-covered ski slopes were carved out of the dense trees. A web of steel ski lifts stitched the sides of the two mountains, and a network of condominiums and luxury mountain retreats pooled at the bottom of them.

Wolf stepped forward onto the flat and took a deep breath. He wiped the bead of sweat sliding down his face and jammed his hat back onto his head, wishing the breeze would pick up again.

The clouds to the south were dark green verging on black. Lightning flickered from within and the air shook with a constant rumble. It was only a matter of time before the skies would open up. Until then, it seemed it was going to be downright hot and humid.

Something made Wolf look back toward the trees on the

left. Something had caught the attention of his subconscious earlier—he was sure of it now.

"What?" Connell yelled from below, seeing Wolf's change of focus.

"I think I found something," Wolf said. He walked over to an oval discoloration in the rocky soil near the tree line. He bent down to inspect his find. It was a darker patch of soil covered with bright-green metallic flies. They burst into a buzzing cloud as he waved a hand.

Wolf heard the shuffles and grunts of Connell below and immediately stood back up, stepped over the spot, turned back toward the cliff, and bent back down. There was no way he was going to leave his back turned to Connell with a forty-foot cliff a few paces away.

Connell charged over the rise at a flying pace. "What? What the hell do you think you found now?" He sucked in air through his clenched teeth and spat off the cliff edge. "Fuckin' Hardy boy." There was a renewed rage in his voice.

Wolf ignored him and eased a fingernail-sized piece of yellow spongy material from the confines of the slightly darker dirt, and then looked at Connell, who was gazing at the town in the distance.

Wolf stood and listened. The ponderosa pines were still. Wolf was thankful there was no wind as he steeled himself for what he needed to do next.

Focusing on his footing, and giving Sergeant Connell a wide berth, Wolf made his way to the ledge. Though the rock shelf was virtually flat, Wolf shuffled carefully forward, not risking a careless foot, a sudden lapse in basic foot–eye coordination that could end in a horrific death.

Connell shook his head and chuckled. "After you."

Wolf looked to the cliff, and back at Connell. That's when Wolf saw it—an unconscious widening of Connell's eyes, and then the façade of a cool expression—a terrible poker face that Connell's small brain had never been able to control in all the years Wolf had known him.

Wolf's pulse quickened as he looked up at Connell with narrowed eyes.

"What?" Connell glanced at the trail below with a lazy expression. The officers were nowhere in sight.

Connell walked toward Wolf slowly.

Wolf studied the scene unfolding in front of him with a surreal interest, as if outside his body. Suddenly, Connell's strange act at the base of the final climb made sense. Had Connell been thinking through this moment? Planning the unthinkable? Was Connell's cork set to pop?

"Well? Do you see him?" Connell was now a few feet away and steadily walking forward, his eyes focused behind Wolf.

Wolf thought about the next few seconds of his life and then looked toward the cliff edge.

Connell's movement was lightning fast.

Wolf hadn't hesitated, though. As soon as Wolf turned away from Connell, he brought himself down into a crouch. The full force of Connell's two-handed shove just missed sending Wolf over the edge. Instead, Connell's palms bounced off the side of Wolf's ducking head, ripping hair and sending Wolf's hat flying over the precipice.

As Wolf reached the low point of his squat, he lunged back toward the tree line, brushing past Connell's legs as he ran the short distance to the trees.

Wolf pulled his pistol, and before he could fully turn around, Connell was already on him, punching with bone-crushing force against his arm, sending Wolf's pistol onto the ground a few feet away.

Connell's massive muscular frame lurched forward with outstretched arms, ducking into Wolf's abdomen.

Wolf had a slight height advantage, but Connell was a shorter and squatter rhino that would have no trouble tossing him ten feet in any direction, given the right leverage.

Wolf sprawled his legs back and grabbed him in a headlock with all the strength he could muster, sending Connell face first into the dirt. Growling low, Connell flailed with animalistic force underneath Wolf's body.

Wolf kept his legs wide and stiff, pushing Connell down, and then dug into Connell's belt holster, clawing at Connell's service Glock. As soon as Wolf got hold of it, Connell went berserk. With a vicious twist, he swung his arm back, knocking the gun off the granite and into a nearby bush.

Wolf let go of Connell's head, pushed off his shoulders, stepped back into the trees.

They both stood still and locked eyes for a moment.

"What the fuck are you doing?" Wolf's voice was barely audible over the thumping of blood in his own ears.

Connell ignored his question and stalked forward.

Wolf scanned the ground for his own pistol. It was nowhere in sight. His eyes swept his surroundings for something he could use to gain the advantage. No fist-sized rocks, no sticks, no weapons of any kind. He cursed himself for leaving his Leatherman multi-tool in the center console of the truck.

He looked back and saw a fallen tree—a thick branchless ponderosa pine log stretching horizontally like an oversized trip-wire a few feet from the back of his legs.

He turned to Connell, who was now approaching with steady small steps. Wolf shuffled backwards in retreat until he felt the wood against the back of his knees. Then he sat, flailing his arms and widening his eyes as he tipped on his rear-end in an uncontrolled-looking fall.

Connell sensed his opportunity and charged like a line-backer, his hands outstretched, eyes focused on Wolf's neck.

Wolf laid back fast, grabbed underneath the log, and pulled himself under to the other side as Connell flew over.

Connell landed with a grunt on the dirt and pine needles, and then turned to get back up.

With all his might, Wolf lunged over the log at Connell's rising form, and landed a head-butt against Connell's nose with a wet crunch.

Connell's eyes became vacant, his thick arms stretched to his sides, and he flopped onto his back with a weak exhale.

Wolf clambered onto Connell's chest and slammed an elbow into his face. Then he punched him with a knuckle-crunching right. Then another elbow. Then another.

...

Wolf stood up, tilted his head back, and greedily sucked air through his bared teeth. His lungs fought for air, burning with each inhale. After what seemed like five minutes of panting, Wolf caught his breath and composed himself. He looked down and bent over, pressing his fingers on Connell's thick neck, now slick with warm blood. Connell's pulse was steady and strong.

Sergeant Connell was going to be tough to move off the mountain. Or maybe he wouldn't need to be moved. Maybe he'd come to and be able to walk himself down. Connell was alive, that's all he knew. He would need facial reconstructive surgery; that was another thing he was pretty sure about. Wolf couldn't remember how many blows he had landed, but he was glad he had stopped before killing the man. *That would have ... complicated whatever the hell just happened.*

A long rumble of thunder echoed from the steadily growing darkness in the south, as if in reaction to his thoughts.

Wolf exhaled loudly, looked down at Connell again, and then stepped away. A glint caught Wolf's eye, and he stepped over to Connell's Glock, almost stepping on his own in the process. Bending to pick up Connell's pistol, he heard a voice in the distance.

"You guys up there?" Rachette said. He followed with a loud whistle.

"Yeah! Up here!" He picked up the gun, removed the magazine and pulled back the slide, ejecting the chambered round. Without thinking, he flung the clip off the cliff, and then tossed the pistol deep in the trees.

The bugs ramped up their hissing. A bird flapped past him and coasted out over the expanse—over the immense drop that beckoned him once again.

To Wolf, the air seemed hotter and more stagnant than before. Sweat trickled down his temples, down his neck and under his shirt collar. He tasted blood and spit, slapping a bright-red dollop on the rock.

He walked back to the edge. His body was humming, his movements fuzzy, body saturated with adrenaline.

Looking, he finally saw what he knew would be there the splayed body of Jerry Wheatman forty feet below, crumpled against jagged boulders. The long drop and the unforgiving landing left little chance that the boy could have survived.

Wolf let his mind run through the scenario. He pictured the teenager slipping up top, tumbling off the edge, deafening wind rushing by his ears, and then slamming into the scree field below.

Wolf jerked away and looked back to Connell's inert form. The man still hadn't moved. Wolf shook his head and rubbed a split on the inside of his cheek with his tongue. He walked away from the potential crime scene and spat more blood into a bush.

"Hey, what's up?" Rachette scrambled up into view.

"Found Jerry Wheatman," Wolf answered, walking back to the ledge.

"Yeah?"

Wolf pointed to the edge with a somber look.

"Oh, man." Rachette's voice trailed off as he looked over the cliff. "Shit." He pulled back from the edge.

"I noticed this here," Wolf said, pointing behind Rachette at the discoloration. "I think it's vomit. You can see the chunks of partially digested food."

Rachette bent over and studied it. "Oh yeah. So what does that mean?"

"What would you say is in that vomit?" Wolf asked.

"I don't know."

"Looks like a ham-and-egg breakfast to me. Yellow pieces of yolk from the egg, pink ham chunks, toast." Wolf pointed.

"Yeah, okay. Yeah, it does look like that. So, what does that mean?"

"I don't know. This person had recently eaten breakfast. Maybe in town. Maybe someone freaked out up here after seeing Wheatman fall off the edge. Puked his guts out and ran. Or maybe he puked his guts out after pushing Wheatman off the edge."

"You think he was pushed?" Rachette turned, expelling a hefty black dollop of tobacco spit in a bush.

"I think it's possible." Wolf flicked a glance to the trees. Connell was still out. "It's hard saying what happened. There are no footprints since it's rock. No indication of struggle."

"There could be some evidence on Wheatman's body," Rachette said.

Wolf nodded and looked down. Two deputies came around the corner and into view on the trail far below. "How about the shoe prints? Three pairs in all?"

Rachette nodded. "There were definitely three pairs of

shoes pointing up the trail, then two pointing down. Three came up, and two ... geez, what happened to you?" Rachette was looking Wolf up and down.

Wolf looked down at his uniform; dust powdered the whole left side of his body. A scrape on his elbow drained blood down the length of his arm to his fingers, and his other elbow was covered in blood that Wolf knew was not his own. His jeans were scuffed with dirt, and a clump of burrs was velcroed to his leg.

"Oh, yeah, that." He slapped the dirt off his pants. "Give me your handkerchief, will ya?"

Rachette gave him his ever-present handkerchief from his rear pocket.

Wolf wiped the blood off his arm. "Sorry, I'll buy you another one."

"What the hell happened?" Rachette suddenly went wide-eyed, then looked again over the ledge, then back to Wolf. "Where's Connell?"

Wolf huffed and nodded toward the trees.

Rachette took a second to find Connell among the underbrush. "What the ..." He swiveled his head back and forth. "Is that Connell's blood?" He finally settled his eyes on Wolf's forehead.

Wolf wiped his head, putting another dark spot on the handkerchief.

"Yeah. I think that's from the head-butt to his nose. He's going to need some medical attention, but I suspect he'll be able to walk his own ass down the mountain when he comes to."

Rachette spat again at his feet and laughed. "Holy crap. I can't wait to hear this."

"Hey, watch what you're doing. Don't spit anymore. Until we know differently, this is a crime scene. Connell and I already messed it up enough. No sense making it worse. And don't worry about what happened here. He deserved it—that's all you need to know for now."

Coming out with the truth was not an option. It was unbelievable what Connell had just tried, possibly in the literal sense to other people. Wolf might come out looking like the crazy one, spreading rumors about the son of an influential council member who happened to be Wolf's opponent for the sheriff's appointment. As much as Connell deserved to be in handcuffs, Wolf's form of justice would have to do for now.

Rachette stepped into the trees toward Connell.

"Is Baine on his way up?"

"Yep, he's right behind me." Rachette let out a long whistle as he looked down on Connell's inert body. "Yeah, that's a broken nose. Hey, Connell! Wow, he's out."

Deputy Baine clambered up into view.

Wolf stepped toward the ledge again. "All right, Rachette, you're with me. We're heading down. Baine, come here."

They all convened one last time on the cliff's edge. Baine peeked over at the body below. "Good Lord. That him?" Baine turned away from the cliff and walked toward the pines.

Wolf grabbed his radio. It was scoured and dusted with dirt, but it still worked.

"All right," Wolf announced, "we've found our victim. Appears DOA, but we've gotta move fast in case he still has vitals." Wolf gave a sharp whistle and waved his hand to the deputies below.

They waved back and doubled their pace.

"Right here, at the base," Wolf said somberly into the radio. "We also have one of ours in need of medical assistance on top of the cliff. Connell is unconscious, and may need to be evac'd off the mountain. We need to move fast. Hilton, Walters." The two men below didn't break stride. "Let me know."

A cacophony of affirmative radio calls barked through their receivers.

Baine was milling about in the trees, staring dumbly at Connell and keeping his distance.

Connell had woken up. His forearm was lying against his forehead, one knee propped in the air

"Baine, when he's up and around, help him down before those storms move in."

"Uh, okay," Baine stammered as he eyed Wolf, then shifted his gaze back to Connell's bloody face.

"Rachette. Get a few pictures of the vomit spot here, and then bag it."

"Yes, sir," Rachette said.

"Then catch up to me." Wolf held up his hand to Rachette.

Rachette shook his head and tossed him his can of Copenhagen snuff. "I thought you quit this stuff."

Wolf took a pinch and put it in on the uninjured side of his mouth, tossed the can back, and turned to the trail. "Not today," he said.

CHAPTER 5

Wolf ended up reaching the parking lot before Rachette could catch up, so he helped coordinate what now had become an extraction of a dead body—Jerry Wheatman hadn't survived the fall.

As Wolf waited for Rachette, he directed two deputies to the top of the trail to help bring down Connell.

"He twisted his ankle bad," Wolf had said. "But bring the full first-aid kit. He might need stitches."

Wolf had ignored the puzzled looks his comments caused, but he was finding it hard to sidestep the questions about his own scrapes and bruises, so he decided to take refuge in his truck.

Wolf climbed into the Explorer with a grunt, his body stiff, muscles stuffed with lactic acid. His adrenaline-injected body had been put through the wringer.

He turned down the radio chatter to a murmur and sat back, settling in for a good rest. It wasn't like him to dwell on the past, but right now he longed for his ten-year-ago physique and conditioning.

"I can't believe you did that to Connell! I wish I would have seen it." Rachette's head was in the open passenger window. He stared at Wolf with a look wavering between reverence and disbelief. "Was that about next week or something?"

Wolf fired up the engine. "Get in the damn car." He waited for Rachette to jump in, then backed out of his parking spot, narrowly missing another SCSD truck.

Rachette held up the bag of evidence he'd collected for Wolf to see, then turned and put it on the back seat. "Where we going?"

"To tell Jerry's parents their son is dead."

Rachette's face dropped.

Wolf couldn't blame him. This was one responsibility anyone in their right mind would not relish. Wolf loathed the prospect of witnessing the last bits of hope fade from the parents' eyes as he broke the news.

"Can you please pour me some of that coffee?" Wolf nodded toward a dinged-up metal thermos and fished an old Styrofoam cup from the floor at his feet.

Rachette stared at Wolf for a second and shook his head, picking up the thermos. "Dammit." He patted at a dark splotch of coffee on his pants as they passed through the deep puddle at the mouth of the parking lot.

"What the hell's wrong with you?" Wolf jabbed.

"Psssshhh."

Wolf chuckled inwardly. He was in his late thirties, ten years in the department, and a candidate to be appointed to sheriff of Sluice County, but somehow he'd found the one person he really connected with to be this second-year twenty-three-year-old.

For too many years, he had observed the disturbing shortfalls of many of the department's deputies. Some didn't step up when the going got tough. Some showed borderline psychotic behavior when given a badge and gun, like Connell. Most of them were good men, but would he trust his life in their hands? Not all of them. Sure as hell not with Connell.

Rachette was different. In his eighteen months in the department, he'd shown Wolf that he was the one within the department that Wolf could count on. In Wolf's estimation, Rachette was the full package—with the attitude, strength, coolness under pressure, reliability, confidence, intelligence, and drive Wolf liked to see in a deputy.

Thinking about all this, while watching Rachette wipe coffee off his crotch, Wolf smiled as he turned his attention back to the winding road to town.

...

The road turned back to the west and dropped in elevation through the dense forest for a couple miles. Massive gleaming, copper-trimmed houses poked out of the trees on both sides of the road. They were well spread apart from one another, leaving vast swaths of dense forest between them; just the way the extremely well-to-do from all corners of the world liked their Rocky Mountain getaways.

Wolf's ears popped as he wound down further still, and finally out onto the dirt straightaway that slung out onto the vast valley floor. Barbed wire lined the road on either side, and cattle grazed in the bright-green fields smattered with wild flowers. They reached the T-junction of Highway 734 that ran north–south and took a left toward town.

Rocky Points was a ski resort town first and foremost, but it hadn't always been. In 1883, some hard-nosed easterners had come to Denver and kept walking uphill, past Black Hawk miners, past Central City miners, over the Continental Divide, and then a little south to try their luck. There they dug, sluiced, panned, found some gold, and set roots. They dubbed their new town Rocky Points, a fitting name referring to the two rocky pointed 12,000-foot peaks to the west of town that would later become the ski resort. Years later, the borders of Sluice County would be carved into the map, running a long sliver north–south, with Rocky Points right smack in the middle.

It had been a rough beginning for Rocky Points, according to the history taught in town schools. There was a good amount of gold to be found at the start, but as word got out, and more and more men made their way into town, it became apparent that the gold wasn't as plentiful as had once been thought. And as competition grew between hard men, things got dangerous. Fighting, murder, and lawlessness ruled for years. That was until a band of four men joined forces to bring law and order to the town. One of those men was Wolf's great-great-great grandfather, the first sheriff of Rocky Points, and then of the larger territory of Sluice County created a short time later. Or so the story went.

Wolf took comfort from knowing he was carrying on his family tradition. He knew that if his father were still alive, he would be proud. *Probably more proud if I could figure out exactly what had happened to the Wheatman boy,* Wolf thought. And probably prouder still if he were to become sheriff.

"Might as well stop by the Mackery now," said Wolf as they approached the northern tip of town. "Maybe Bill can shed some light on where his daughter is. I need to fill up anyway."

The Mackery gas station sat right on the north end of Main Street, past which each and every day-tripper from Denver drove on the way in and out of town. A perfect location for a gas station. However, Ruth Beal ran the Mackery, which handicapped the Mackery's potential.

Wolf pulled off the highway and docked the SUV next to a

clean gas pump, the only part of the Mackery one could consider up to date.

Before Wolf could shut off the engine, Ruth was out of the small shack of a convenience store, yelling at the top of her lungs.

Ruth wore dirty jeans and a dirtier denim jacket to match. Her hair was twisted every which way like a nest, and she looked like she was just in the middle of eating, because there was a yellow dollop of mustard on her lip.

"Did you find the bastards?" she yelled.

Wolf opened his door and got out. "Hi Ruth. What are you talking about?"

"The hippies who stole the gas!"

Wolf looked at her with a blank expression. "I'm not sure what you're talking about."

"What? I called it in just now! A couple hippies just drove off without paying for fifty bucks worth of gas! Probably too high to remember to pay. Damn hippies—"

"Did you get the license-plate number?" Wolf asked, swiping his credit card, and then inserting the gas hose into the tank.

"No, I just went in the back when they pulled up, then I came back out and they were gone."

Rachette opened the door and leaned out with a concerned expression. "What kind of car was it?"

"A gol-darn hippie mobile! One of those gol-darn mini-vans." She was becoming red in the face.

"You mean a bus? Like a Volkswagen bus-type van?" Wolf asked.

"Yeah, I guess. If that's what they call 'em." She muttered to herself and looked into the distance, like she was spotting hippies in the trees.

"Ruth, is Bill Mulroy here today?" Wolf asked.

"Nope. He's in Frasier ... I think."

Wolf met eyes with Rachette, and then turned back to Ruth. "Why's that?"

"Why? What do you mean, why?" She stared bug-eyed at Wolf.

Wolf was confused. "Why is Bill Mulroy in Frasier? Why did he go there?"

"Oh," she said. "I don't know why." She scrunched her face, thinking about it.

The gas pump clicked to a stop and Wolf pulled the hose out. As he did so, he noticed a sign hanging from the tank. "Ruth, what's this sign all about?"

All three stood frozen. Rachette got back in the car and shut the door.

"Pre-pay?" Wolf asked. "Isn't it impossible to fill up unless you turn on the tank after someone gives you money or they put in a credit card?" He pulled out his credit-card receipt and waved it before putting it in his pocket.

Ruth stood with a sparsely toothed open mouth. "Huh. Oh mercy. What the hell am I thinking? I don't know what happened then!" She burst into a cackle, which ended in a brief coughing fit that made Wolf hope he wasn't going to have to perform CPR on her.

"So, there weren't any hippies who stole your gas?" Wolf opened the driver's-side door.

"No, I guess not. Sorry, I don't know what the hell's goin' on ..."

Wolf smiled. "Talk to you later, Ruth. Stay out of trouble and try not to harass too many people coming into town, all right? They are good for your business," he chided her.

Wolf noticed that she looked slighter than usual, which was a usual twig-thin to begin with. He got in the truck and turned to Rachette. "Why don't you run in and make sure Bill really isn't here?"

Rachette ran in past Ruth.

Wolf waved Ruth over.

She swayed over, concentrating hard on each step.

"Are you doing all right, Ruth?" Wolf asked.

She nodded and sighed. "Oh, you know. Ever since Ed died, I'm just countin' the minutes."

Rachette came back out of the building. He ran over and jumped in, jostling the truck.

Wolf looked at him, and Rachette shook his head. Bill was apparently in Frasier for the day.

"You take care of yourself, okay?" Wolf said, reaching out the window and patting Ruth on her bony shoulder.

Ruth nodded absently and returned to her shack.

Wolf started the truck back up and turned onto Main Street.

Rachette leaned toward the side-view mirror. "She's not looking too good."

"Yeah, we'll need to keep an eye on her. And we need to keep up with Bill. To ask him about Julie when he gets back."

Rachette nodded. "So, what's the plan? Off to be the bearer of shit news?"

"Yeah, off to tell the Wheatmans."

"Fun stuff."

"Yep. Fun stuff."

CHAPTER 6

It took Wolf and Rachette two hours to get to the Wheatmans' home, tell them the horrid news about their son, console them little to none, and return to the office building on Main.

Wolf and Rachette stood in the vast doorway of the department squad vehicle garage and stared into the deafening deluge of rain. Lightning flashed and a crack of thunder followed immediately, but Wolf didn't have the energy to flinch. He was whipped—physically and mentally. The day had thrown a lot at them. At him.

Wolf knew there was going to be more to come. What kind of aftermath could he expect with Connell? What was Connell going to tell people when he got back from the hospital trip he was on now? What was Connell telling people right now? What should Wolf tell people about it? Wolf felt like he'd missed the boat on some right action he should have taken after the fight. But what that action was he couldn't figure yet. He was trusting that he and Connell were in this thing together, and that they were going to deal with it like men. Maybe that was putting way too much trust in Connell.

"Been quite a good day." Rachette said taking a pinch of Copenhagen and throwing the can to Wolf.

He caught it, relented to the urge, took a pinch and threw it back. The tobacco juice burned the cut inside his lip, which was now swelling, but the warming sensation of the nicotine was instant, a welcome feeling that counteracted the pain blossoming everywhere else in his body.

I have to quit this stuff.

The wind swirled inside the door and sprayed them with mist from the downpour.

Rachette spat onto the frothing puddles. "Are you going to tell me what the hell happened up there or what?"

"I'm really not sure what happened." He was still running through options for how this was going to play out.

"You are going to get the job next week, right? I mean, that's pretty much a done deal, right? We can't have that guy as sheriff."

"It's not up to me," Wolf said.

"Yeah, but ... come on. That guy has been pretty much abusing the rest of the department for the last few months. I saw him slap Baine the other day."

He looked at Rachette and raised an eyebrow.

"I'm serious," Rachette said. "The guy is a crazy meathead."

"And you didn't report this to Sheriff Burton? Baine didn't?"

"Yeah, right."

Of course they didn't. It was an unwritten code of conduct for men in uniform worldwide—you didn't rat out a fellow deputy.

Wolf stretched his neck with a grimace and looked at his watch. 3:39 p.m. "I'm heading home early today."

"I don't blame you. Go get some rest, and you might want to ice that cheek."

Wolf felt his bulging cheekbone. "Yeah, good idea. If Burton comes round looking tell him he can call me. And let me know what comes of the evidence, and especially let me know if Julie Mulroy shows up."

Rachette scoffed and held out his hands. "Of course. What am I, an idiot?"

"Eh, no comment." Wolf got in the Explorer, fired it up, and drove out into the pounding waterfall of a rainstorm.

...

The SUV's wipers wrenched back and forth at the top setting, still not affording Wolf much of a view out of the windshield. Lightning spliced the sky in all directions; with thunder so close it shook the vehicle.

This storm and his inability to see what was coming more than a few feet ahead seemed to parallel his life at the moment.

Wolf mused on how there was a good chance he would run into Gary Connell when he got home. After all, Gary Connell had every right to visit his own ranch, and often did so unannounced. What would Wolf tell him? *Hey, sorry, I just beat the crap out of your son because he tried to kill me.*

Wolf didn't know if he had the heart to do that to Gary. Unlike his son, Derek, Gary Connell was one of the sweetest men Wolf had ever known. Following the death of Wolf's father, and the family's ensuing financial ruin, Gary Connell had stepped in to buy the ranch and rent it back to the Wolfs, for nothing.

Wolf would still be living rent-free on the ranch if not for his pride. In the end, Gary had been a good enough man to realize he needed to respect Wolf's wishes—that he had to take monthly rent payments from Wolf. Not that the great Gary Connell needed the money. That wasn't the point. The Wolfs paid their own way. They always had, and always would.

Something occurred to Wolf. Could Derek Connell have been willing to kill Wolf because of Wolf's relationship with Gary? Was that it? Connell was jealous and had decided that terminating Wolf would set things right?

The thought was jolting, and, for a split second, Wolf allowed a tiny vibration of sympathy for Derek Connell to enter his mind. Then Wolf thought of plunging off the cliff and, as quick as it came, the sympathy was gone.

Well, if Gary Connell were at the ranch, Wolf would tell him they'd been in a fight, and leave it at that. Wolf didn't have the heart to hurt the man by telling him his son was a monster.

Wolf was out of the southern end of town now, so he hung a left on the unpaved county road to the ranch. He could feel the truck careen a little sideways in the mud as he rounded a bend, so he coasted to slow down.

The rain was still heavy, but the sky was lightening ahead, and he even saw a patch of blue for a brief moment.

It was the blue of Sarah's eyes. *Sarah.* The thought of her made his heart skip. She was probably back in town at this point. What was Wolf going to see in those beautiful blue eyes this time? A brightness he hadn't glimpsed in years? Would she have an interest in life again? Or would it be that same lazy, defiant look he'd seen take root over the past six years?

He hoped it was the former. He hoped it so much for his son's sake that he dreaded seeing Sarah. Wolf could barely remember being twelve years old, but he knew his life had been much easier than Jack's must be right now—with a mother whose love for pills trumped her love for him. Life as a twelve-year-old that had him staying half the time with his grandparents, and the other half with his father.

The air in the truck was muggy and suddenly stifling. He hit the air-conditioning button and turned the radio to the local bluegrass station, a welcome distraction.

At least he wasn't lying dead at the base of a cliff next to Jerry Wheatman. At least he could be grateful for that.

CHAPTER 7

SUN STREAMED through the clouds and glared off the windshield as Wolf drove his way up the final stretch to the ranch. The truck bumped and sloshed through new potholes and small streams that dissected the muddy road. It had held up well through the storms of the past few weeks, but it would need a new grading before fall. That would be something to take up with Gary.

Wolf crossed the cattle guard that marked the northern edge of the ranch property, and continued up the hill. Then he reached the top of a low plateau just above the meandering Chautauqua River and took in a majestic view that never ceased to inspire him.

The three-hundred-acre property was part forest, part grassy meadow, and all rugged beauty. Once through the arched wooden gateway, the road continued straight ahead through a grass field a couple of hundred yards to a roundabout in front of two separate buildings: an understated one-story, three-bedroom house laid out in an L-shape with large windows to capture the panoramic views, and a small red barn that stood easy walking distance from the house. The multi-use barn gave Wolf adequate space to store outdoor equipment and camping supplies, garage his dirt bike and small John Deere tractor, and still have a decent space for a shop.

It was a great property and a great home, though not nearly in the tip-top shape it had been when his father was alive. Shortly after his father's death, Wolf's mother, who had never fully embraced the Rocky Points lifestyle, moved to Denver to be near her sisters. Wolf's brother had followed suit after high school, leaving for college and becoming a journalist, returning to Rocky Points only as an infrequent tourist.

It was only Wolf, and Jack for half the week, who lived here now and had any real connection to it. And Wolf couldn't shake the feeling that he was letting the place rot into the ground. There was always too much to be done for one man to keep on top of.

If he did get the job as sheriff, there would be more money—money for repairs; money for bringing in a handyman for occasional help; and money for substantial payments toward owning the property outright.

As he always did, Wolf grabbed his cell phone from the center console when the house was in sight, as driving up to the plateau on which the ranch was situated meant driving back into cell reception. With all the action that had happened during the day, he looked at the screen with anticipation.

Four missed calls, one from Rachette, and three from his mother. One voice message. From his mother. Rachette could wait.

Clearly his mother was itching to talk to him. He briefly considered not calling her, not wanting to add more drama to his day, but three attempts to reach him was a little out of the ordinary. *What had her sister done to her this time?*

He dialed her phone number, not bothering with the voicemail. She answered after a half ring.

"Oh, David. Where have you been?" She sniffed loudly into the phone. She was crying.

"Mom, what's wrong?"

She breathed into the receiver for a few seconds with shaking sobs.

"Mom? What happened?"

She didn't answer.

Wolf slowed the truck to a stop, wondering if he'd lost phone reception. "Mom? Can you hear me? What happened? Hello?"

"John's dead," she said in a tiny voice.

Wolf's skin flushed hot and his vision swirled. He took off his seatbelt and opened the door. He stepped out, and the truck lurched forward, slamming into the small of his back. He reached over and pushed the gear stick into park. "What? What are you talking about?"

"He's dead. He died this weekend."

Wolf stared in shock at nothing, not seeing the shining land moist with the passed rainfall, now bustling with birds. He let out a long breath.

"I guess Friday night, they are saying," she said.

"Who is saying? What happened?"

She sniffed and then let out another string of sobs.

"Mom. What happened?"

"He killed himself."

CHAPTER 8

Wolf stirred his fourth cup of strong coffee and glanced at his watch. Almost one in the morning. The computer screen was the only light in his darkened study besides the slivers of moonlight entering the open blinds.

Wolf stretched his arms high, yawned, and re-read the email.

Hey Bro, what's happening? How are you doing man? How's Points? How's Jack doing?

I just wanted to catch up. I know it's been a long time since we've connected, but ... eh, you know how it is.

Lately things have been going well. My blog is kicking ass, and I've finally got everything squared away with my third book —it was picked up by Nordberg Publishing, and they are going to release it in mid-October. It's a great deal for me. They say it's going to be in airports everywhere. Can you believe that shit?

I was in New York a month ago meeting with them, and they are projecting some numbers that I don't even want to talk about ... at least until I see it happen. No sense jinxing it. But I'm excited to say the least.

Italy is going well. I'm finding the life here really pleasant and great for productivity, as I've been writing non-stop since I got here. I've been hanging out with the girl who lives right above me, and have met a few people around town. It's fun, but I miss Colorado. I'll definitely be coming back for a little while at the beginning of the year. Then, who knows?

So how about you? I hear from Mom that you are a shoo-in for the sheriff job. Although I didn't need to hear that from her to know that. Because you are. I can't wait to come home and tell everybody my bro is the sheriff ... plus, I'll pretty much be above the law. Maybe I'll start growing some weed again, haha.

We'll have to have a serious talk about the ranch too. If this book deal goes like they are saying, well, again, I don't want to jinx it. But I'd like to help out buying the property so it's back in the family.

Talk soon, brotha.

John

This doesn't make any sense, Wolf thought for the thousandth time since the phone call he'd received from his mother.

Wolf was hit by a wave of exhaustion as he stood up and looked at his watch. It was finally just after one, which would have been nine in the morning Italian time, the time he'd decided to make his call to maximize his chances of speaking to the right person—for said person to be on duty.

He exhaled and picked up the phone, then thumbed the piece of paper with the number he'd gotten from his mother earlier. He dialed and then listened to a series of clicks, then a long one-tone dial sound that he remembered was typical of many foreign countries.

"*Carabinieri.*" The voice sounded distant, like an old vinyl recording.

"Hello, my name is Sergeant David Wolf of the Sluice County Sheriff's Department in the United States. Do you speak English?"

"David Wolf?" *Dahveed Vowlf* a young male voice pronounced it. "I am not very good with English, no. Un momento ..."

Before Wolf could respond, he heard the phone clunk, as if dropped on the top of a desk. For ten minutes, he heard the bustle and muffled voices of what sounded like an active police station a few thousand miles away.

"Pronto? Carabinieri." It was the same voice, this time slow with boredom.

Wolf blinked. "This is Sergeant David Wolf of the Sluice County Sheriff's Department in the United States. Who am I talking to?"

"Yes, this is Tenente Tito, sir," he said.

"I need to speak to your superior officer right away," Wolf said.

"Yes," Tito said, and the phone clunked again.

Wolf used mind-relaxation techniques he'd learned in the army for withstanding torture as another five minutes passed.

"Pronto?" Tito said again.

Wolf sighed. "Tenent Tito—"

"Tenente, sir."

Wolf clenched his jaw and spoke slowly. "I need to speak to your captain, to your colonel, to your sheriff, to your general. Do you have—"

"Yes, sir. I will connect you now. Please hold un momento."

Wolf pulled the phone from his ear. Just as he was about to throw it against the wall as hard as he could, he heard another single dial tone through the earpiece.

Wolf pushed his phone back against his ear.

"Rossi," a husky male voice answered.

"Hello, my name is Sergeant David Wolf of the Sluice County Sheriff's Office in the United States. Do you speak English?"

"Ah, yes. Sergeant Wolf. This is Maggiore Rossi." His accent was thick but clearly understandable. "I am sorry we could not get in touch with you and your family sooner. It took some doing. I am very sorry for your loss." There was warm concern in his voice.

Wolf was silent for a beat. "Thank you, sir. So you are aware of my relation to the deceased."

"Yes," Rossi exhaled. "Your mother told me about you. I've been expecting your call."

Wolf didn't respond.

"I found your brother," Rossi continued. "I was one of the carabinieri first on the scene at his apartment."

"You told my mother he had committed suicide. That he had hanged himself. I need to know details, please."

"Yes, of course," he said in an apologetic tone. "We were called by a person who lives at the apartamento ... er, apartment, who suspected something was wrong, a young woman who was dating your brother. She called us, we came and went inside, and found him on the floor. It was clear he had hanged himself."

"He was on the floor?" Wolf paused. "But you say it was clear he hanged himself? That doesn't make sense to me, Maggiore."

A car horn blared in Wolf's ear, from somewhere near the man Wolf talked to five thousand miles away.

"Yes. I understand. I am sorry, please, my English is ..." Rossi paused. "It was a chandelier. He tied himself to it, and then hanged himself. He and the chandelier fell from the ceiling after he die and that was how we found him."

Wolf shook his head and leaned forward. "And what was the time of death?"

"Friday night, declares the coroner. And there was ..." Rossi cleared his throat. "Sergeant Wolf, we also found drugs ... cocaine? How do you call—"

"Cocaine?" Wolf stood up. "That doesn't make sense." His brother wasn't the type to do hard drugs. Marijuana? On occasion he used to. But not often. That's what made the reference to growing weed in his email a joke. John knew that Wolf knew he never did the stuff anymore. He'd watched his brother refuse it on many occasions for years. So to say he'd upped the ante and started snorting cocaine? It didn't ring true.

"Yes, sir. We found evidence of cocaine," Rossi said into the silence.

"I hadn't heard about that. You didn't tell my mother that."

"Ah, yes, sir. I apologize. I wanted to speak to you about it first. Your mother was so upset. Like I said, she told me you were a police officer, and I hadn't told her about the drugs, so I just ... I just figured I would talk to you about it. There is no sense in making matters worse with this type of news."

Wolf paced back and forth. "Okay. Thank you for that, I guess. Was this cocaine found during the autopsy?"

"No, sir. Actually the drugs were found at the scene, and residue was found on his nostrils," Rossi said.

"What did the tox screen in the autopsy show?" Wolf asked.

"An autopsy was not called for—"

"No autopsy?" Wolf almost yelled. The static on the phone hissed and popped.

Rossi made a non-committal noise followed by a long breath into the phone.

"I'll be coming over on a flight tomorrow."

"I understand, Sergeant Wolf. You'll want to bring your brother home."

I'll want to investigate his death. "Yes. I'd appreciate any help your ... department can give me." Wolf didn't know what the regional department of the carabinieri was called. Didn't know a thing about Italy other than it churned out good food and cars. Research into the operation of the carabinieri was tacked onto his to-do list for the night.

"Of course, Sergeant Wolf."

Wolf talked with Rossi for another few minutes, arranging some specifics, and then hung up.

He went to the kitchen and set his coffee cup in the sink, then stared out at the dark forest behind the house. Something about John's death wasn't right. Correction: everything about John's death wasn't right, and there was no way Wolf could learn anything useful about what had happened over a rickety phone connection from five thousand miles away.

He imagined his mother staring sleeplessly at the ceiling of her bedroom, wondering where she had gone wrong and blaming herself for her son's death. Thinking about her inability to instill the will to live, to persevere, in her baby son. After first losing her husband years ago, and now her son, perhaps she was even entertaining thoughts of ending it all herself.

He took to pacing a groove into his carpet.

The email.

John had been too positive, too excited about the future. Plus, Wolf had known his brother, really known him. His kid brother was a fighter, mentally and physically. There wasn't a single instance in his life where he could remember John giving up on something or backing down from a challenge. The man had been a lifelong systematic goal-achieving machine. He ate up challenges, no matter how big, and shit them out, leaving them behind for even bigger ones. Suicide just didn't fit.

And Wolf was going to Italy to prove it.

CHAPTER 9

WOLF WAS WRENCHED awake by the alarm clock on his phone. He grabbed a cup of coffee and his fur-collared Sheriff's Department jacket and went to the front porch. It had only been a few hours since he'd collapsed onto his bed and caught a couple hours of restless sleep, and his mind and body felt sluggish. Slow. Depressed. But determined nonetheless.

The sky was a blue glow behind the eastern peaks, and his breath was smoke in the bitter cold early morning air. Elk milled about in the field, and they all turned to look at him as the screen door slammed shut. Animal and man stared at one another for a few seconds, and then Wolf sat on his patio chair and thumbed on his cell phone.

Despite the pre sunrise hour, his mother answered after the first ring. "Hey," she said in a hoarse voice. Probably worn out from crying.

"Hey. I spoke with a *carabiniere* last night. A cop from Italy. He was first on scene to John's apartment. He's going to help us with getting John released and brought to Colorado."

She responded with an exhale.

"You doing all right?" he asked, immediately regretting the

question. "Never mind. Stupid question." They sat in silence until Wolf spoke softly. "We are going to get through this."

Silence.

"I'm going to go to Italy to get him."

"You are?"

"Yeah, I am."

More silence.

"Listen, Mom. I'll keep in touch, all right?"

"You'd better." She sniffed and hung up.

Wolf got dressed and headed into town.

...

Sarah Muller's parents lived in the pines a mile and a half west of town. The house was stoutly built with logs and wood beams. Large and well windowed, the home afforded its occupants spaciousness and a beautiful view of pine trees and meadows in the foreground, and majestic Rocky Mountain peaks in the background. The best a generous amount of money could buy.

Wolf pulled up the dirt road and saw the house, lit inside and out in the dim early-morning hour. The Mullers had always been early risers.

Venus gleamed just over the pines in the eastern sky. The sun would be following close behind, having to scale the eastern peaks first.

He rang the doorbell and heard muffled conversation inside. Sarah's face appeared in the ornately frosted window set in the hand-crafted wood door. She opened it a crack.

"Hi David."

Her blond hair was askew, like she'd just woken up, but her sky-blue eyes were clear and bright-looking. Wolf couldn't remember her looking so vital and beautiful. She wore sweat-pants and a white T-shirt, both fitting snug to accentuate her perfect body, a rare place in the universe where time had always stood still.

"Hi Sarah. How are you?"

"Good," She said.

There was a mumbling behind the door, and she looked down and then tucked her head back inside.

"Is that Jack?" Wolf craned his neck.

She leaned back and turned sideways. "Uh, no. Jack! Your dad's here!"

He heard the faint yell reply from somewhere in the interior.

"Who is that behind the door? Are your parents here?"

"Umm, yeah, my parents are here."

"Oh," Wolf said. Apparently they weren't behind the door, though.

In answer to Wolf's curiosity, just then a man came behind Sarah and placed a hand on the small of her back. She looked down and stepped out of the way. He was dressed in sweat pants and a T-shirt as well.

"Hi, how you doing? My name is Mark." The man extended a long arm over Sarah. "Mark Wilson."

"Hey. Nice to meet you." Wolf shook his hand.

"Dad!" Jack burst out of the doorway.

Mark stepped aside and ducked back in, as if to respect their distance. Wolf watched as Mark persuaded Sarah to shut the door to leave Wolf and his son alone.

Wolf gave Jack a hug and ruffled his hair. "Hey, bud. What's happening?"

"Not much." He stayed latched tight to Wolf. "Just watching toons and having breakfast."

"Cool. Hey, I've gotta leave town for a little bit, so—"

"Where? Where you going?"

Wolf paused. "I'm actually going to Italy."

"What? Are you serious? Are you going to see John?"

"Yeah, I am buddy." Wolf nodded.

"Tell him he needs to call me. When is he coming back?"

"Listen, buddy. We'll talk more when I get back. I think I'll be gone a week. Are grandma and grandpa here?"

Jack nodded. "Yeah, you want to talk to them?"

"No, don't worry about it. Never mind." Wolf relaxed a little bit, his worry about the strange man inside diminishing. Sarah's father had guns, and a concern for his grandson matched by no one but Wolf. "So how's your mom doing?"

Jack nodded. "She's actually doing well."

Wolf nodded, trying to ignore the hopeful expression on his son's face. *She had better be doing well. This kid deserved a good mother.*

"Listen, buddy," Wolf said, "John's not doing ..."

Jack frowned in confusion.

Wolf didn't have the heart to tell him what was going on. But he had no choice. It had to come from him. Right now. Otherwise, he would know from some other person in town before the morning was through. It was just how it worked in Rocky Points.

"John died this weekend, buddy."

Jack's face fell. He stared at Wolf with glassy eyes, and his lip started to quiver. "What?"

Wolf nodded and hugged Jack. "Sorry, buddy. I have to go get him and bring him back home. That's where I'm going."

Jack hugged Wolf again and shook softly with sobs.

"I know, buddy." It was all Wolf could think to say. "I know." They hugged and cried, Wolf letting the emotional floodgates go. After what felt like an hour of wallowing in tears he pushed Jack back and knelt down. "All right, bud. Be good.

Go back inside. Tell your mom I need to speak to her again real quick, all right?" Jack wiped his eyes and stared at the ground. Wolf wiped his own face and pulled Jack's chin up. "Hey, buddy, I love you. You know that, right?"

Jack nodded.

"All right. I'll see you soon, okay?"

Sarah opened the door. She looked at Jack wiping his tears and shot a questioning look at Wolf, which turned quickly to an accusing one.

"Bye, Dad." Jack turned and walked inside.

Wolf stood straight. "So, how are you doing, Sarah?" This time Wolf put the full weight behind the question.

"Fine, David. I'm doing just fine," she said.

Wolf had to admit, she looked fine. He felt a stab of jealousy for the new guy now skulking somewhere behind the door.

She crossed her arms and watched Jack walk inside. "What was that all about?"

"I have to go out of town. I'll be gone all week, all right?"

She shrugged her shoulders and looked down.

Wolf saw the shadow in the door window. "Hey, Mark, come here for a second?"

Sarah glared at Wolf.

Mark stepped around Sarah, out onto the front porch.

"Can I talk to you for just a second?"

"Of course, David. Of course." Mark nodded his head to Sarah, who stepped in and closed the door quietly.

Wolf turned and walked a little way down the massive front deck, and Mark followed next to him. Wolf stopped and placed his hands on the railing, and then looked out into the pines, now brightening as the sun threatened to crest the peaks.

"What do you do, Mark?"

"I'm a builder. Custom homes," he said blowing into his

hands and rubbing them together. "Man, starting to get cold overnight already."

Wolf nodded. "And do you know what I do?"

"Yep. Up for appointment to sheriff, from what I hear."

"And you're shacking up with my ex-wife, who's one day fresh out of rehab, at her parents' house, where my son happens to live."

Mark shifted and scratched his head, smiled, then let it die. "Yeah, I guess that's exactly what's going on. Look, I met Sarah in rehab. I'm ... I wasn't in the rehab myself. Well, not this time around. I was before. I'm an addict, but I'm clean, and I have been for over six years. I spend a lot of time helping out at the center as a counselor. Sarah and I met, and we've become close."

"Okay," said Wolf, feeling another jolt of jealousy. "How's she doing? Did she kick it this time, or what?"

Mark crossed his arms and shivered a little. "She's doing very well, David. Now is a critical time of the process, but she made some serious breakthroughs, and I'm confident she has more than enough momentum to keep clean this time. For good."

Wolf nodded. "And this isn't the beginning of a toxic relationship between you two, where one of you falls back into the drugs, and the other follows, and you end up huffing meth in a shack in the woods?"

Mark's hearty laugh echoed back from the forest. "No." He looked at Wolf's expression and sobered his own. "No, David. This isn't one of those relationships. In fact, she wants to help out at the clinic for the foreseeable future. She has devoted parents to support her, her loving son ..." he looked at Wolf and looked at the ground.

"And she has you," Wolf completed his sentence.

Mark pursed his lips and nodded. "Yeah."

"Look, I don't want to threaten you with violence if you end up hurting her or my son, so I won't. You seem like a good guy who's smart enough to figure that out for himself."

Mark laughed again.

Wolf couldn't think of anything else to say, so he shook his hand.

They walked back to the door and Sarah cracked it open and let Mark inside.

"Sarah, can I talk to you?" Wolf asked.

She stepped out and the door closed softly behind her.

Wolf nodded at the tall shadow behind the door's frosted glass. "He seems like a good guy."

Sarah nodded, avoiding eye contact. "Yeah, he really is a good man."

"Well, I just wanted to let you know ... John died."

"What?" Sarah's eyes went wide and met Wolf's.

Wolf nodded. "Yeah. I'll be going to Italy. I'm thinking for at least a week. I just wanted to let you know. You know, before you heard it from someone else."

Sarah nodded and opened and closed her mouth.

"You guys will have to take Jack for the week. You have keys if you need to get into my house for anything of his."

She nodded, unable to disguise her shock.

Wolf turned and stepped off the porch. The gravel under his boots scratched with each step until he reached the truck. As he got in, he glanced back to the front porch and couldn't help but notice a tall man hugging a beautiful sobbing woman against his chest.

CHAPTER 10

THE SUN HAD FULLY RISEN over the peaks of the Continental Divide, and was blasting a glare off his windshield as he headed east down the hill. When he reached the highway, he hung a right and headed into town.

There were a few deputies already at headquarters, and a few who had been there all night, so the parking lot was almost half full.

He pulled off Main Street, into the gravel lot of the building and parked his SUV. Leaving his travel bags in the back seat, he walked to the main entrance. The front doors of steel and glass were warm to the touch.

Tammy, the receptionist, call operator, radio dispatcher, and general ass-kicking motherly figure of the department, sat still behind the reception desk looking down at an open file. She raised her eyebrows over her red plastic frames and smirked. "Sergeant Wolf. You have been a naughty boy, I hear." She dropped her voice to a whisper and leaned forward. "About time that piece of shit got what was coming to him." Then she sat down and resumed perusing the file in her hands.

Wolf rolled his eyes and scanned his card to enter.

The loud chatter in the Squad Room was snuffed to silence with the clack of the door shutting behind him. Every deputy in the room looked in his direction, then awkwardly to files, or computer screens, or a dirty fingernail.

Wolf stood still and scanned the room. Somewhat with relief, he didn't see Connell. With everything on his mind, he would be just fine if his short stop-in was without confrontation.

He ignored the stares, and one hearty pat on the back, and walked over to Burton's office. He gave the heavy wood door three solid knocks.

"Come," called Burton, barely audible from outside the door.

Sheriff Burton didn't look up as Wolf entered. He was filling out a 10 04-D form. The "D" was for disciplinary, Wolf knew, though he hadn't filled one out before.

Wolf kept his eyes averted from what was being written, or which deputy, or deputy sergeant, the form was for, and sat down. When Burton ignored his presence, Wolf stared out the window at a few birds chasing each other through the pine trees.

Burton slapped his pen down and scraped the form into a manila folder, then creaked back in his chair. He spent a long few moments bouncing and swiveling, pondering Wolf with a disappointed grimace, then stood and looked out the window, leaving his chair spinning in a lazy half circle.

"I don't know what the hell happened between you two, yesterday," Burton said, "but I know you. And I know Derek. And I know you probably won't tell me that Derek started whatever the hell happened up there, so I won't ask." Burton turned and pointed at Wolf. "You have to keep yourself under control. You need to play nice with Derek if you see him this morning. In fact, you need to play nice for the rest of your career here."

Was that an admission that Wolf had the job as sheriff?

Burton sat back in the seat with a heavy sigh.

Wolf knew the sheriff's old bones were ready to call it quits. He didn't need any of this so late in the game. Wolf felt almost sorry for the old man.

Sheriff Burton held out his hands. "Well?" he said, leaning forward on his elbows. "You wanna tell me what happened?"

Wolf smiled and looked behind the sheriff again, this time focusing on the resort with its dormant ski lifts. Wolf considered it, then fixed his gaze on Burton and shook his head.

Burton sat back, wheezed through his walrus mustache and crossed his legs. A faint satisfaction gleamed in his eyes. "All right, all right. But I hope this little scuffle doesn't hurt your chances with the council."

"Me neither, sir." Wolf said.

"And now you have to go?"

"I need to go over there to get John."

Burton put his elbows back on the desk and buried his face in his hands for a second. "I was so sorry to hear about your brother, son." He had a look of deep sorrow. "Keep in touch. I don't see how my old ass could help, but, if you need anything, just holler. I'll try to keep you in good standing with the council while you're gone, but ... it would be much easier if you were here."

"I know, sir. But something isn't right over there. The John I knew wouldn't consider suicide an option, much less the answer. If he truly did this, I need to be convinced, and that won't happen if I stay here. I can't take a half-way-around-the-world-stranger's word on something this big."

Burton nodded and stood up. "Well, at least you don't have to worry about the Wheatman case while you're gone. You'll have enough to worry about over there as it is."

Wolf narrowed his eyes. "What do you mean?"

"What do you mean, what do I mean?"

"The Wheatman case? I don't have to worry about it?"

"You didn't hear about Julie Mulroy and Chris Wakefield?"

"No."

Burton's chair squeaked as he sat back down. "I thought Deputy Rachette gave you a call yesterday to fill you in on the whole thing."

Wolf remembered the missed call from Rachette along with the three missed calls from his mother. "Well, yeah. I think he called, but I never did talk to him. He didn't leave a message, and I forgot to call him back with all the—" Wolf interrupted himself and sat forward. "Just tell me what happened."

"Julie Mulroy and Chris Wakefield showed up yesterday. They were scared shitless, talking about how they were with Jerry Wheatman when he fell."

Wolf sat back. "Chris Wakefield? He was with Julie and Jerry?"

Burton just nodded. They both knew Chris Wakefield well. He was the sixteen-year-old son of the mayor of Rocky Points. Whereas the mayor was a good man in every sense of the word, Chris was regarded as a bit of a rebel. He was the kind of kid that you would have avoided eye contact with if you passed him on the street. For a couple of years, he had dressed in all black, wearing headphones and shutting out communication with anyone. Save for a couple friends he had had in town, he spoke to no one. Not even Wolf.

Recently, however, Chris Wakefield appeared to integrate himself back into society. Over the past year, he had changed his attire to "fit in," and he seemed to lose some of his animosity toward the town and for life in general. Wolf had theorized that it was no coincidence the kid's metamorphosis had coincided with his father's run for mayor a year ago.

"Okay," Wolf said. "So according to Julie and Chris, Jerry

fell. How? Why wait so long to report it? What angle are we taking on these two?"

Burton stayed silent for a second and then blinked. "We're not taking any angle."

"All right."

Burton sat motionless.

"So what's their explanation of what happened?" Wolf asked.

Burton shrugged. "They say Jerry was dickin' around up top and fell. End of story."

Wolf was unconvinced. "Details, Sheriff. Details."

Burton took a deep breath. "Apparently, Julie and Jerry go up top together. Alone. Jerry shows off to Julie on top of the cliff, messing around near the edge, and slips off. Julie watches him plummet to his death, freaks out, and freezes up on top. Now, she can either call the cops or her friend. She opts for the friend, thinking we'll think she pushed Wheatman off. So she calls Wakefield. Wakefield drives out to the trailhead, walks to the top of the trail, and helps her down the mountain.

"Wakefield says Julie was catatonic on top of the mountain. Puking everywhere. In bad shape. He tries to convince her to go to the cops, but she's having none of it, freaking out, thinking we are going to lock her up and throw away the key. Wakefield takes her to his house, and finally succeeds in convincing her to come to us. So they showed up yesterday." Burton held up his hands like he'd just finished tying a rope on a steer.

"So they don't check if Jerry is okay? They just leave him to die?" Wolf was incredulous.

Burton held up a hand. "Chris says he ran down to the body. Checked Wheatman's pulse, and he was dead."

Wolf stared for a few seconds, just shaking his head. "Julie drove to the trail."

Burton nodded. "Julie drove to the trail. And Wakefield

drove to pick her up. Then they both drove back to Chris's house."

"And Julie was okay to drive to Chris's house, despite having just been catatonic. That's quite a story." Wolf got up and paced. "What about the mayor? Did you talk to him? What does he say about all this? He just lets his sixteen-year-old son bring home a girl to spend a couple of nights at the house?"

Burton's face went red—whether out of anger or embarrassment, Wolf couldn't tell. "Of course I talked to the mayor," he said in an even voice. "He says he didn't suspect a thing out of the ordinary. He says Chris told him that Julie needed a place to stay on account of her drug-addict parents, and he believed his son. And, of course, I believe the mayor. As you should, too."

Wolf waved a hand. "Okay, okay. But this just doesn't add up. These kids are hiding something, and you know it."

"Sit down," Burton said. "Sit."

Wolf did.

"We don't have any evidence to contradict these kids' stories. Nothin' on Wheatman's body, no defensive wounds, nothin'. What do you suppose we do? Accuse the girl of murder? That would make the mayor's son an accomplice to murder, without any evidence to back it up. Personally, I'm *real* attached to the prospect of getting my pension. And I'm sure you're real attached to the prospect of becoming sheriff next week."

"I understand," Wolf said, standing. He didn't need further explanation. Getting on the bad side of the mayor was professional suicide, but Wolf still didn't like any of it. It would have to wait, though. There were more pressing issues that Wolf needed to take care of.

There was a knock on the door.

"Come in," Burton said.

Rachette poked his head in and did a double take at the

sight of Wolf. "Sirs. I was actually just going to let you know, Sheriff, that I'll to be taking Sergeant Wolf to the airport this morning down in Denver."

Burton stood up and squeezed Wolf's shoulder. "Son. Again, I'm sorry, and let me know if I can help in any way."

He shook Burton's hand and walked out of the office with Rachette on his heels.

CHAPTER 11

WOLF WAS JOLTED awake by the ping of the seatbelt sign and a loud voice in Italian over the Boeing 777's intercom. He was in Milan. *Milano.* He looked out the window and saw green fields and countless red-roofed buildings. Anything tall enough to be hit by an aircraft was painted in a red-and-white candy-cane striping.

While in the army, he'd been to Germany on many occasions, en route to the Middle East, and that was the extent of his experience in Europe. He was more familiar with countries further east of the Prime Meridian, or south the Middle East, China, Vietnam, Laos, the Philippines, Central and South America.

And when he was in another culture, it was usually on missions, taking in the sights from a helicopter at night or through the scope of a gun. Ever since his final day as an army ranger ten years ago, he hadn't set foot outside the United States, so it was safe to say he had no clue what to expect in Italy.

He'd seen the pictures on his brother's blog, read a few of his posts about life there, but he really didn't have a sense of what he was getting into at all. For him, the word Italy conjured up thoughts of pizza, spaghetti, meatballs, and calzones. Ferraris and Ducatis and Mario and Luigi.

The plane came to a halt at the Lufthansa gate at Malpensa International Airport.

"Ciao," a pretty dark-haired flight attendant said to Wolf as he stepped off the plane. The air was warm and startlingly humid inside the jet bridge, and his Colorado-dried skin drank the moisture like a sponge.

As he reached the main terminal, the air was still thick, and whatever was in the air, probably smog, tickled his throat. Looking out the terminal window, past the docked planes, revealed a flat landscape with a dense hazy sky. Any direction he looked seemed to present the same thick copse of deciduous trees beyond the airport. He knew the Alps were close by. He'd gotten a good look at the Matterhorn before the rough dive into Milan, but the Alps hid behind a veil at the moment. His mental compass was spinning. At home it was easy. Rocky Points had the Rocky Points to the west, and Denver had the towering mountains to the west. Gauging direction without landmarks was proving difficult, and his inability to get his bearings exacerbated his uneasiness.

A sea of people chattered all around him in a language he had little experience with other than one semester class in high school before he changed to Spanish. Everyone was using the same voice intonations along with the same hand gestures. *Grandiose* was the word that came to his mind when he watched the people speaking around him.

Passing through the customs line, the officer asked him why he was in the country.

"Vacation," he said. No sense causing any confusion.

The customs officer said something else to him, looked at him expectantly, rolled his eyes, and then shooed him onward.

Wolf walked on, into a vast terminal, coming up blank when he tried to figure out what had just been said. The language resembled Spanish in many ways, but was spoken in such a rapid staccato that he had no chance of picking out a single word.

Signs throughout the airport were in Italian with English underneath. He concentrated on listening to the people around him, listening for other English speakers, and heard none. He thought back on the phone calls and how difficult it was to communicate with the few people he'd spoken to.

What was he expecting here? Sure, he was getting John's body and bringing it home, but he had much larger aspirations for this trip. *How the hell was this going to go down?*

He set out to find the train.

CHAPTER 12

THE NEXT TWO hours were an exercise of faith and following the poor directions from Maggiore Rossi of the carabinieri. Not once was he completely sure he was on the right train or going in the right direction. The train app he'd gotten for his iPhone was rendered useless the moment he'd stepped off the plane, as he didn't have an Italian SIM card for his phone. The sky outside was a dull gray, no shadows. Coupled with the flat landscape and towering buildings everywhere, there was no way to get a bearing on direction.

Two trains later, however, he was reasonably sure he was on the right route. Twice he caught a glimpse of the word *Lecco* on signs—the city where John lived, and where the carabinieri awaited Wolf's arrival—and the Alps finally came into view amid the haze ahead, indicating he was at least heading north. The train stopped often, slowly weaving its way into the green hills. A large slow-moving river flitted into view on the left-hand side. There were boats pulled up along the shore on the dry riverbank, the waterline seemingly a few feet lower than it had been in the recent past. Still, the amount of water sliding by looked to be more than a few of the largest Colorado rivers combined.

Brightly painted buildings of sorbet orange, sky blue, purple, lemon yellow, and other electric shades were everywhere—next to the river, halfway up the steep inclined hills, even directly on top of the mountain peaks. Nature was choked out by thousands of years of settlement, but the foliage was rampant at the same time. It was thick, dense, wiry, and thorny. Grass grew in feet, not inches.

Vibrant shades of painted stucco gave way to a consistent powdery gray stone color as the train continued north. Each roof on the thousands of buildings of all shapes and sizes was topped with the same tangerine-hue clay tile.

As the train slid steadily north, the gaping river widened into small lakes, then narrowed into a tighter bottleneck before ultimately opening up into a gigantic body of water.

Towering steep mountains lined all sides of the blue expanse. They were densely green with deciduous trees, and there were chalk-white cliffs where the land had slid into the water at some point in time thousands of years ago, or last week, as far as he knew. Straight ahead, the lake continued until it faded out of sight in the muggy air.

Thanks to his Google searches the night before, he recognized it as Lake Como. The lake was one of the deepest in Europe according to the internet, and, looking at the steep mountains that dove straight into the edges of the lake, it wasn't hard to imagine the limestone slopes continuing for another thousand or so feet down under the water.

The train arrived in the city of Lecco, where his brother had lived for the past five months. Wolf recalled that Lecco sat on the geographical lower right tip of the lake, which itself was in the shape of an enormous upside down Y. They were on the southeastern tip, and the northernmost end was somewhere far ahead.

He was to get off at the train station and wait for his contact to find him. Wolf looked at the "No Service" indicator on his phone and hoped to God they held up their end of the bargain.

After an uneventful debarkation of the train, he walked a short distance to the front of the train station and sat on a steel bench that was riddled with graffiti.

For fifteen minutes he sat thinking about SIM cards for cell phones and with a cursory glance around the area came up with zero ideas as to where to get one. He would settle for an internet connection and Skype, but all he saw was a small hole-in-the-wall looking place that said "bar" above the door. A carabinieri officer would help, he assured himself.

Thirty-five minutes later, he decided to begin walking, *somewhere*, when a uniformed officer approached him.

"David Wolf?" The carabinieri had a phone pressed to his ear.

"Yes."

The officer was no older than twenty-five, dressed in a dark-blue, sharp-looking uniform that had a red stripe down the leg, with a glossy white leather belt from which hung a Beretta pistol. He held a shiny-billed military-style hat in his left hand, and his cell phone in the right.

"I am Tenente Langoria," he said not offering a shake, since both hands were full. "You may call me Tito." Tenente Tito put the phone back to his ear and waved Wolf to follow.

Wolf thought back on the phone conversation he'd had with Tito when he was in Colorado and resisted the urge to drop kick him. Following dutifully, he studied the young man. Tito's hair glistened in the sun as they stepped out of the station—hat still tucked under his arm. His sideburns were shaven to a precise point halfway down the sides of his face, and a pencil-thin goatee was etched on the skin around his mouth. It looked like it took him well over an hour to get ready in the morning.

Wolf felt his own hair. It was a greasy mat that left his fingers slick. Then he pulled his hand over the sandpaper stubble on his face, and decided to take his mother's advice and not pass judgment on others.

Tito continued an animated conversation on the phone, bending to plead at the ground and standing straight to yell at the sky as he did so. It was a painfully slow march down the street, but they finally reached and stopped at his sleek Alfa Romeo carabinieri cruiser. It had a V-configuration of three cylindrical lights on top and was painted a shiny jet-black with a white stripe.

They slowed at the vehicle and Tito fished in his pocket, pulled out some keys and then clicked open the locks, all the while talking incessantly. Wolf dropped his bag on the back seat and slid onto the warm leather passenger seat. The interior was nice, equipped with what looked to be a top-of-the-line dash computer mounted in the center between the bucket seats.

Tito fired up the engine with a roar and pulled out of his parking spot with a jolt. A car screeched to a halt behind them, its driver leaning on the horn for a few seconds. Tito merely glanced in his rear-view mirror while he spoke and peeled down the street.

The leather seat creaked under Wolf as he was pulled back from the acceleration. With reflex speed, he reached for the seatbelt and put it on.

Ten minutes later, with three near collisions of which Tito seemed oblivious, and two pedestrians who were lucky to still be alive, they reached their destination. Tito, still talking to some lucky human on the other end of his phone call, clearly regarding unprofessional matters, pulled into a parking lot behind an old building and parked.

The building stood on the eastern shore of the lake. It was square and gray, four floors high, reminding Wolf of any number of communist-era buildings he'd seen throughout the world.

He stepped out of the car and pulled his bag from the back seat. A damp breeze came off the lake, smelling vaguely of fish, and the air was clearer than it had been just a few miles away, on the train. There was a line of crisscrossing sails in the distance moving at high speed—kite surfers and sailboarders.

They walked the short distance to the back of the building and entered through a thick metal door set in worn marble.

Wolf almost gagged as the spicy odor of human sweat filled his nose. He appeared to have just entered hell, or at least the waiting room for it.

People were jam-packed in a room to the right and had spilled out into the lobby he'd just entered. People inside faced front in dense lines, waiting for something that didn't seem to be coming nearly fast enough. Apparently the gatekeeper of that something was a uniformed man behind bulletproof glass who was stamping a stack of paper.

The people looked to be immigrants from places south or east of Italy, if Wolf had to guess. Many leaned up against the cracked and dirty yellow walls of the lobby, fanning themselves with stacks of paper. Next to them hung black-and-white pictures of various buildings in rubble, as if after an earthquake or an aerial shelling. An infant's muffled shriek was their soundtrack.

Welcome to Italy.

Across the vast room was another entrance with a metal detector. An armed carabinieri officer interrogated an Asian couple with a baby, while people streamed in behind them, tripping the alarm. No one of authority seemed to care about the blinking light and incessant beeping, so Wolf guessed he shouldn't either.

Directly above them was a vaulted ceiling, and, to the left, a spiral stone stairway corkscrewed to the upper levels. To his relief, Tito was already halfway up the first flight, wrapping up his phone conversation and waving to Wolf to follow.

They climbed two flights of marble stairs and entered into a large light and airy room with numerous desks and people in uniform. The windows of the great room offered an unobstructed view of the lake, and were all propped ajar, letting in the pleasant breeze, which carried mouthwatering aromas Wolf couldn't put his finger on.

Tito stopped and looked to his right. He sucked in a deep breath and pulled down his uniform jacket with both hands, as if to steel himself for what he was to do next.

Wolf followed his eyes. He was staring at a door with the words *Colonnello Marino* painted in black on the frosted glass. Someone inside the office was yelling, and the deep voice seemed to shake the door.

Tito finally stepped to it and knocked gingerly.

"Dai!" the voice boomed.

Tito poked his head in and then entered, opening the door to let Wolf in behind him. The man who was apparently Colonnello Marino had a phone up to his ear and was staring toward the windows behind his desk. He waved his hand at two chairs against the wall without looking, then yelled in rapid Italian, slamming his fist into his leg.

Tito sat and squirmed in his chair. His face was draining of blood, turning white as sweat beaded on his forehead and slid down his manicured hairline.

Marino finished his conversation and twisted in his chair. Tito flinched, and Marino held up a finger, still not resting his eyes on his new visitors. He pushed his finger on the plunger of the phone, then dialed a number and twisted to the window again.

Wolf watched Marino bounce his head, speak in pleasant tones, laugh heartily, hand gesture animatedly, and mumble niceties into the phone for another few minutes. He was beginning to wonder whether anyone spoke to one another without the aid of a telephone in this country. Wolf checked his watch, which showed 7 o'clock in the morning, Colorado time.

Eight minutes later Marino swiveled back to the phone again. The colonnello brought his non-phone hand to the ancient rotary, pressed the switch again, then dialed another number and held up a finger as he swiveled slowly toward the window.

"Excuse me," Wolf said. "I've come a long way and would like to speak to you about my brother."

Marino pulled the handset from his ear and glared at Wolf. After a moment his face broke into a sympathetic smile. "Ah, yes. Mr. Wolf. I am sorry about your brother. And I am sorry about my English. It is terrible." It *was* terrible; Wolf was having trouble making out the words.

Marino gently hung up the phone, and then launched into a hurried monologue to Tito in Italian.

In turn, Tito translated for Wolf.

"He says he is waiting for final authorization to release your brother's remains. It should be in the next two days. You will be allowed to transport his body at that time."

Marino folded his hands and leaned forward on his desk with a sympathetic expression.

"Okay, thank you," Wolf said. "I spoke with a Detective Rossi on the phone earlier in the week. As I told him, and as I'm sure you are aware, I am a sheriff's deputy in the United States ... a police officer. I do not question the carabinieri's resources or integrity. I hope you will understand my desire to learn all that I can during my short visit. I respectfully request permission to see my brother's body, review the police report, and speak to the investigating officers. And, of course, I will need access to his apartment to retrieve personal items."

Tito conveyed Wolf's request to Marino, using far fewer words and little emotional inflection.

Nonetheless, Wolf nodded as Tito spoke, watching the colonnello's reaction closely.

When Tito was finished, the colonnello smiled and lit a cigarette in a practiced flourish. He pulled a deep drag and spoke on his exhale. "Mr. Wolf. I understand your concern with your brother's death," he said in nearly unrecognizable English.

Marino placed his cigarette on the lip of his ashtray, and a smooth stream of smoke rose in front of him, undisturbed in the hot, still office.

Wolf glanced at the large window and wondered why it was shut.

"I can give you Tito for a day. He'll go with you tomorrow to see your brother." Marino nodded, picked up his rotary phone and dialed a number. He plucked his cigarette from the ashtray, swiveled to the window, and spoke into the receiver.

Clearly relieved, Tito stood and opened the office door, where he turned and waited for Wolf.

Wolf sat for a few seconds. Then he got up, walked to Colonnello Marino's desk and pressed the phone switch.

Marino looked at the handset as he processed what had just happened. Realizing Wolf had disconnected the call, Marino's gaze rose to Wolf's face, fell to Wolf's finger, and then rose again.

Wolf stood his ground, leaving his finger in place. "I need more than Tito for a day. I need to see my brother, I need to see the police report, my brother's apartment, and to speak to the officers who discovered the body," Wolf said.

Marino's face brightened to a glistening tomato red in a matter of seconds. "You don't tell me what to do!" He then snapped a quick order to Tito, who relayed the message in a loud voice to the room outside.

An instant later, two officers slammed into the office, each taking one of Wolf's arms and wrenching them back. Then one of them kicked the back of his knees, landing him hard on the tile floor. A third showed up and wrapped Wolf in a chokehold, pulling him up to his feet. Wolf fought his instincts to free himself or fight back and stared at Marino.

"You want to tell us how to investigate? American cowboy?"

Wolf could hear a group gathering in the office doorway behind him, officers shuffling to get in on the action.

"Sir," Wolf coughed, struggling to breathe. "No, sir."

Marino motioned for the officer to release his chokehold.

Wolf sucked in a breath. Though the chokehold on Wolf had been hesitant and weak by the officer behind him, Wolf made a show of how mentally and physically destroyed he was.

"Colonnello Marino," Wolf said, realizing he needed to shift tactics fast, "please help me. My mother and I need some answers about my brother's death. We need to know what really happened. I'm not saying your department conducted the investigation poorly. I am saying there is no way you could have known my brother like I did, and I know he didn't kill himself. I am only asking for some help from you and your department, and for permission to go over the case evidence."

Marino seemed to contemplate his words for a few seconds, and then he looked to the rest of the now crowded room with a grin. "Non ho capito niente!"

The room exploded in laughter.

A female voice interjected over the noise, speaking rapidly in Italian directly behind Wolf. He turned to find a young woman, a startlingly good-looking young woman, explaining something in reasonable tones, gesturing to Wolf as if he were a prisoner on display—a prisoner she looked to be arguing in defense of.

When she'd finished, Marino squashed his cigarette and lit another, looking Wolf up and down. The room was silent, as if awaiting an emperor's decree.

Marino put his cigarette into the ashtray and stood directly in front of Wolf. "Okay."

Marino looked at the other officers and waved them out of the room. He barked a long order at the woman, who had now pushed her way to standing attention next to Wolf. Her flowery scent counteracted Marino's blend of body odor and stale smoke.

She listened intently without making a sound or moving, and finally answered in a curt affirmative when the colonnello was through.

Marino turned to Wolf. "I will give you until Friday, the end of the week. We cannot spare much, uh ... help, so I will give you Officer Parente. She will assist you. Then, you must leave here after this week. Take your brother home. Comfort your mother," he said with a sympathetic look.

"Thank you, sir. I appreciate your help."

"Via! Via!" Marino swept them out of the room with a flail of his arms.

Wolf picked up his backpack and watched the dark haired officer disappear through the door. He left the office and looked around, not seeing her amid the crowd.

Tito stood near and saw Wolf's confused look, then pointed down a hallway behind him.

Wolf saw a slender backside receding briskly with the gentle sway of a dancer. A tight brown-haired ponytail bobbed back and forth between firm shoulders.

He nodded to Tito and walked after her. Before he could catch up, she turned an abrupt right and was out of sight again.

He followed fast and almost slammed into her as she picked up her hat and coat from her desk, which was right around the corner.

She huffed at Wolf's chest, which was now blocking her path, pushed past him, and retraced her steps down the hallway.

Wolf stood still, unsure what to do.

"You coming?" she said over her shoulder.

"Yep." He strode after her.

Wolf followed her down the steps, watching her take them one at a time with athletic grace, swerving between people at full speed, all the while pulling a few loose coffee-colored strands of hair behind her ear.

Outside, they walked to a replica of Tito's car, though parked in a different spot and much dirtier. She waved for him to get in, so he did, brushing aside a crumpled up napkin off the seat.

It was warm inside and smelled of perfume.

She got in and stared out of the windshield. Her eyes were aquamarine with long eyelashes. She bit her lower lip, revealing a perfect set of upper teeth. She seemed to be weighing a serious problem.

"Hey, I don't know what you said in there, but thanks," he offered.

"Yep." She fired up the engine and gunned the Alfa Romeo out of the parking lot, directly in front of a fast-moving truck.

Wolf fished for his seatbelt and put it on. "I'm David, by the way."

She kept her eyes forward. "Lia."

Wolf sighed in resignation as she ignored him, picked up her cell phone, and dialed.

CHAPTER 13

Lia hung up after a short conversation and dropped the phone in front of the stick shift.

"I have to admit, I'm glad your call was short. Tito was on the phone the entire way here from the train station," he said. "I never did get a chance to even—"

"Tito's an idiot," she said.

"Yeah ..." He looked at her expressionless stare out through the windshield. "Anyway, thanks." Wolf turned to the window and studied the long procession of pedestrians walking along the lakeshore.

Just then, she downshifted and accelerated into a traffic circle, threading in between two cars, then shot out the other side. A second later, she swerved into oncoming traffic, looked to her left at a convex mirror that was mounted on a stone wall, jammed the brakes and cranked the wheel in a sharp buttonhook right turn.

It took Wolf only a moment to realize he was riding shotgun with a gifted Formula One driver. He loosened his white-knuckle grip on the door. "Could you take me to my brother's apartment?"

"Yes. We have to meet a colleague, and then we'll go to the apartment."

"Okay, thanks. I wasn't sure. I really haven't been able to communicate with people that well so far. It's nice to know what's going on." Wolf sat in silence for a minute. "Your English is very good, hardly any accent."

"Thanks," she said with a lazy blink of her eyes.

"You're welcome," he said.

...

They parked in a cobblestone alley shadowed by ancient-looking buildings that were attached to one another, delineated with different shades of paint. Getting out, Wolf heard the thrum of people somewhere in the distance, and as they walked up a road and through an archway, Wolf saw why. They entered into a crowded football field-sized piazza. Water shot out of the ground a few feet away and small children screeched in delight as they splashed in it. Cafes with four or five rows of outdoor seating lined the entire length of the open amphitheater-like space, and old ornate-looking residential buildings were stacked five or six floors high on top of the eating establishments.

Wolf's mouth watered at the sights and aromas of crisp pizzas, forks heaped with pasta, and handfuls of French fries. He realized his stomach was empty, and he would need to be sitting down at one of these restaurants soon.

Lia stopped and Wolf stopped alongside her, watching her eyes. She had spotted a male carabinieri officer across the piazza.

The two met eyes and nodded, and Lia walked swiftly toward the man.

Just then, a cacophony of noise stirred the piazza. Four kids on motorbikes came through, gunning their tinny engines. The bikes were all similar, two-stroke dirt bikes with street tires. The 50 cc engines were un-muffled and loud, and the boys were having a good time causing unrest with each flick of their throttles, bringing each and every conversation to a halt, and drawing the resenting glares of everyone within earshot.

After a few seconds, three of them killed the motors and leaned their bikes up against a side-alley wall, while another circled back and revved hard in front of a group of people, scaring them into a frenzy of stumbles and shrieks. Wolf's stomach sank when he realized it was a group of young disabled people.

Lia slowed down and Wolf came up alongside her. She was watching the officer in the distance march with determination toward the four riders, who were now taking off their helmets and laughing. The fourth kid still sat on his bike, leaning against the wall with the engine shut off, peeling off his helmet.

He didn't see it coming.

The officer walked up and slapped his bare head, a smack that was clearly audible over the noise of the piazza. Then he ripped the kid off the bike and pushed him up against the wall. He type-writered the boy in the chest and gave him a vigorous speech that, by the looks of the kid's white expression, was one of the scariest things he'd ever heard in his life. Releasing the boy, he said something to the others, and they all pushed their bikes up the alley and out of sight. Done with that, the carabinieri officer straightened his pants, turned, and walked toward Wolf and Lia.

"That's good police work right there," Wolf said.

"Detective Valerio Rossi." He shook Wolf's hand. "We spoke on the phone. I'm sorry for your loss, Officer Wolf." His English seemed better now that they were face to face.

"Thanks. I appreciate it. Thank you for all your help so far."

"Ready?"

"Yeah," Wolf lied.

"His apartment is right here. Just off the piazza. Let's go."

Wolf followed Rossi and Lia, all the while watching them have a conversation in Italian. Lia seemed to be confiding something to him, and Rossi was shaking his head in disbelief, consoling her with a fatherly, or brotherly, pat on the back.

Wolf turned his attention from the two officers' relationship dynamic to the prospect of going to see where his brother had died. He felt more than a twinge of regret that he hadn't kept in better touch with John, hadn't made an effort to visit him more. Maybe they would have had a good time drinking a few beers in this piazza together.

Wolf followed the two officers off the piazza and up a narrow road. It was hemmed-in by old buildings that towered above, some probably dating back five hundred years. Maybe even a thousand, for all he knew.

Rossi and Lia walked to a large open courtyard and stopped. Security fencing surrounded the property—iron spikes filed to thin deadly points topping each tall iron bar. Rossi pushed the intercom button and spoke to the onsite property manager, who buzzed them in.

A short man walked out of a door and into the courtyard to meet them. He was portly, and finishing a mouthful of food as he approached them. He wiped his hands on his denim pants and held out a hand to Wolf.

"Buon giorno." He had a sullen expression.

"Hello, do you speak English?"

"Uhhh, no."

"Okay." Wolf glanced at Lia and Rossi. "Thank you for meeting us."

Lia stepped in and began translating.

"You were the one who found my brother?"

The man answered, and Lia translated.

"He and the girl, Cristina, who lives above your brother found him. The property manager, here, called the carabinieri," Lia said.

Wolf nodded. "Okay. Let's just head up."

CHAPTER 14

THE MANAGER TOOK a set of keys out of his pocket and inserted the top key into the door of apartment twenty-two. He turned it four or five complete revolutions to the left, then put a smaller key in and turned it five more times before the door popped open a crack.

The manager stepped back and let the door creak open. They all looked to Wolf, who stepped forward and entered the dim apartment.

Wolf noticed the pungent smell of lemon disinfectant. Rossi walked around Wolf and went to the small balcony off the main room, sliding open floor-to-ceiling shutter doors. Bright sunlight poured in, revealing a spacious room with high ceilings.

There was a dark wood table and four chairs, a recliner seat, television stand, small flat-screen television, two-person couch, and a couple of folding chairs along the wall. No coffee table or end tables. Black-and-white photographs hung on the walls. Frameless. They looked to be John's work, perhaps blown up at a local supermarket, or photo shop, or whatever they had here that did that kind of stuff.

"Apparently your brother went out Friday night with a

friend, came home, and the girl living above heard a noise. She said she was concerned after not seeing him all day Saturday, or Saturday night. They were supposed to have a date on Saturday night. She became concerned midday Sunday and told the manager.

"The manager came with keys and opened the door, which apparently was difficult because the keys were in the top lock from the inside. He somehow pushed them out and got it unlocked, then they found the body ... sorry, your brother."

"Did you talk to the person he was out with that night? What was his name?"

"No, we did not. I do not know his name," Rossi answered with a pained face.

"You didn't look into that?" Wolf asked.

"No, Mr. Wolf. The keys were in the lock, locked from the inside, with only your brother inside." Rossi held out his hands with an apologetic look.

There was a small hole in the ceiling with a capped wire sticking out. He glanced at the floor and noticed a scratch on the wood veneer right below the hole in the ceiling. Wolf bent down and rubbed it. "This is where the chandelier fell and hit the floor?"

"Yes," Rossi said. "He was underneath it."

Wolf had heard the story over the phone. *They walked in, found him underneath the chandelier, a leather belt around his neck still fastened to the chandelier. Drugs found at the scene.*

"Where did you find the cocaine?"

"There was a small bag here on the table," Rossi said, "and residue on his nose. We have the bag in evidence at the questura, the station, I believe you Americans would call it."

The manager said something and Lia translated. "He says he cleaned yesterday. He emptied the trash, got rid of some food, and cleaned up the debris in the main room here."

Wolf noted the shiny, clean table in the main room as he left to walk to the kitchen, which was a narrow galley with small appliances, a few small cupboards, and a little counter space. At the far end of the kitchen was a small balcony. Stove burners glistened and the countertops shined. It was perfectly clean. Classic John, Wolf thought. The manager probably hadn't had to clean too hard. His little brother had always been anal-retentive when it came to keeping his space neat.

Wolf pictured his little brother's room growing up—how the bed was always made, everything hung in just such a way on the wall, and his clothes always tucked and hung in their places in the closet. Wolf allowed himself a small smile at his brother's memory.

He walked back to the main room and out to the balcony. They were high above the piazza, looking directly down on it from three floors up. A vast section of Lake Como was in view over the rooftops. Kite surfers and wind sailors still whipped back and forth over the white-crested water. The air was fresh and crisp. *Not a bad place to live.*

Wolf walked inside and through the apartment to the bedroom in the back. It was dark like the main room had been when they came in. Wolf pulled the shutter doors open to another balcony, and sunlight blazed in, revealing a completely different breathtaking view. The opposite side of the apartment overlooked the rooftops of Lecco, jutting at all angles like frozen waves in a sea of orange-clay tiles.

One of the clay-tiled roofs butting up against the balcony extended into the distance. It looked like one could step out onto the rooftops and walk all the way across the city, if one didn't mind the thirty-plus degree slope of the first roof here. He studied it for a moment, then craned his head over and looked up to an identical balcony above.

Ducking back in, he noted that the bedroom was as sparsely

furnished as the rest of the apartment. A queen-sized mattress lay directly on the floor with no bedside tables. One reading lamp stood next to it, surrounded by a smattering of paperback books—mostly old-looking literary stuff Wolf wasn't into. A flimsy-looking wood table was tucked in the corner with an open Mac computer perched atop it, a wireless router hooked into the wall.

Wolf went to the computer, swiped his finger, and then pushed a few buttons. It was dead.

The small closet was filled halfway with hanging clothes, separated into different color schemes.

Wolf raised his voice. "The girl upstairs, what was her name? Cristina?"

"Yes." Rossi walked to the bedroom doorway.

"I'd like to go talk to her."

"Let's go."

They left John's apartment and went upstairs, found the door for Cristina and knocked. There was no answer.

"How about the apartment below his apartment? What did they say? Didn't they hear anything? The chandelier hitting the floor?"

"Nobody lives there." Rossi shrugged.

"Okay, this girl isn't home. Do you guys know where she is? Where she works?"

"I do not know," Rossi said.

Lia shook her head.

"Did you question her on Sunday?" Wolf asked.

"I talked to her," said Rossi. "I asked if she heard anything. It was apparent that she was having a tough time, and she needed support. She was very upset. We called in a person, but she had disappeared before the ... person could arrive."

"A counselor?"

"Yes, a counselor. But she left before the counselor arrived."

“Okay.” Wolf sighed heavily. “Did you ask her about the drugs?”

They walked down the stairs to the outside of John’s door.

“No. It really was not an interrogation. We were dealing with the delicate task of removing your brother’s body. Knowing what the evidence inside was presenting us, it was more a matter of comforting the girl.”

“And this neighbor?” He pointed to the only other door that was on his brother’s level. Number twenty-one.

The manager said a few sentences, and Rossi took the reins with translation. “They were gone, and have been for over a month. A lot of people go on vacation for August here, and they have been gone all of August, and all of September so far. They weren’t here.”

“Okay.” Wolf suddenly felt a little lightheaded. He needed food, and he needed sleep. Two things he would have time for later.

The manager said something to Rossi and Lia while pointing at Wolf. He held up the keys and shrugged his shoulders.

Rossi waved his hands as if declining something, then looked questioningly at Lia, who then looked skeptically at Wolf.

“What’s going on?” Wolf asked.

“He is saying you can stay here if you like. The rent is paid for the month, and he can give you the keys,” Lia said.

“Thanks, that would be perfect.” Wolf took the keys from the manager’s outstretched hand. “What is your name?”

“Giuseppe.”

“David. Thank you. Grazie.”

The manager showed Wolf the different keys for the outside gate and door locks, then left. They all looked at their watches. It was 5:38 p.m. local time.

"Is it too late to go see my brother?" Wolf asked, ignoring his urge to collapse on the mattress in his brother's room.

"I have to leave for other commitments," Rossi said, looking at his watch.

Lia nodded. "The morgue is open twenty-four hours. We can go right now."

CHAPTER 15

Wolf sat in silence on the way over to the morgue. Glancing at his watch, he did a quick calculation. He'd been up since midnight Colorado time when the plane landed at 8 a.m. in Italy, with just a few hours sleep before that on the plane. So what did that mean? It meant he was tired as hell.

"I'm sorry I was so angry earlier," Lia said, looking at Wolf. Her tanned olive skin coupled with her luminous eyes in the evening sunlight was startling to him, and he wasn't easy to startle. He unconsciously rubbed his face, noting the long stubble—way past a five o'clock shadow.

"No problem. I would have been pissed too," he said.

She shot him a suspicious look.

"I couldn't tell if your boss was just a terrible English speaker, or a terrible bigot. I take it he's a terrible bigot. 'We have important work to do and can't spare anyone of importance, so I'll give you Lia for two days,' is, I believe, the gist of what he said. Yeah, that would piss me off too."

She gave him an unreadable look and resumed driving.

"I know that what your boss thinks is important to you, and you think that he thinks he's put you on an unimportant case.

Maybe that pisses you off; I'd be pretty angry, too. But, the thing is, my brother didn't kill himself. I'm one hundred percent sure of that. So that leaves only one explanation. He was murdered."

They drove in silence for a few minutes. In his peripheral vision, he could see Lia glancing at him.

"I was really sweating being paired up with Tito there for a minute," he said, breaking the silence. "So thanks again."

"Yeah, like I said, Tito's a dumbass." She laughed and smiled. "You would've been pretty screwed with him."

It was the first time he'd seen her smile. *She was beautiful.*

...

The morgue was another building that looked straight out of the Mussolini era—square, gray concrete, and non-descript. It was in sharp contrast with the rest of the city, which was full of statues, elegant curved lines, and natural stone. Lia pushed a button on a state-of-the-art electronic keypad next to the heavy steel door.

"Si?" said a tinny male voice.

"Siamo noi."

Buzz. Click.

"Ciao," a voice said from a doorway down the hall. A bald man, looking over pushed-down glasses, peeked his head out of a doorway and waved at them to come.

They walked down the hall to where he was. The room was cold and smelled of formaldehyde, just like any other morgue room Wolf had been in. Two rows of four refrigeration units lined the far wall. The lower right-most one was pulled out, displaying a sheeted lump of a figure. *His brother.*

His heart skipped and his breath caught as he looked down; then he turned to shake the hand of the pathologist.

"Ciao. I am Vittorio." The pathologist blinked rapidly behind thick glasses while stretching his neck muscles as if his collar was itchy.

Vittorio and Lia had a brief exchange in Italian, Vittorio speaking quietly and rapidly with intelligent eyes that never looked in Wolf's direction. Then the man left the room quickly, and Wolf turned to the pulled-out refrigeration unit.

Suddenly, he was anxious to get everything over with, but he knew he should probably wait for the pathologist to return before looking at his brother. Besides, Wolf realized, he wasn't in that much of a hurry to look at his brother's face, a face he hadn't seen in real life for over five months, other than in tiny pictures on a blog.

Lia stood beside Wolf, put a hand on his shoulder, and gave a gentle squeeze.

"Sorry." Vittorio moved swiftly into the room. "I have the records all here now." His accent was vaguely British. "Are you ready, Mr. Wolf?"

He wasn't. "Yeah, go ahead."

The sheet was pulled back in a well-executed, not-too-slow/not-too-fast technique, revealing his brother beneath.

John's skin was a bluish white, and he wore a peaceful sleeping expression on his face. His hair had been closely cropped, and a large straight-line bruise was on the right side of his head, angling from the top of the forehead to his ear. There was a deep black bruise lining the circumference of his neck, indicating where the belt had been wrapped around his throat.

"Why was no autopsy ordered?" Wolf asked, keeping his eyes fixed on his brother's lifeless face.

"We determined the external evidence on the body to be consistent with suicide," Vittorio said quietly. "And we normally do not perform an autopsy for a suicide, unless ordered by the coroner in collaboration with officers on the scene."

"How do you explain the bruise on his head?" Wolf asked.

"We determined the bruise was ante mortem ... how you say?"

"Sure, ante mortem."

"Bruising from the chandelier falling on his head," Vittorio said.

"Okay." Wolf shook his head. "So how did he die? Are you saying he died from the hanging, then the chandelier fell on his head, causing a bruise?" Wolf looked skeptical. "Once the heart has stopped beating, isn't it impossible to bruise?"

"It is actually entirely possible to bruise shortly after death. If he died while hanging, then shortly thereafter the chandelier gave way and fell on him, it could have bruised his head. There was also pooling of blood on the left side of his body, as you can see by the bruising, consistent with the position he was found in underneath the chandelier."

"What was the evidence of drug use?"

Vittorio produced some photos from the file. "Since we didn't do an autopsy, we did not do a complete toxicology report. But I did an exterior exam, and found residue on his nose that was confirmed to be cocaine. I have some photos of your brother's body at the scene."

Wolf took the photos and looked. There were close-ups of John from every angle. He was covered in small glittering slivers of glass, apparently from the chandelier.

"You can see, there, a bar on the chandelier lines up with the bruise on his head." Vittorio dug for another photo and pointed at the wooden chair that was tipped over, five feet from John's dead form. "I am not completely sure, but I feel the chair was kicked out from under him with a spasm, which could have begun the process of the chandelier falling." He flipped to another photo. "And here is a close-up of his right nostril, with cocaine residue."

Wolf smiled humorlessly. "You don't think this is grounds for ordering an autopsy? At best, we have a manufactured manner of death, as if you made up the story first and then pieced together evidence to support it. What if the bruise was caused by someone else?"

The pathologist looked at Wolf with a look that said it all. "It is not my decision, but, in my opinion, I think it could have gone either way, the decision for an autopsy, that is. But we have other pressures here, Mr. Wolf. Your brother was not a resident here, and the comune pays for the autopsy—"

"The comune?" Wolf asked.

"Yes, the municipality, I think you say?"

"Okay, I get it. You guys looked at the whole scene with worry about money?" Wolf shook his head in disbelief, but also knew the same thing could happen in Rocky Points if a foreigner died from an apparent suicide.

Vittorio offered a solemn expression in response.

Wolf took a deep breath and silently studied the pictures. John was wearing jeans and a long-sleeved button-up shirt. The jeans had small stains on each leg. Like oval mud stains.

"Do you have the clothing he was wearing?" Wolf asked.

"Yes, I do. I will go get his belongings."

Vittorio gently placed the sheet back over John's face, again with a well-executed touch, and left the room. Wolf stood up and paced in thought.

Lia stood in silence.

Vittorio returned with a sealed large plastic bag and put it on a steel table against the wall, motioning to Wolf to go ahead and look. He took the bag and began laying the contents out on the table. Vittorio and Lia had a quiet conversation in Italian, walking to the other side of the room.

Wolf dug in the bag for John's jeans first. Pulling them out, he looked at the knees. There were two large, faint circles, as if he'd been kneeling in wet, muddy grass. Next he pulled out a pair of black Puma low-top canvas shoes. The bottom sole pattern held a bit of mud, and the canvas was streaked light gray with the same.

Two belts were in the bag—one would have been used for the hanging and John would have been wearing the other one, Wolf guessed. He took another look at a picture and saw that the black belt was the one John had been wearing, and the light-brown leather belt had been around his neck. Wolf took the light-brown belt over to John's body, and motioned for Vittorio to pull back the sheet again. Wolf ignored Vittorio's show of being insulted. The belt was the same width as the marks on John's neck. Wolf felt a faint shudder as he realized he was holding a murder weapon.

He returned to the table and rifled through his brother's pants pockets. Nothing, but he took his brother's wallet out and looked through it, pulling out the driver's license and finding a dated receipt from a pub tucked in the main pocket; it puzzled him for a second, until he realized the different way Europeans wrote dates *day, month, year*. It was from Friday night. The last night his brother was alive.

His iPhone was in the bag as well, but the battery was dead.

Wolf stood straight and felt lightheaded. With a crash, he stumbled into the table and bent over, breathing deeply a few times to stop himself passing out.

Lia and Vittorio rushed over and patted his back.

"Should we go? You need to rest after such a long day," Lia said.

"Sure. Can I take these belongings with me?" Wolf asked.

"They must be released with your brother's body as soon as

the paperwork is finished." Vittorio scooped his brother's cell phone off the table and placed it in the clear bag.

After a few more minutes, Wolf and Lia thanked the pathologist and they left.

"They don't do many autopsies here in Italy?" Wolf stared out the car window at the tall mountains surrounding the city, now black against the glowing orange sky.

"If determined it is needed, then they will order the autopsy."

"Do you think there should have been an autopsy?"

She fidgeted uncomfortably, then shifted the car. "I don't know. It looks pretty cut and dry. Italians don't do well with complications. If the shoe fits, they put it," she said. *They poot eet.*

"Wear it. And it's cut and dried."

"What?"

"Never mind."

They sat in silence for a few moments as she drove.

"Look, I guess I'll go sleep. I am dying here." Wolf pressed his hand against his eyes. "Are you still with me tomorrow?"

"Yes, I will help you until the end of the week."

He looked at his watch. It was 6:54 p.m., Wednesday night. That gave him two days. *No pressure.*

CHAPTER 16

Wolf dug into his backpack, filled the inside of his lip with a pinch of snuff, fetched a plastic cup spittoon from his brother's kitchen, and plopped down on the couch with a grunt. He pulled off his shoes. His entire body ached from a long, long day, and then ached some more from the cliff-top fight with Connell. When had that been?

Shit. His mom. She would be worried sick, and he still didn't have a SIM card for his phone. He thought of the laptop in John's room and walked to get it. Thankfully it was already hooked to an electrical adaptor for Italian plugs, something that hadn't crossed his mind until that moment.

He plugged it in, switched on the computer and rubbed his eyes when he was presented with a login screen.

He typed in *B-e-r-n-i-e.* The name of their first dog. Nothing.

That was the extent of his hacking skills, especially in his current state of mind. He left the computer to recharge and returned to the main room, feeling thoroughly dejected.

He burrowed deep into the couch, settling his gaze on the hole in the ceiling, then to the second chandelier that was still hanging in the room. He put down the spittoon and pulled a chair underneath it. Reaching high up the center of the brass chandelier trunk, he grabbed it and pulled down with his right arm. Then harder when nothing happened. Then harder still.

Finally, he straightened his arm and sagged down, putting the entirety of his weight on it. With a crack, it jolted free from the ceiling, sending him in a sudden free fall. The chair sputtered sideways from underneath his feet, and he landed hard on his side, instinctually pointing his shins and forearms upward to block himself from a plummeting light fixture of yet undetermined weight. When nothing hit him, he rolled on the ground to get out from under it. Only then did he finally steal a look upward.

The light fixture swayed violently from side to side, hanging by two wires. A fleck of white plaster landed on the floor.

Just then he heard a soft knock on the door. He took stock of his injuries as he struggled to his feet. He'd have some bruises in the morning, but otherwise there was no damage.

He opened the front door, which revealed the second strikingly beautiful young woman of the day. She stood outside with wide, timid, chocolate eyes and a puzzled expression. She had brownish blond hair, chiseled facial features, and a slender athletic body. Her scent was flowery, all femininity, and she was dressed in a skimpy white T-shirt, flannel pants and slippers. She asked something unintelligible, and Wolf gave a confused stare in response.

"Who are you?" she tried in English.

"I'm David Wolf. Who are you?"

"I'm Cristina. I live upstairs."

"Oh, I came to your apartment today ... you weren't there. I'm John's brother. I was hoping to talk to you."

"Are you okay? I just heard a loud noise." She was excited, looking behind Wolf at the still rocking chandelier.

She didn't speak English in an Italian accent. She spoke well, but not like Lia. It sounded Eastern European.

"Yes, I'm fine," Wolf said. "Listen, will you come in? I'd really like to speak to you."

She backed up a few feet with a look of horror.

"Uhh, sorry. Here, I'll show you my passport." He hurried to his backpack leaning up against the wall, pulled out his passport, and brought it back to her.

"No, I can see that you're John's brother. You look just like him. I just don't want to come in there. You can come up and talk if you want." She turned and padded up the stairs.

"Okay, I'll be right up."

...

Her apartment was in stark contrast with John's. While he went with the interior design of a minimalist, six-month stay, one stop at Ikea, whatever you can pack in a suitcase look, she was all about decoration and permanence. Every square inch on the wall was meticulously decorated in a way that took a lot of thought and creativity—pictures of her, her family, and landscapes from exotic forests in countries he'd never seen; flowers on shelves; hanging dried flowers; rows of bookshelves; and a myriad of other collectibles. The volume of knickknacks reminded him of the pub in Rocky Points, though nothing could match the pub's gaudy interior-of-a-ski bar décor.

Ambient jazz was playing softly in the background, and he recognized it as Pat Metheny. A few candles were lit, filling the apartment with a flowery aroma.

She offered him a seat on a comfortable chair, and bent down to close what looked to be a journal she'd been writing in.

He sat, eyeing the patterned blanket draped on the back of the chair. It was reminiscent of Navajo designs he'd seen countless times in his grandmother's house, but with more vibrant colors and flowers lining the edges.

She saw him looking at it. "It's a traditional weaving from my home. I am from Romania."

"Oh, okay." He struggled to picture where exactly that was.

"It's directly east of here. You travel to Venice and keep going east, through Slovenia, Hungary, and into Romania," she said, apparently reading his mind.

"Ah, I see." A deep silence fell between them. "Were you dating my brother?"

She stared at her hands folded in her lap and began to shake. The beginning throes of a good cry, he recognized from recent experience.

"Y-yes. We have been seeing each other for a few months." Her hair drooped across her eyes. "Had been seeing ..." she corrected herself. She lifted her chin and her face brightened with a smile. "We met on our balconies. He was sitting there on the computer, and I accidentally threw a cigarette on him because of the wind." She burst into laughter.

Wolf couldn't help but laugh with her.

"I heard him shuffling and grunting, and he poked his head out to yell at me. Then he forced me to go out with him as payment for ruining one of his shirts. It was a piece of crap T-shirt." She smiled and laughed, then broke into another fit of crying.

He looked away and steeled his gaze on nothing in particular. They sat in heavy silence for a few seconds as the music changed tracks.

"I have a few questions," he said finally. "Firstly, do you think he killed himself?"

"You don't think he did?" She looked at him with wet, wide eyes.

"No, I don't. I just don't think he was that type of person, and ... there's just something going on."

"I have been thinking all along there is no way that he would do that. But then I kept thinking maybe I didn't know him that well anyway, so then I wasn't sure. I've been so confused." She looked back at her hands.

"Well, I don't think he did," he said. "Do you do drugs, Cristina? Did you and John do drugs together? Just tell me. I don't care either way. I just need to know."

"No," she said quickly. "We don't do drugs ... didn't do drugs. Not even pot. We talked about how it made us both paranoid, so that's why we didn't like it. Why are you asking?"

He studied her reaction, her eyes. He believed her. A woman trying to hide her drug use was something he was intimately familiar with, something he'd learned to read on a woman's face just as plainly as a track in fresh mud.

"Because there was cocaine found on the table in the living room, and in his nose."

She looked genuinely surprised. "I never knew him to take drugs. He and I never did. We would drink wine, and he would maybe have a cigarette with me every once and a while ... but that's it."

"Do you know anything about the night he died? That Friday night? What was he doing? Who was he with?"

"He was supposed to go out with a friend," she said. "His astronomer friend, who works at an observatory."

"What's his name?"

"Matthew. Matthew Rosenwald."

"Okay," Wolf said leaning forward, feeling a jolt of energy. "Where is that observatory? What's it called?"

"It's in a town just south of here. In Merate. It's just called the Merate Observatory, I think, or the Osservatorio di Merate, I guess it would be named in Italian."

"Do you have Matthew's phone number?"

She shook her head. "No, I don't."

"Have you heard from him at all?"

"No."

"Okay. How about what he was doing with Matthew that night, do you know that? Did he tell you about it?"

"He said they were just going out for a few drinks. They usually went out about once a week together. Matthew's from Australia, and they met through a friend of mine. They kind of hit it off because they could speak English together, and they both like to drink beer." She laughed.

He pulled a slip of paper from his pocket. "Do you know this bar?"

She looked at the receipt for the Albastru Pub. "Yes. It is actually a Romanian bar."

"Have you been there?"

"Once with John." She sucked in a breath. "And, actually, Matthew was there too."

Wolf's thoughts were burning through the fog of jet lag, and he felt excited to have a good direction to take the next day.

He put the receipt back in his pocket. "The carabinieri said you heard something downstairs that Friday night."

"I did. I heard a crash and went downstairs and knocked on his door. But it was dark underneath his door, and it was locked. I just started to think I probably heard something else, outside, or from across the hall, or something. I just went back upstairs and went to sleep." She seemed to be staring back in time, shaking her head at the horrific thought.

"When was that?" Wolf asked gently.

"It was 1:15 in the morning. I remember looking at the clock when I heard the crash."

"There's nothing you could have done," he whispered.

She nodded her head, staring at her hands again.

"So you talked to the carabinieri the next day?"

"Ummm ... no. I talked to them on Sunday. When he didn't call me, or respond to my texts, or answer his door all day Saturday, I started getting worried."

"Oh, yeah, okay. Sunday." He rubbed his temples. His mind was struggling to keep details straight. His body demanded sleep. "What did you tell the carabinieri?"

She looked to the ceiling. "Not that much. One guy was just asking if I saw or heard anything that night. I just told him what I heard, and how I came down and knocked. I told them how he didn't answer my calls, or my knocking, and how he stood me up for our date, and that's why I was concerned. Then ... well, that was pretty much it. A couple of officers were just waiting outside my door. They said they had a special counselor coming for me to talk to. I didn't want to wait around to speak to some government worker who doesn't know me, or didn't know John. I just walked out."

"Yeah, I understand. I don't blame you," he said. "Did they ask about drugs?"

She looked confused. "No, not at all. I didn't know about the drugs until just now."

A warm blanket of exhaustion wrapped around Wolf again. He'd had enough. His body needed rest. There was no use fighting it anymore.

"Are you going to be around in the next couple of days?"

"I have to work during the daytimes, but I am usually home at night."

"All right. I may need some help with some things over the next two days, and maybe this weekend." He thought once again about the Friday deadline Marino had given for Lia's assistance.

"Let me know. I'll be glad to help."

"Thanks."

He let himself out and walked back down the marble stairs to his brother's silent apartment, trying not to think about the ghost of his brother as he went.

CHAPTER 17

Wolf picked up his backpack and went into his brother's room, ready to finally succumb to the exhaustion. Putting down the bag, he pulled the comforter back, surprised to see there were no sheets on the bed. He found a set on a shelf in the bathroom closet, but there were no pillowcases.

Looking in John's bedroom closet bore no fruit. Wolf stood, shaking his head and marveling at the anal-retentive organization. The assortment of clothing was meticulously separated into dark and light segments, coats in a separate section still. John had set out six pairs of shoes in a straight line along the closet wall floor, ordered from darkest to lightest. A cheap, hanging plastic rack housed belts and ties along the right side, and a robe hung from a hook on the other side. But no pillowcases, so he decided he would live without one.

As he spread out the clean bottom sheet over the mattress, Wolf stopped with a jolt. He went back to the closet and pulled the clothes over to get an unobstructed view of the belt and tie rack.

There were four belts, an empty space, and then four ties. A perfect spot to put the belt John had been wearing the night he'd died. *So where was the space for the belt he'd hanged himself with?*

CHAPTER 18

Wolf had been up for four hours when Lia picked him up at 8 a.m. Despite his exhaustion the night before, his jet-lagged body had rebelled against sleep in the early-morning.

They met outside the apartment-building gate and headed into the piazza, where Lia said she had parked.

She shot a couple of appraising glances at Wolf as they walked. "You look better this morning."

He had shaved, showered, shampooed the grease mat that was his thick dark-brown hair, and put on some fresh clothes. He *felt* better. Wolf looked at her and smiled. "Thanks."

He'd always been confident in his good looks. The old adage, or whatever it was, of tall, dark, and handsome applied to him. He was six-foot-three, taller than most men he came into contact with, had spiky dark-brown hair, a complexion that tanned if the light bulbs were too bright, dark walnut eyes, thick eyebrows, and a mole on his upper right cheek that women in his life had often referred to as a beauty mark ... not that he considered himself a heart throb, but he wasn't an idiot either.

He stole a glance at Lia. She was walking fast with her chin up, chest out, and slender athletic body bouncing lightly on her feet. She wore the same tight ponytail, swaying underneath the back of her carabinieri cap. She looked the same as she ever had to Wolf.

"You look nice this morning too," he said, meaning to sound nonchalant. It was impossible to do so with such an understatement. He caught a whiff of her lavender scent and cleared his throat, snapping to his senses. "I talked to John's girlfriend last night; she was home."

"And?"

"She had the name of the guy he was with the night before. I'd like to go talk to him. His name is Matthew Rosenwald and he works at the Merate Observatory. Do you know where that is?"

"Yes, I do. I've been there a few times. For high school ... I was in Liceo Scientifico."

"What does that mean?"

"In Italy, you choose your vocation early in life, and go to school for it. Or you choose the ... how would you call it ... the track."

"The major? Like in college?"

"Well," she said, "it's much earlier. It starts in high school. But I guess it is kind of like a major for college. Anyway, I was Scientifico. We studied natural sciences and I went there a couple of times for astronomy."

"Great," he said. "But we also have to go back to the morgue. And I want to do that first."

She gave him a puzzled look as they climbed in the Alfa Romeo cruiser. "Why?"

"I have to see the belt he hanged himself with again."

He explained what he'd seen in the closet the night before.

"Okay," Lia said. "Definitely sounds interesting. Do you want to get a coffee before we go over?"

"Yes. I've been thinking about coffee since I woke up four hours ago."

They pulled up to a bustling "Bar," as it was called on the sign, and Wolf followed Lia inside. A herd of people were standing up against a long elbow-height counter, packed three-people deep, barking fast orders to the two men behind the counter. Lia expertly wove her way to the front of the crowd and made eye contact with one of the baristas.

"What do you want?" Lia yelled back at Wolf.

"Just a ... I'll have what you're having."

She whipped her head toward the barista. "Due caffè e due brioche alla marmellata."

A few seconds later, a thimble of coffee and a jam-filled croissant were pushed in front of him. He took a large bite of the croissant and a small sip of the coffee.

"Buona?" She nodded at Wolf.

"Uh, si."

He felt the glares of people waiting behind him for the countertop real estate he and Lia were occupying. He shoved the rest of the croissant in his mouth and downed the coffee with two hearty sips. She followed his actions, slapped down her cup, went to the unoccupied cash register, laid down some coins and threaded her way out the door. He followed her, wondering what the hell had just happened.

"Good Lord. Felt like my first time all over again," he mumbled to himself.

"What?"

"Nothing."

They continued walking for another few seconds.

She turned with squinted eyes. "Are you saying that was like your first time having sex?"

"What? Uh ... yeah. That's what I meant."

She looked down and resumed walking. "So, your first time was that crowded? I don't understand."

"No, more like standing, uncomfortable, and over before I knew what had happened." He looked into the distance at nothing in particular. "Never mind. I ... regret what I just said now."

She burst into a high-pitched natural laugh that magnified his caffeine buzz.

Lia drove at speed through the tight streets and swirling traffic circles, keeping both hands on the wheel when she wasn't expertly shifting.

"So, how the heck do you speak such perfect English?" Wolf asked, trying once again to sound nonchalant as she swerved into the oncoming traffic lane and blew past a long truck.

She laughed. "My mother is from New York. She spoke only English to me and my brothers when we were kids. It just comes second nature to me. And I went for two years of college in North Carolina ... Wake Forest."

"Aha. Okay, that explains it ... And you and Valerio?" He braced himself as she dove full speed into another traffic circle. "You seem like close friends."

"Yes. Valerio is kind of like a brother to me. Our families have always been close. I have three older brothers, and he has a brother, and they were all friends growing up."

"Wow. Three brothers? Older brothers? That must have been rough."

"You could say that," she said with a smirk. Then her expression turned serious. "I had to fight for independence from my brothers. Two of them were overly protective of me. I hated it. I didn't need the protection."

She paused, glanced to the right, and then cranked the

wheel left. This caused Wolf to look to his left so hard it was more a convulsion, before realizing she was using another convex mirror.

She looked at him and laughed softly. "I fought and gained the respect I deserved from my brothers."

They rode in silence for a minute.

"So, you feel this job ... the colonnello ... you aren't getting the respect or the chances you deserve?"

She glared out the windshield. "Yeah. Something like that. Valerio was a friend of the family. He grew up with us. He knows I can handle myself. He knows I'm better than what they think. And I know it's also a matter of paying your dues. But the dues are much more expensive for a woman in Italy."

Wolf nodded and looked out the window as they drove along the lakeshore. Waves glistened in the sun like crystals.

"What do your brothers do? They cops too?"

"Ehh," she exhaled. "Let's see, one is a lawyer in Roma, one is a carabiniere in Bergamo, and one is Guardia di Finanza."

"What's Guardia di Finanza? Finance guards?"

"Yes. They are part of the military, kind of like the carabinieri. They patrol the territorial waters of Italy. Working against smuggling, illegal immigration, that type of thing. Among a lot of other duties. Valerio's little brother is also in the Guardia."

Wolf nodded.

"Luca," she said with a fond smile.

"What's that?"

"Sorry. Luca is my brother in the Guardia. I am most close to him." She blushed and looked at Wolf, a tinge of regret in her eyes, as if she had just realized she was flaunting a toy that he didn't have.

She was, but he knew she didn't mean anything by it. They drove on in silence.

CHAPTER 19

Wolf and Lia were buzzed into the morgue, this time by a female voice. He met the morning pathologist on duty, Bianca. Lia explained the situation, and Bianca left briefly, returning with the bag from the night before.

Wolf brought the bag into the room where his brother lay, and set it down on the steel table. Lia followed close behind, intrigued. He removed both belts and laid them side-by-side on the table. The brown belt that had been found around John's neck was noticeably longer. The holes still lined up, but the wear marks were at least five inches apart.

"This brown belt isn't John's. It's from someone with a waist band that is at least five inches bigger."

"Yeah, but couldn't the belt have stretched from him hanging on it?"

Wolf looked closely at the leather. "It's not stretched at all," he said. "There's a thread pattern on the edges that would be broken with significant stretching. There's not one broken thread."

"Okay, so what are you saying?"

"I'm saying that my brother was found on the floor of his

apartment. Not hanging from the ceiling. The chandelier couldn't hold his weight—there was irrefutable evidence of that. So you tell me which is more likely.

"One, he borrowed someone else's belt, or stole it for the purpose of killing himself, did some cocaine, then hanged himself with the belt. He hangs there until he is almost dead, kicks the chair out during a convulsion, which sets off a slow drop of the chandelier. But a perfectly timed drop, mind you, because the hanging has to *kill* him. Otherwise he would have just gotten up later with a bad bruise on his head. So, the chandelier stays hanging, *just* until he dies. Then it falls within a time frame brief enough that he's still bruised after death. Because, like the pathologist said last night, bruising can occur for only a short period after death.

"Or, scenario two, someone strangles him with the belt, probably in a fit of rage. In an effort to cover it up, he strings him up, or, rather, *they* string him up to the chandelier."

"They?" Lia asked.

"There's no way one man could hold a another's dead weight and string the belt from the chandelier at the same time. There had to have been two people. So, they are trying to cover up the murder with a hanging. They string him up, and all goes wrong when the chandelier won't hold him. He drops. The chandelier drops. It makes a loud noise, and they freak out. They lock the door and turn out the lights. Cristina said she went downstairs and saw that the lights were off underneath the door. John wouldn't have hanged himself in the dark. That wouldn't have made sense." Wolf saw everything lining up in front of him. "And the door was locked from the inside, keys still in the top lock. So whoever killed my brother had to have still been in there. They probably freaked out after the loud crash ... probably didn't want to go out the front door in case the neighbors came knocking to see what had happened. So they turned off the lights and sat quiet. Then they heard the knock at the door. They knew they had to leave some other way, like out John's balcony and along the rooftop next door. They couldn't have left from the front door because, like you guys said, the door was locked, and his keys were pushed out of the door by the manager when you guys went in."

Lia was staring at him with raised eyebrows.

He caught her expression and stopped talking.

She looked down at the floor, then back up at Wolf. "I think that there was another man's belt found around his neck." Her voice was soft and controlled. "I believe *that*."

"Good," Wolf said. "And how do you explain it? How does he have a heavier man's belt around his neck?"

She looked at him. "I don't know."

Wolf stared wide-eyed at the floor, envisioning the night with perfect clarity. Doubt stabbed his mind, and the story he'd constructed began to waver and swirl apart. "We need to go talk to an astronomer." He walked out of the room.

...

Lia kept silent for the twenty-minute journey south, allowing Wolf to shuffle the thoughts in his brain.

He stared out the window with an unblinking gaze. In his mind he was there the night of John's death, one minute seeing exactly how he was killed, the next not so sure. What had really happened? Was it conceivable that John had killed himself? Had he given up on life? *He waits to become a mega successful blogger and author, only to end it all after snorting a bit of cocaine?*

What if he actually *had* given up on life? Maybe his

apparent successes to the outsider's point of view were actually a hollow reminder to John of something he didn't have in his life. What the hell that could have been, Wolf had no idea.

Wolf thought about a bitter Colorado mountain winter day in middle school when the school bully, Billy Tranchen, and his three buddies stole John's winter hat. John had slogged all the way home on foot that day, come into the house, grabbed a hat, gone to Billy's, knocked on the door, asked for Billy, and beaten the crap out of him right there in front of his own mother. Then he'd taken back the hat and left.

Wolf had marveled at that story in the years to come, and had never spoken about it with John, but for one time. John told him, "The guy had it coming." And that was that. John Wolf was a tough, stubborn, hard-nosed son of a bitch, just like himself, and just like their dad.

"Look, David," Lia said, "I am sorry. I know it must be so difficult. I can't imagine having to go through this with one of my brothers. If you say he didn't kill himself and didn't do drugs, and he was murdered ... then I believe you. But, we must have some indisputable evidence to change the minds of those who have already opened and shut this case."

He nodded. "Let's just go talk to this Matthew guy and see what we can find out."

CHAPTER 20

The Merate Observatory was three buildings and two telescope domes sitting on a small hill. Tall spindly pines and an iron fence topped with Roman spearheads lined the entire perimeter, which looked to be about five or six acres in area. Dense foliage of all types filled in the property surrounding the structures within.

The European Union and Italian flags hung limply from the pole next to the wrought-iron gate. Lia jerked off the main road in front of a slowly approaching truck and leaned out the window to push the button in one move. A small sign read "Osservatorio Astronomico di Merate — European Astronomical Society."

"Chi è?" A male voice crackled through the speaker.

"Carabinieri. Possiamo parlare per un minuto con il direttore dell'osservatorio?"

"Si, ehh, parla inglese?"

"Yes, I do," Lia answered.

"Please pull up to the guest parking lot, and I will meet you outside," said the metallic sounding voice in a well-mannered English accent.

Two lights flashed yellow as the gate swung jerkily open to the inside. Lia waited patiently, then shot through with precise timing to miss the side-view mirrors with an inch to spare.

They parked and got out. Wolf had been studying the foliage of the area, and could only come to the conclusion that nature looked confused. There were palm trees, pine trees with long drooping limbs, stiff spiked trees with red flowers that looked like fruit, large-leaved prehistoric looking bushes, pine trees you might see in Colorado, and a variety of exotic-looking foliage he'd never seen. The lawn was lush green, full of grasses and thick-stemmed wild flowers with tiny yellow and blue blossoms, and at least a foot tall. One thing was certain—this area got a lot of rain.

The surrounding area seemed densely populated—cornfields lined with dense pockets of apartment buildings and villas of all sizes, much like the part of northern Italy he'd seen so far. Definitely not the best location for observing stars.

A tall, lanky man with thick glasses approached with clicking shoes. He was disheveled looking—pants too tight, too high, and one side of his collared golf shirt tucked in. It looked like he'd just finished using the bathroom and re-dressed in haste.

Wolf hoped that wasn't the case as they shook hands.

"Hello, I'm Stephen Wembly," he said with precise Queen's English and a squint-eyed smile. "I'm the director of the observatory. What may I have the honor of helping you with today?"

Lia stepped forward and offered her hand. "Hello. We are looking for an astronomer, Matthew Rosenwald, who we understand works here."

"Oh, yes. Well, he isn't here. I haven't seen him all week."

"Do you mean he hasn't been to work all week?" Wolf asked. "Or that you just work at different times?"

"I mean he hasn't been in at all." Deep lines formed on

Wembly's forehead. "Quite frankly, I was wondering if something dreadful had occurred ... *has* something ... dreadful occurred? Oh my. Is that why you're here?"

"We just want to talk with him," Lia said.

"Well, we can go inside and I could get his phone number for you if you like?" Wembly said. "He hasn't been answering for me."

...

"This is the Zeiss one-meter telescope, installed in 1926." They entered the large dome-ceilinged room. "Light pollution for this area is considerable nowadays, but the telescope is still used for University of Milan students on clear nights. Otherwise the observatory complex is now a leader in X-ray optics development, and ground-based gamma-ray astronomy."

The telescope was painted off white and lime green, the paint scheme of a 1950s Colorado house.

Wembly stood beaming at the telescope for a few seconds, then seemed to snap out of his tour-guide mode. "Ah, yes, sorry. This way please. I need to get my mobile from my office."

They followed closely behind Wembly. Outside of the main telescope dome room, the rest of the building was not large by any means. Wolf counted five offices through the hall, some with open doors, and all with nametags that read like an international phone book. *Chang. Izhutin. Rosenwald. Egger. Vlad.* Wembly had an office at the end of the hall and around a corner. Wolf looked over his shoulder as they walked onward. There looked to be a similar wing in the opposite direction.

Lia got the number from Wembly and called Matthew Rosenwald.

"Dr. Rosenwald is our one and only representative from the southern hemisphere here at the observatory," Wembly told Wolf, rocking on his heels.

Wolf heard movement from the *Vlad* office and glanced in that direction. The scientist was kicking the rubber doorstop with his heel, trying to shut his door.

Lia pointed to her phone with the universal *No luck happening with this call* facial expression, and Wembly read it.

"Vlad! These two are looking for Dr. Rosenwald. I was telling them about how he hasn't shown up in the last few days." Wembly turned to Wolf. "This is Dr. Vlad. He knows Dr. Rosenwald on a more personal basis."

"Uhh, yes, I do not know where he is." Vlad's voice was raspy, like he hadn't used it in a day or two. He cleared his throat for a few seconds.

Vlad was a short, large, and sweaty individual. His jet-black facial hair was sporadic, denser on the neck, and he had not shaved recently. Whether or not he had showered within the last week was a toss-up. His dark-gray shirt had darker still finger-sized grease stains, the result of eating potato chips from the bag splayed open on his desk. Four haphazardly placed and partially crushed Coke Lite cans cluttered the desktop. He wore dirty jeans and flip-flops. A hand wasn't offered as introduction, and Wolf thanked God for that.

"Have you talked to him this week at all?" Wolf asked.

"No, I have not," he said as he shook his head.

His accent was Eastern European, sounding similar to Cristina's, John's girlfriend he'd met the night before.

Vlad's shifty eyes darted between Wolf's clothing, the wall behind him, and Director Wembly. "I have not spoken to him all week." His glance rested on Wolf's eyes for a split second before jumping to the wall behind him again.

"So, you know Dr. Rosenwald on a personal basis? Do you guys spend a lot of time with each other?"

"We have gone to have a beer or two after work a few times before," said Vlad.

"Have you met my brother before? His name is John Wolf."

"Oh yes, I have." Vlad's voice was suddenly quiet.

"How did you meet him?"

"I believe he has, eh, come out with Matthew with us for a beer after work a time or two." Vlad's forehead was glistening with sweat. "Why do you ask?"

"I'm asking because my brother was killed this weekend, and I'm looking to Matthew for some answers."

Vlad's eyebrows shot up. "Oh, that's terrible. I ..."

Wolf waited. "You what?"

"I, I ... that's terrible. What happened?" He looked Wolf in the eye, then wiped his forehead with the palm of his hand.

"He was killed in his apartment, and someone is trying to make it look like suicide."

"Oh, wow ..." Vlad looked down, shaking his head. "That's terrible. And you think Matthew has something to do with it?"

"That's what we're checking. Was there a particular bar you guys went to for beers?" Wolf asked.

"Yeah, well, no," his face flushed red and his eyebrows rose for a split second.

"Did you guys ever used to go to ..." he fished the receipt out of his pocket, "the Albastru Pub?"

Out the corner of his eye, Wolf saw Lia turn and look at him.

"Uh, yeah. We've been there before," Vlad said.

"What were you doing Friday night?" Wolf put the receipt back in his jeans pocket.

"I was working in the office, actually. I was here quite late on Friday night."

"You weren't with them at the pub, getting a beer that night?"

"What? No." He was excited now. "I was at work all night."

Wolf paused for a few seconds and stared at the scientist. "Okay. Thanks, Dr. Vlad. And you didn't see Matthew or my brother at all last weekend?"

He shook his head. "No, I'm sorry. I haven't."

"So what do you do here? Are you an astronomer as well?"

"Me? I, uh, I work for the EAS. I am overseeing the refurbishment of the Zeiss telescope."

"Vlad is an important man in the world of astronomical equipment, Mr. Wolf," Wembly said. "In any given month, a lot of equipment is exchanged between countries and continents, and Dr. Vlad has become the top man for the EAS to oversee its logistics. We are lucky to have him here." Wembly wore a proud expression.

Vlad nodded with closed eyes and held up his hand—as if he was a movie star and Wembly a raving fan.

Wolf nodded back to Vlad. "Where are you from?"

"I'm from Romania."

"What part?"

"Cluj."

"And what about Dr. Rosenwald? What does he do here?"

"He works on our gamma-ray astronomy team," Wembly answered behind them, "with Dr. Chang there." He pointed toward the center of the building.

"Okay. Mr. Wembly—"

"*Doctor* Wembly ... never mind, sorry, it doesn't matter." He shook his head and squinted his eyes in apology.

"Dr. Wembly," Wolf said, "how did he get to work? By car?"

"Yes, he drove a car."

"And what is the make, model, and color of it?"

"It's a, um ... oh, you know better than I, Dr. Vlad. What did he drive?" Wembly asked.

Vlad was pulled from deep thought. "He drives a blue Fiat Panda."

Wolf looked back to Dr. Wembly. "Do you mind if we question Dr. Chang? And can we please have Dr. Rosenwald's address? Do you have that on file?"

"Yes, I believe I do. Let me fetch it for you."

"Thanks, Dr. Vlad. We'll be in touch if we need anything else."

Vlad stuck out his hand to shake, and Wolf walked out the door.

...

Dr. Chang was three doors down the hall in his office, cradling a teacup with both hands, looking intently at his computer screen.

"Dr. Chang?" Wolf knocked on the open door.

"Yes?" Dr. Chang looked up through steamy glasses.

"You work with Matthew Rosenwald, correct?"

"Yes." He put down his cup and turned to them.

"Have you seen him or heard from him in the last few days?" Lia asked.

"No, I have not."

"Is that usual?" Wolf asked. "Not to hear from him for days?"

Chang furrowed his brow and stood, crossing his arms. He wore a white lab coat unbuttoned and draped over his blue T-shirt and tight jeans. He wore large Buddy Holly-style glasses that looked way too big for his face, and had tall spiky hair. "No, it is not usual. We usually keep in touch, and he missed some important milestones for our work earlier this week, in fact."

"And what is that work exactly?" Wolf asked.

"We were, uh ..." he hesitated.

Wolf didn't blink. "What's the matter?"

"Well, I don't know how to explain it, other than in a way that won't make sense to you, I'm sure."

"Try me."

"We ... we were shaping X-ray beams via deformable mirrors. We have been analytically computing the required mirror profile for a series of telescopes."

Wolf looked blankly at Dr. Chang. "Do you have a relationship with Dr. Rosenwald outside the work place?"

"No. Not at all, actually," he said pushing his glasses up the bridge of his nose, as if realizing it for the first time.

"Were you with him at the bar this weekend getting beers? Or did you see him this weekend?"

"No. Like I said, I didn't ever socialize with Dr. Rosenwald outside of work." He looked to Lia and Dr. Wembly. "What's this all about?"

"Never mind. Thanks for your time, Dr. Chang. If you hear from him, can you please call this number?" Wolf looked to Lia, and she gave him a phone number.

They said goodbye to Dr. Wembly and left mid-morning with Dr. Rosenwald's address in hand.

CHAPTER 21

"WHAT WAS that all about with Dr. Chang?" She revved the RPMs to pass two trucks. "Why were you pressing him about his work?"

"I wanted to ask him that question before asking him about Dr. Rosenwald ... to see his reactions. He wasn't hiding anything. Not like Dr. Vlad was. That guy was a comical liar. I'm surprised he didn't start dry-heaving right in front of us."

"Yeah. He was acting strange." She eyed him. "And, where did you get that receipt?"

"I picked it up at the morgue."

She turned to him with a wide-eyed glare. "You took that when you pretended to almost pass out!"

"I wasn't pretending. I almost passed out."

...

M. Rosenwald and a number were written on a call box that hung outside the wrought-iron gate. Lia pushed the button and waited.

"No answer." Wolf smacked a mosquito on his neck.

The apartment building was a short drive north of the observatory, along the same wide river that dumped out of Lake Como —which meant it was brutally muggy. Thick foliage covered every nook and cranny of the surrounding area, all the way to the water. The building seemed to pop up from underneath the greenery. It was large, containing thirty or more apartments.

"I don't think he is home," Lia said.

Wolf bent forward. "Is there a building-manager button?" He waged war on two more mosquitoes hovering around his ears.

"I don't see one." She shrugged.

"Okay, you do the talking." Wolf pushed five buttons in quick succession.

She put her hands on her slender hips and gave Wolf a dirty look.

"Chi è?"

"Chi è?" Two people answered almost simultaneously.

"Buongiorno. Siamo i carabinieri. Lasciateci entrare?"

The gate buzzed and clicked open, then buzzed again.

"Okay, now let's go get a closer look." Wolf pushed through the gate.

"Is this how they do it in Colorado?"

"Nope. We don't have fences like this where I come from."

They walked through the courtyard, up a series of steps outside, and pulled open a large door into the apartment building. The air was steamy inside, and smelled of simmering tomato sauce and searing meat. Wolf swallowed so he wouldn't drool.

They climbed the stairs to Dr. Rosenwald's floor and ran into a concerned-looking old woman poking her head out the door.

She and Lia had a brief conversation.

"What did she say?"

"She hasn't seen him."

They continued down the hall and stopped at Rosenwald's apartment. Wolf knocked four times against the thick wood door. The sound echoed through the marble-encased hallway they were standing in. There was no response from inside, no sounds at all.

"Would you object to me picking this lock?" Wolf raised an eyebrow.

"I ... could you do that?"

"I could. They don't teach that here in your military?"

"I don't remember learning that skill, no." She smirked. "Well, in Italy, we do not need a warrant for drugs to search a person's property. Since your brother had drugs in his system on the night of his death, and he was with this person on the night of his death ... then I don't see any problem with us entering this apartment on suspicion of drugs."

"Okay, good. I'm going to need some things. I need something that's long and thin and made of metal, and I haven't seen a lock like this in my life. I say let's go to the old lady's apartment and see what we can get there." He turned to walk down the hallway.

Lia reached down and turned the doorknob. With a soft click the door creaked open to the inside.

She swept her hand at the door. "They don't teach that skill in the American military?"

"Huh. No I don't remember learning that." He stepped in.

The apartment was dimly lit. A corridor hallway inside the

entrance was lined with a body-length mirror and a framed painting that looked to be Australian aboriginal art.

Two doors were closed on the right-hand side and a brightly lit bigger room was at the end of the narrow hallway.

"Hello?" Wolf called into the apartment.

Lia flipped a switch and the hall flooded with yellow light. She shut the door, suffocating any outside noise.

He smelled her sweet breath as she turned toward him, and then the lavender scent of her hair. The apartment was completely silent save the gentle rustle of her clothing.

Wolf was aware that he'd passed beyond the act of looking to staring at Lia, so he sprang into action. "I'll check in here." He turned and opened the nearest door, revealing Rosenwald's bedroom. A queen-sized bed was unmade with two shirts strewn across it. A wicker dirty-clothes basket was full to the brim, giving the room a musty body-odor smell. The screenless window was open a crack, and Wolf felt another tiny sting and slapped his forearm.

Distant thunder rumbled outside, shaking the building deeply. Light dimmed by the second.

"Pretty nice place!" Lia said from somewhere else in the apartment. He left the room and followed her voice down the hall and into a large living room with vaulted ceilings. There were two massive windows set in an exposed brick wall that looked out onto the river, filling the room with subdued natural light.

The opposite wall was painted Italian-flag green. From it hung a medium-sized flat-screen television. Australian landscape photography and paintings adorned the rest of the wall space. It was thoughtfully and tastefully designed, with attention to detail. There was a leather couch, dark wood end tables, and a kitchenette with a table where Lia was digging in a backpack.

"Notice the coffee table over there?" She nodded her head toward it.

Wolf looked and saw a small pile of euro coins, a few pieces of paper, and a tiny white bag. It looked like a bag of cocaine. He picked it up and studied it closely, then opened it. It looked and smelled like it at least.

"So, Matthew here is also using cocaine," she said.

"I don't think my brother was using cocaine."

"Sorry." She gave him a sideways glance. "So ... how do you explain the coroner's report?"

"It said there was residue on his nose. There weren't any blood tests done."

"True."

He closed and pocketed the tiny bag and they began a thorough search of the apartment. Nothing seemed out of the ordinary for a single male from Australia living his life as a gamma-ray astronomer in a foreign country. Other than the bag of coke, that is.

Receipts were piled on the kitchen counter against the tile backsplash, all of them looking like they were for gas or groceries.

"There's no phone. That reminds me, can we look at phone records for my brother and this guy? There may be some clues there. We should have the cell-phone company ping his phone as well to see where it's at, if there's any charge left in it. Did it go straight to voice mail when you called it earlier?"

"Yes, it did."

"Okay, that says something. He's not charging his cell. Maybe he knows someone could trace his phone if he charged it. Maybe he took out the battery. Maybe he's running. I don't see his car keys anywhere. What about his passport?"

Lia twisted and raised her hands. "Let's look for it."

They split up, Wolf returning to his bedroom and Lia staying in the living room and kitchen. Wolf got up close with the contents of every drawer and nook in the room and came up empty.

"Nothing," Lia said when Wolf returned.

"Nothing in there, either. So he has his passport on him. Can we trace his movement with it?"

"Probably not. At least, it's not easy. Schengen rules allow free travel between most European countries. Most countries don't even have electronic passport control of any kind. There will be a guard, and he will look at the passport, and done." She swiped her hands together as if wiping off crumbs. "We can check, of course, but we shouldn't expect anything. Credit cards and the cell phone are a better bet."

"You have a person in the carabinieri that does all this stuff?"

"Yes." She smiled. "There is a guy who does all this stuff. He is the technical genius of the office."

Nearby thunder rumbled for a long time outside, and a deluge of raindrops began hitting the roof and windows.

"We'll have him check on Dr. Rosenwald's car as well," she said. "He can get the registration."

"I wonder if he could hack into my brother's computer at the same time."

"If it can be done, he will be able to do it."

"I'd also like to take a thorough look at the police report, or whatever you call it here," he said. "All after we go to the Albastru Pub."

"Is that all?" She looked at him facetiously.

"No."

A white flash of lightning lit the interior of the apartment, followed by a deafening boom that rolled into the distance.

"Whoa. We'd better get to the car." They walked down the hall and out of the apartment. "So what else do you have planned for us, Mr. Wolf?"

"Food." Wolf said. "Food."

CHAPTER 22

LIA CUT a chunk off her pizza and stuffed it in her mouth. "So, what's it like in Colorado?"

"It's a beautiful place. There aren't nearly as many people as here, at least where I come from in the mountains. Some days you'll see more animals than other people. I love it."

They sat inside a crowded pizzeria along the river while it poured with rain outside. They ordered pizza, water, and Cokes, a meal Wolf liked anywhere in the world, but he was looking forward to tasting the authentic thing. Wolf dug into the savory pizza and he wasn't disappointed.

"Have you been there your whole life?"

"Most of it. I was in the military for a number of years right out of high school, then I returned. Otherwise, yeah. Born and raised."

Her eyes lit up. "Really? Where did you serve?"

"I was stationed in Washington."

"Where did you go?"

He laughed at her intense interest. "Middle East. Pacific Rim, mostly Asia and Australia."

"Oh, wow. That must have been amazing." She shook her head and sipped her Coke. "Did you see any action?"

"Nah, not much," he lied. "I saw some in the Middle East, but otherwise, it was more a nice tour of the world."

She stared at nothing for a beat, then shook her head. "What is your position on the police force there?"

"I'm a ... deputy sergeant, in the Sheriff's Department."

"Is that a bad subject or something?" she asked, studying Wolf's face.

"Well, it's an interesting time for my career at the moment. There's a possibility I'll be appointed to sheriff on Monday."

She paused. "Really? Monday? Wow, congratulations."

"Yeah, no congratulations yet." They sat in silence as he swilled another small glass of water. "That's if a few things go right."

"What do you mean? Do you not have the job already?"

"No, I don't. I have to be appointed by a council of the top political officials in our county. I have to have the majority vote of all the members."

"And ...?"

"Well, I hurt a guy pretty bad before I left, and his father happens to be on said council."

"Uh oh." She leaned forward on her elbows. "And you are a bit worried?"

"Well, yeah. They could be persuaded to vote for another person as sheriff instead. Because of what I did."

"Oh, okay. So, is there another candidate for the job?"

"Yes," he said. "The guy I hurt pretty bad before I left."

Her eyebrows shot up. "Ah, I get it," she said. "He may try to convince the others to vote for his son, especially since you just beat the crap out of him. Also, of course, there is the matter of your brother here, which you want to make sure is taken care of before you go home."

They both resumed eating.

She paused. "So, you think that the council member would have voted for *you* before you hurt his son? Wouldn't he have pushed the council to vote for his own son anyway? I'm confused."

He laughed. "Yeah, it's confusing as all hell. But, no, he wouldn't have, I don't think. He probably would have voted for me over his own son. In fact, that's probably the reason his son and I got into it the other day."

She nodded her head as if all was crystal clear, and then she finished her last bite and wiped her mouth. "All right. So let's figure this whole mess out soon so you can take your brother home and go win your job."

He liked this girl more and more.

CHAPTER 23

Lia parked the Alfa Romeo right in front of the Albastru Pub, which sat in a piazza in the heart of Lecco that looked otherwise restricted to vehicle traffic.

The pub had a large dark wooden sign with hand-carved lettering above the front door, and a blue, yellow, and red square flag hanging from a pole above it. A single deciduous tree grew thickly from a small square of brick in front.

"Romanian." Lia pointed at the flag as they got out, answering Wolf's forthcoming question.

They entered the pub, and Wolf noted the nautical-looking clock on the wall that said 2:10 p.m. It looked like the bottom-rung customers were there at the moment—a few older men slumping over a yellow beer or a brown opaque liquor in their glasses. Punk-rock music Wolf didn't recognize buzzed out of the large wall-mounted speakers. Two muted televisions showed the same soccer highlights.

No one was behind the dark wooded bar, nor was there any indicator bell on the door or anything to telegraph their entrance.

Lia took off her hat and brushed the stray strands of her dark hair from her forehead. "Buongiorno!" she called toward the rear of the bar.

A thin face with buggy cobalt eyes peeked from around the corner at a surprisingly tall height.

Almost imperceptibly, the man's eyes widened, then a stringy arm appeared, holding up a finger. "Buongiorno! Un momento, per favore." The second half of the sentence retreated away from them behind the wall. There was a fast clipped conversation just audible over the music somewhere in the back, a door closing, and then the man returned.

The bartender was tall. What Wolf thought to be a man standing on a step stool and peeking around a corner was in fact a man that stood well above Wolf's own six-foot-three frame. His head was shaved on the sides all the way to the skin, with a spiked hairdo on top that shone with copious amounts of gel, making the man look even taller than the already circus-height he was. His ears protruded from the side of his head like two open car doors. He had a large nose, and a tight small mouth with spittle built up on the corners. A gold necklace jostled around his neck, well displayed on his bared chest above his mostly unbuttoned white silk shirt.

He hurried over and extended a huge hand across the bar to Wolf. "Ciao, sono Cezar."

Wolf shook his hand, eying a pattern of five dots in between the man's right forefinger and thumb, like a five on a dice. He'd seen the tattoo countless times around the world. Always on bad people. It seemed that each culture, or country, or region, had different meanings for the universal mark. Some men in the Far East would get the tattoo in prison; some would get it to signify that they'd killed another man. Wolf assumed Cezar's mark represented something similar, and didn't represent his prowess for dice games.

"Do you speak English?" Wolf asked.

"Yes, I speak English. Why?" The faint sound of a car engine fired up toward the back of the building, revved, and gradually faded.

"Because I don't speak Italian. My name's Wolf."

"Wolf! What is that, German?"

"No, actually it's not," he said. "Do you mind answering a few questions for us?"

"Of course I do not mind! I'm Cezar." He slumped down on his elbows giving Wolf his undivided attention. "How can I help you?"

Cezar blinked long and hard while turning his mouth downward, ending the move with a hard sniff. Reaching in his pocket, he pulled out a pack of Marlboros in a black box, a type Wolf didn't recall ever having seen. He pointed the box in Wolf's direction. "Would you like one?"

"No thanks." He held up his brother's driver's license, which he had also pocketed from John's belongings at the morgue. "Have you ever seen this man before?"

Lia cleared her throat.

Cezar looked at the license with an unreadable face. "Yes! I know this guy. He and his friend come in sometimes."

Cezar pulled out his cell phone, apparently all his undivided attention used up on the one question.

"You own this place?" Wolf asked.

"Yeah, it's mine, all mine." He raised his arms out, showing off his pterodactyl wingspan.

Lia stepped forward and put her elbow on the bar. "Did you happen to see him this weekend? On Friday night?"

Cezar paused for a few seconds, swiping his finger on his phone.

"Cezar?" Lia reached across and put her hand over his phone screen.

Cezar inhaled a sharp breath and glared at Lia, a dark side

showing itself for a brief moment. With a forced smile, he said, "Friday? I don't think so, I normally remember everyone who comes in, and I don't remember seeing him that night."

Wolf pulled out the receipt and laid it on the bar counter.

Cezar glanced at it, then back at his phone. "He might have been in here, I don't know. It was pretty busy that night."

"This is my brother's receipt from that night—"

"Yeah, I get it. Look, I didn't see him that night, okay? Sorry to disappoint you." He stared with a sad look on his face, head tilted to the side. A shrug was added for good measure.

"Yeah. Okay." Wolf stared icily. "Hey, you have a bathroom in that back room I can use?" He looked over Cezar's shoulder to the back hallway.

His eyelids drooped lazily as he pointed to the far wall. "The toilet is over there."

Wolf stood still, glaring at Cezar

Cezar held up his arms in a defensive gesture, a vaudeville look of fear twisting his face, then laughed through his tiny spit-ringed smile.

...

"He knows something," Wolf said as they got into the car.

"That guy is creepy."

"Yeah, that too."

Lia's phone trilled. She picked it up and talked for a minute.

"Valerio is going to meet us at the station with the police report. Let's go pick up your brother's computer and head down there."

CHAPTER 24

WOLF FOLLOWED Lia into the carabinieri station. She darted up the stairs to the left without a glance at the chaos below, which Wolf saw had escalated to biblical status.

Upstairs was light and smelled refreshing after the midday rains. The lake in the distance was white capped once again, and more aquatic boarders rode the winds back and forth across the vast expanse. He shook his head, looking back at the stairway, like it was a wormhole into another universe.

The room bustled with activity—officers on phones, paperwork being shuffled from desk to desk. A few unanchored sheets fluttered to the floor on the breeze coming in the windows. Colonnello Marino's room to the right was closed, and once again his booming voice rumbled from within. Detective Rossi stood up from behind a desk in the distance and waved them over.

"How are things coming along, David?" Rossi folded his arms.

"There have been some developments for sure." He looked to Lia, who sat comfortably on the edge of Rossi's desk. "We found that the belt around my brother's neck was not his own."

"What do you mean?"

Wolf explained the length of the belt and how it couldn't have been stretched, and therefore couldn't have been his brother's belt.

"That *is* interesting, indeed. About your brother," Rossi said. "I am working on getting all this paperwork done to release him and his belongings as fast as possible. And did you find this friend he was out with the night before?"

"No, we just went to his place of work and his apartment, and no luck at either place. It looks like he's been missing since John died. Or, at least he hasn't shown up for work all week."

"Interesting again." Rossi raised an eyebrow. He waved them to the chairs in front of his desk and sat back down. Wolf sat gratefully and stole another glance out to the shimmering water behind Rossi.

Rossi handed a manila folder to Wolf. "Here is a copy of the police report. If you would please not let Marino know that I gave you that, it would be much appreciated."

"All right." Wolf took the folder and put it on his lap. He looked around the room, noticing the piles of paper on each desk. It seemed mountainous compared to what he was used to. Every single person at a desk was dealing with paperwork, or holding a piece of paperwork while on the phone, or handing a stack of paperwork to someone else.

Rossi seemed to sense his curiosity. "What?"

"Oh, I was just noting the vast amounts of paperwork on everyone's desk. I thought we had it bad in Colorado."

Rossi and Lia giggled. "Really? This is a lot of paperwork?"

Wolf nodded. "Yes. This is a lot of paperwork."

They laughed like school children, Rossi slapping his hand on the desk. "Paperwork is in the DNA of all Italians. We cannot get out of our mothers' wombs unless we have the proper paperwork."

Rossi leaned forward and frowned, as if remembering the sober reality of Wolf's visit. "David, all that paperwork is the reason it can take a lot of time. But I've been keeping on top of your brother's release papers. They are sitting on Marino's desk now for final approval. In the meantime, I see you have your brother's computer?"

"Yeah." Wolf nodded. "I can't get into it. I was hoping to get your guy to help me."

"Good, give it to Paolo. He will be able to help you. If he can help me with this pig," he slapped the side of his dirty cream-colored desktop monitor, "then he can help you with a brand-new computer like that!"

"I hope," Wolf said.

CHAPTER 25

"*PORCA MISERIA*." Lia plucked a slip of paper off her desk. "I have to go see Marino. Let me get you started with Paolo."

"Ciao!" Paolo stood up from behind two giant flat-screen monitors on his desk.

Wolf estimated his age at about fifteen years old, but then again he wasn't good at estimating ages past twelve years old, Jack's current age.

Paolo was dressed in plain clothes, wearing a black T-shirt that had two 1950s-style American hot rods smashing into each other. His jeans were faded, baggy in the mid-section and skin tight in the legs, a popular look Wolf had noticed propagating through the youth of Italy. He wore thick red plastic-framed glasses and had a spiky hairdo. Silver rings on three fingers and a bright-red plastic watch adorned his arm, which extended to shake Wolf's hand. It was a firm handshake, and he held Wolf's gaze as they shook.

"Piacere," Paolo said.

"Hello. Uh, do you speak English?" Wolf asked.

"Yes, yes! I am not very good," he said with an impressive American accent. "But, I learned in university."

"Great." Wolf wondered if college for Paolo was done pre or post puberty.

"Well, what's up?" Paolo pointed at the computer bag slung on his shoulder.

"I would like to get into this computer, but I don't have my brother's password." Wolf wore a pained expression as he pulled out the thin Mac laptop.

"Pffffffft, okay."

"Do you think you can do it?"

"Yes, no problem."

Lia looked satisfied. "Paolo can do anything with computers — programming, the internet, and all things that confuse the rest of us."

Paolo was blushing ferociously but also tilting his head back proudly. He opened the computer and pushed a few buttons simultaneously, all the while his attention unwavering from Lia.

"He'll take care of you," she said, slapping Paolo's back. "I have to go talk to Marino. I will be back, hopefully soon."

Wolf looked around. "Okay, sounds good. I'll be here."

Lia walked away back across the room and down the hall. Wolf caught himself staring and turned back to Paolo, who was now standing at his desk watching Lia leave the room.

"Mmmmmadonna." Paolo breathed, turning to Wolf with a conspiratorial look. "She is beautiful, eh?"

"Yes, she is," Wolf agreed with a resigned smile. "Okay, what's happening?"

"Oh, yes, you can pull up that chair there. I am going to create another administrator account on the computer. It takes a few seconds. Then I can go in and access all the files."

"Okay, sounds good."

Wolf waited and watched Paolo work his magic with the computer. The screen looked to be displaying lines of code, a sight Wolf was completely unfamiliar with. He felt proficient enough with a computer, but he was watching a master mechanic rip the hood off of a car and dig into the engine. A tweak here, a command there, and soon they were inside with a normal view that Wolf was more accustomed to.

"Okay, I've created a new admin account, and changed the password to your brother's account, allowing me to log in as him. I'm going to fire up a few of his programs. Otherwise, what would you like to do?"

"I'd like to look at his documents, I guess. His emails, the latest activity. Try to find some clue as to what was going on before last Friday."

Paolo tapped the keys for a few minutes, opening windows and programs. "Well, wait a minute, this is interesting." Paolo was looking in Skype.

"Why?"

"Well, you haven't logged in on this computer at all since you got here? Obviously not ... never mind."

"No, I haven't. It was closed when I found it in John's room. I tried a couple passwords to hack in. No luck. So I gave up and just left it to charge."

"Okay, okay. Well, there are messages on Skype from another person to your brother on Tuesday. Two days ago."

"Okay," Wolf said expectantly, "and what does that mean?"

"Well, okay. Look here." He pointed toward the little logo on the bottom of the screen. "If there was someone who was trying to get hold of your brother with some messaging on Skype, say, on Tuesday, then I would have just logged into his account and a bubble would have shown up on the icon telling me how many messages he had missed since he last logged in."

"Okay."

"But there was no bubble that popped up on the icon." Paolo was tilting his head with wide eyes. "But, if I go into his account and look at his recent conversations here on the left, look what someone is saying to him."

–Hey man, you there? 9:12 p.m.

–What's happening? Are we doing this interview or what? Let me know ... 9:53 p.m.

–You okay? You there? 10:09 p.m.

Wolf shook his head, not getting it yet.

"So, the most important part is here," Paolo pointed. "Look at the date these messages were sent. This was Tuesday, September 18th, three days after your brother's death, at 9:12 p.m. local time ... or, how many hours behind is Colorado?"

"Eight."

"Okay," Paolo looked at the ceiling for a second, "so that means between one and two in the afternoon, your time, on Tuesday, someone was trying to get hold of him, looks like for an interview. But he wasn't answering. However, Skype is telling us these messages *have already been looked at*, because there was no indication on the icon that there were unread messages!"

Wolf nodded. "Which means someone was on the computer looking at these messages at some point *before* we just looked at them, otherwise there would have been unread messages." Wolf was finally getting the significance. He sat back hard in his chair, putting his hands on his head.

"Exactly," Paolo said. "Someone has opened this computer and looked at Skype in the past few days, *after* your brother's death. So, what do you think they were looking for on this computer?"

"I honestly have no clue," Wolf said. "Can you somehow tell? Can you see what they did on it?"

"No, not unless I had pre-loaded key-stroke recognition software on his computer. But, we can infer some things, like we did just now."

"They probably got on the computer to erase something, right?" Wolf asked.

Paolo raised an eyebrow and nodded. "Okay, let me check. It's actually more difficult than people think to erase all evidence of a file off a computer. We'll see if this hacker knew more than just the log-on trick, which is actually quite basic." He rolled his eyes as he dove back onto the keyboard in a flurry.

Entering commands on the screen, Paolo's fingers were a blur. Wolf marveled at the strange sequence of letters, numbers, and punctuation this wunderkind was commanding at Mach speed.

"Ahhhh." Paolo had a pained expression. "Well, either they cleaned it completely, or they simply didn't erase anything. There's no trace of any files that were recently erased. It's more likely they didn't erase anything."

Lia came around the corner and walked to the desk. She looked pained, avoiding eye contact with Wolf. "So, any luck?"

Wolf gestured to the laptop. "We're in, and we've seen that someone else has been looking at the computer in the last couple of days."

"Really?" She leaned forward, pressing her firm stomach against Wolf's shoulder.

"Yeah. According to Paolo, these Skype messages tell us that someone was on the computer sometime Tuesday night or later."

"*Ma-donna*. What else?"

"Well," Paolo said, looking down at the way Lia leaned on Wolf, "we can't find any indication that anyone erased anything. We have to get online and do some work. Your brother was what, a blogger?"

"Yes," Wolf answered.

"Okay, he probably did things more online than off. What's his email address? A Gmail account?"

"Yes, it is."

"Good. Give me a few things, and I'll do some work. I want your email address, his email address, his blog name, your Facebook account login ... you do have a Facebook account, right?"

"Uh, yeah." He squirmed. "I don't remember how I log in, though."

Lia smiled at his obvious discomfort.

Paolo shook his head. "Just give me the blog name." And with that, Paolo shooed them away.

Wolf and Lia walked away. "How was your talk with Marino?" Wolf asked.

She avoided eye contact. "It was fine."

"Is everything okay?"

"Yes. It's fine."

"Okay," he said. She was preoccupied with something.

Wolf left her to her thoughts and went to the window. He opened the manila folder containing the police report and his stomach sank. It was all in Italian. *Of course.* He would need a lot of translating done for him. And things were always lost in translation.

"Twitter! Haha!" Paolo blurted.

Wolf looked to Paolo, who was holding up his arms in triumph.

Wolf shoved the papers back in the folder and joined Lia at Paolo's desk.

"I went into your brother's Gmail account and checked the activity. Looks like someone erased a few messages on Tuesday night at 11:37 p.m. So, the question is, what was erased? So I went onto your brother's blog, thinking there might be a hint there. Nothing. It looks like he hasn't done a blog post in a couple weeks. He has a different contact email address on his blog. He runs it through Gmail as well, so I checked that email account. Nothing there either. They could have erased some stuff there. I could probably hack into his blog, but ... well, let me move on.

"I checked his Facebook account through his blog. It looks like there wasn't any activity on there. But, that could have been erased also. The login and password information was, again, stored in the browser—"

"Paolo." Lia smacked him on the shoulder.

"Sorry, yes. But, Twitter!" His eyes lit up. "It looks like he tweets a lot. A lot. Your brother was a pretty big deal online, I take it. He has 172,839 followers on his account and he's following 320 people."

Wolf shrugged.

"It' means he's popular. So, anyway, I logged into his Twitter account, and it looks like someone removed some of his tweets.

"But you can't just erase tweets from the web. Especially if you have 172,000 followers. People are constantly retweeting his stuff, or replying to it. All traceable, and never erasable. And on the night of your brother's death ..." He punched a couple keys and a tweet was displayed from someone who was apparently a cat wearing a hollowed watermelon on its head.

"It's a response to your brother's tweet. It looks like he posted a picture, but it's been erased from his account. But it was a picture of Jupiter by the description he gives and the responses, and he says he was at the Merate Observatory."

"You can't show the pictures?" Wolf asked.

Paolo shook his head. "Can't. They've been erased."

"But he was there at the observatory that night," Wolf whispered.

"At 11:17 p.m., according to the original tweet," Paolo added.

Wolf stared at the screen and shook his head. "How about phone records? Can we get access to both John's and Matthew

Rosenwald's phone records to see what they said that night? Or earlier in the week as well? We'll also need to find Rosenwald's car."

Paolo sat back and looked at them. "Yes, I'll call the phone companies to get the records next, and I'll see if I can get a triangulation of where his phone is at. I'll check credit-card activity for both of them as well. I'll look up the car registration too. These things could take the rest of the day. I'll get started."

"Give me a call when you have more information." Lia walked to the front of his desk and leaned both hands on it.

Paolo lit up. "Of course I will, mi amore!" He added a quick sentence in Italian that caused Lia to roll her eyes.

"Shall we go?" she asked Wolf.

"Sure. I think we need to go back to the observatory."

Lia bit her lip and looked at her watch. "It's just after 5:00 p.m. What are the chances he's still there?"

"Vlad seems to be a late worker. I'd say pretty good."

CHAPTER 26

As they exited the main room to the stairway to hell, a voice called from across the room, "Lia, David!" Rossi put his phone to his ear, said a quick goodbye to someone, and waved them over. "What are you guys doing?"

They explained the situation to Rossi as quickly as possible. He stopped them numerous times, asking them to expand on points, and go over others again before egging them on for more details. Finally, he looked to Wolf with folded arms and a furrowed brow. "Okay, so what are you going to do at the observatory?"

Wolf was taken aback by the question. "Well, we're going to get the real story from this son of a bitch, Vlad. He's hiding something from us about Friday night."

"What did you and Marino just talk about, Lia?"

"Uh, he was wondering about what was happening." She glanced at Wolf, then the desk.

"And?" Rossi asked.

"He said ... he said that David's brother would be released tomorrow, and he wanted him out of the picture." She pointed at Wolf.

Wolf stood still, not reacting.

"David," Rossi glanced at Marino's closed door, "we have to be careful about your next moves. Your brother's remains are released tomorrow. That means you can get the belt with the belongings, right?"

"Yeah, I guess," Wolf said. "When will the body be released?"

"Marino said first thing in the morning," Lia said. "Then he wants to talk to you after that, to try and persuade you to go home ... cooperatively."

"I'll go home cooperatively when I find out who killed my brother. And it's looking like Vlad had a hand in this whole thing."

"David, let me finish." Rossi put his hand on Wolf's shoulder and stepped closer. "Marino has pressure from higher-ranking officials to make this situation go away. They don't like that a police force from another country is coming in and helping with a closed investigation. I know that is not what is happening," he said quickly. "I'm just telling you what Marino must be thinking about right now behind that door.

"It is important that we do this right. Right now, you have the testimony from a worker at an observatory that he didn't see your brother the night of his death. That's it. He could be telling the truth—he could have been locked in his office the entire night, never seeing a single soul. However, if you had the belt, and we could show that it was Vlad's somehow, then we actually have a piece of evidence. Or we need to find Matthew, which Paolo is working on right now, like you said. But at this moment, you are risking some sort of ugly international incident if you go over there *right now*."

Wolf took a deep breath. "So what do you propose I do instead?"

"Eat," Rossi said with zero hesitation.

"What?"

Rossi touched both of them on the arm. "You and Lia come to my house, this second, and have an excellent meal with my family. We will talk this out, on full stomachs!"

Wolf stared at Rossi's motionless bug eyes and broke a smile. He looked to Lia, who seemed all on board with the idea, then nodded. "All right. That sounds good, I guess."

"Oh-kay!" Rossi pulled his coat off his desk chair. "Now let's get the hell out of here before Marino's office door opens." He marched between them, out of the room, and disappeared down the stairway.

CHAPTER 27

Two miles into the tunnel, Wolf's back pressed into the seat, letting him know they were gaining altitude at a good rate. He leaned discreetly, keeping a white-knuckle grip on the ceiling-bar, to catch a glimpse of Lia's dashboard gauges.

No more than five car lengths behind Rossi, she was doing one hundred sixty kilometers per hour, a straight one hundred miles per hour. He held his breath when the car rocked from side to side as they blew past another train of cars traveling the other way.

They slowed to a breathable speed as a series of flashing signs indicated a sharp turn, which turned out to be the end of the tunnel. The view was stunning, looking down on Lecco from what was at least a thousand feet up the steep Alpine mountain. They continued onward and upward for another few minutes, switching back and forth along a tight-cornered road gouged into the side of a steep green slope lined with tall pine trees of a kind Wolf had never seen.

Wolf craned his head to see the distant valley floor through the trees. "This seems to be far from town, and a really nice area."

"Yes, they moved here a few years ago, when Valerio's father died. He and his family were left an inheritance, and they didn't hesitate to move to this nicer area. You'll see his house. It's quite beautiful."

Wolf couldn't help but think for a moment about his own father's death, and how it had caused quite the opposite effect on his own family.

Rossi finally slowed as they pulled up to a bush-lined property. They waited as gate lights flashed yellow, and an ornate weave of wrought iron slowly swung inwards.

A dog pranced with wagging tail in front of Rossi's Alfa Romeo, and Wolf sucked in a breath as Rossi pulled in, pushing it aside with the bumper of his car.

Lia stopped and they stepped out onto the cobblestone driveway. The air was crisp and clean, smelled of pinesap, and was noticeably cooler than it had been on the distant valley floor. As they followed Rossi along the side of the house to the entrance, they had a fantastic view of the city below. Lecco sprawled like a model city on a gleaming Lake Como. It was so steep that Wolf imagined he could run, jump, and land smack in the middle of the lake below.

The yard of the house was perfectly manicured, and surprisingly flat for how steep the surrounding area looked. The stucco concrete house was one story in front, with a walkout lower level on to a stone patio, where two boys were playing soccer below.

"Ciao ragazzi!" Rossi bent over the railing, then yanked open the door to the side entrance.

"Ciao!"

"Ciao, Daddy!"

Inside, a male Italian singer was belting out high vibrato notes from an unseen speaker system. Smells of cooking Italian food saturated the moist air inside. A slightly disheveled-looking woman wiped her hands and kissed Valerio quickly, then gave a loud welcome to Lia as they kissed each other's cheeks.

"Ciao, sono Maria." She extended a hand to Wolf.

"Ciao," he said. "I'm David."

"Nize-a to meet you," she said, laughing. "I am terrible Eenglish." She pointed to herself with a red-faced smile.

"Not as bad as my Italian," Wolf replied.

The first order of business for Wolf was to use a computer with internet access. His mother would be distraught at Wolf's lack of contact. Wolf explained as much to Rossi, and Rossi immediately pulled him through the house to remedy the situation.

Rossi's home office had dark-green ceramic tiles on the floor and color photos of vineyards adorning the bright-yellow stucco walls. Rossi turned on the tall floor lamp and ripped open the shades, revealing the incredible view below. The sky outside was now bright orange behind white-stoned peaks, and the city below speckled with lights. Rossi plopped down at the dark wood desk, fired up his computer, signed into Skype, and plugged in some headphones with a microphone.

Rossi opened the door to leave, letting in the loud music from the rest of the house. "Take your time. We'll be having aperitivo."

Wolf picked up the headset and took a seat. "Thanks. I appreciate it."

…

"Hello?" His mother answered her cell phone after the first ring.

"Hi, Mom, it's me."

"Oh, thank God. Where have you been?"

"Sorry. I've been having phone trouble. I'm just taking care of everything. Getting John on a plane home."

She paused. "So?"

"Well, I really haven't got any news yet, Mom." He debated whether to say anything until he had definitive proof, but then she sniffed, and it was clear her nose had been running. That she had been sobbing for who knew how many hours before he'd called. He said, "I don't think he killed himself, Mom."

She didn't answer.

"Mom? You there?"

"Yes. I'm here." Her sobbing echoed in the headphones.

"In fact, I'm sure of it."

"Good. Good," she whispered.

"Yeah."

"Have you seen him?"

"Yes, I've seen him."

A rustling sound filled the headset. "How did he look?"

"He looked ..." *Dead.* "He looked fine, Mom. How are you holding up?"

"I'm doing all right. I think I'm going to go up to Rocky Points tomorrow."

"Good, Mom. Go see Jack."

"Of course. I hear Sarah is back," she said.

Wolf sighed. "Yeah, she is back. Look, I have to go now. I'm sorry for the short call. I'm at another person's house, on their computer. I'll try and get back in touch tomorrow. Keep your phone on."

She sniffed. "Okay. Catch the bastard that did this, David."

"That's the plan," Wolf said.

They said their goodbyes and hung up.

Next Wolf called Jack and didn't get an answer, so he left a message. He was a little disappointed, but thankful his son wasn't answering his "emergency cell phone" when he was supposed to be in class.

He dialed another number.

"Hello?"

"Hey, it's Wolf."

"Hey," Rachette said. "I was wondering what this random phone number was. I hoped it was you. How's it going over there? You find anything out?"

"Well, maybe. It's taking some time. There's definitely something going on that doesn't look right."

"Really? What's happening?"

"A lot. Too much to explain," Wolf said.

"Yeah, I under—" Rachette's voice cut out.

Wolf turned up the volume a little on the keyboard. "You there?"

"I'm here. Can you hear me?"

"Yeah. Listen, anything new going on?" Wolf asked.

"Yes. A lot." Rachette's voice was excited now.

"What do you mean?"

"Do you know a girl named Lisa Hardwick?" Rachette asked.

"No. Why? Should I?"

"Apparently not. No one really knows her at HQ. She's a sixteen-year-old junior at Rocky Points High, new in town this year. Her family moved in at the beginning of the summer."

Wolf nodded. "Okay, yeah. I think I've heard of the Hardwicks. The father works at the golf course."

"Exactly," Rachette said. "He's the new head pro at Pine Meadows. Moved up from somewhere in Denver."

"Okay."

"Lisa came in and talked to us yesterday," Rachette continued. "She claims to have spent a lot of time recently with Jerry Wheatman."

Wolf frowned and swiveled in the chair to look outside. The orange glow behind the Italian Alps was dying.

"That's interesting," said Wolf.

"Yeah. And it gets more interesting." Rachette spoke fast. "She said she thinks Julie killed Wheatman. She says she's sure of it."

Wolf turned back to the computer screen. "And why does she say that?"

"She says Julie was furious about her and Jerry spending time together. She says Jerry talked about breaking up with Julie."

"To be with this new girl, Lisa?"

"Yeah."

Wolf stayed silent.

"So?" Rachette asked.

"So what?"

Rachette blew into the receiver. "So we have motive for Julie Mulroy killing Jerry Wheatman, that's what. And something else."

Wolf stayed silent.

"Lisa told us Chris Wakefield is madly in love with Julie Mulroy, that it's common knowledge around school that he always has been."

"Okay," Wolf said. "So you think Wakefield was in on the whole thing. How?"

Rachette sighed. "Well, it fits now why we found both of their footprints coming down the mountain. We have motive for these two to commit murder. Julie does it for revenge against Jerry, and Chris helps so he can please Julie and be with her after all is said and done."

Wolf thought a moment. "And what does Burton think?" he asked, already knowing the answer.

"He doesn't seem too impressed by the whole thing. But I think they did it. They killed Jerry Wheatman. Had to."

"Well, if anyone could come in off the street accusing someone of murder, and law enforcement acted on those accusations without proof, we'd live in a pretty messed-up country." Wolf was suddenly famished.

Silence filled Wolf's headphones. He could sense Rachette's disappointment from halfway around the globe.

"But that's not to say I don't appreciate the heads-up," Wolf added. "I think something's not right about Julie and Wakefield's story, the way they tell it now, that's for sure. But the bottom line is, we need clear proof of any wrongdoing, or our hands are tied."

Rachette sighed. "Yeah. I guess you're right."

"So get some proof."

"How do you think I should do that?" Rachette asked.

"Carefully."

Rachette sighed again.

"I have to go," Wolf said. "Thanks for the update. I'm going to give Burton a quick call. Maybe he can shed some light on some next steps."

"There's another thing," Rachette said hesitantly.

"Yeah? And what's that?" Wolf didn't like Rachette's tone.

"It's Connell. He's been telling people you jumped him the other day."

Wolf clenched his fists. He should have filed an official report. He should have said something to someone. Hell, he should have been quicker, gotten to his gun and shot him dead before any of this happened.

"Wolf?" Rachette asked.

"Yeah. All right. Thanks. I'll talk to you later."

"You want me to patch you through to Burton?"

"Uh, yeah. Good idea. You know how to do that?"

"What? You think I'm an idiot?" Rachette asked, and before Wolf could answer, a ringing filled Wolf's ears.

"Sluice County Sheriff's Department."

Wolf didn't recognize the voice behind the garbled connection. Apparently Rachette *didn't* know how to patch him through.

"I was trying to reach Sheriff Burton," Wolf said. "Can you please patch me through?"

There was a long drawn-out pause. "Who's calling?" *Who's callink.* The reception cleared, and Wolf realized it was Connell, sounding like he had a nose plugged with gauze.

Wolf gritted his teeth. "Patch me through to Burton."

"This *is* Burton. Well, at least you've reached his office." Connell used the tone of a jovial secretary. "Can I help you with something?"

"What the hell you doing in his office?" Wolf asked.

"Just covering for him for a bit. We're a bit short handed with deputies skipping town and whatnot."

Wolf paused. "You telling people I jumped you, Connell?"

"I'm just telling people what happened, Sergeant Wolf," he said. "Doesn't look too good what you did to me, then skipping town right before the appointment. Not too good for you, at least."

Wolf's face went hot.

Connell chuckled. "Damn good timing for brother John to kick the bucket over in Italia," he said. "Aaaaaaanyways, have fun over there. I hope you enjoy your vacation."

With a *sploosh* sound, the Skype session ended. Wolf stared at the screen and ripped off the headset.

...

. . .

The dinner turned out to be a much-needed distraction. Pasta, crispy bread, meat sauce, and savory red wine. It was some of the best food he'd tasted in his life. Valerio and Maria Rossi's two boys seemed like good kids, despite Wolf not understanding a word they said.

He was happy to sit and watch, not feeling in the mood to have to speak after the Skype call, and found it fascinating to observe the spoken Italian language and animated gestures. They would all laugh, and Lia would stop to translate, and then he would smile, well after the magic of the moment was gone. Nonetheless, he appreciated the effort from her and he enjoyed the company.

"Lia used to try to be one of the boys," Rossi explained. "Growing up, we would be playing *soccer* as you Americans call it, or *calcio* as we call it, and she would insist to play all the time."

Lia was concentrating on her meal with a quickly ripening face.

"She, of course, was better than everyone," he said. "Except me!"

Lia kept her gaze on her food.

"No, she really was. All the boys were so confused by her. Here is this beautiful young girl who wanted desperately to kick their butts at every chance she could get."

Lia jutted her head forward. "I didn't want to kick anyone's butts. I just wanted to be treated like anyone else with good skills."

"It is the same today. She is one of the best soldiers we have in the carabinieri." He held his hands up. "And the boys are confused by her once again."

"They are not confused. They are all ..." She looked back at her meal and resumed eating. Tension fell on the table, and everyone ate in silence until Rossi spoke.

"They are confused." Rossi used a quiet tone. "They don't know what to do with such a talented, beautiful, strong, and vicious young woman. You have already been recognized for your talents. We have a saying in Italy," Rossi looked to Wolf, "'Il tempo viene per chi sa aspettare'—which means 'All things come to those who wait.' Isn't that right, David?"

Wolf took a sip of wine. "In a perfect world, I guess."

Rossi studied his expression. "What is your job at home? Are you an officer? A captain? How do you say?"

"I'm a deputy sergeant for the Sheriff's Department. We're a small department, in a small county in the state of Colorado."

"Deputy sergeant." Rossi emphasized each syllable, scrutinizing the words. "I'm not familiar with your ranking system. Who's your immediate superior?"

"The sheriff. We're a little unconventional with our simplistic ranks. We have deputies, sergeant deputies, who act as undersheriffs, and then the sheriff."

Rossi nodded and took another bite. "Do you wish to be sheriff some day?" he asked.

"My father was the sheriff when he was killed in the line of duty." Wolf took a deep breath and rolled some spaghetti. "I would very much like to be sheriff."

The table went quiet again. All concentrated on their plates, except for Rossi, who stared at Wolf.

"I, too, lost my father," Rossi whispered. "A few years ago. It was his time. He had a long life. Your father was taken from you at a younger age. It must have been difficult."

Wolf nodded. "I'm sorry about your father," he deflected. "I heard about it from Lia on the way up here." He stopped himself, suddenly self-conscious of his conversation with Lia on the way up. Like they had gone behind Rossi's back in some way.

"Yes. My father was a good, hardworking man. At least,

that's the way I remember him. He and my mother split when I was a child. He helped my brother's family and my family tremendously after his death. He was never around, really. We had no idea he had amassed such wealth. He never taught us about how to invest or save the way he did. He just quietly did it himself. It was a surprise for the entire family to get such a large inheritance." He raised his hands and looked around. "It gave us this. And gave my brother a place to call his own in Liguria, as well."

Rossi's eyes glistened as he pushed his pasta in an aimless circle on the plate. Maria rubbed his back and gently set her head on his shoulder.

Lia reached to Wolf's leg under the table and gave it a soft squeeze, looking at him. She pulled her hand away, rolled her eyes and resumed rolling her spaghetti on her fork. She looked up suddenly. "I'm not vicious!"

Hearty laughter evaporated the tension. Rossi's two boys joined in, giggling and staring wide-eyed at Lia.

When they had finished dinner, Wolf tried unsuccessfully to help Maria clear the dishes and clean up. Rossi pulled him to the back porch instead, where they sat on the patio overlooking the lights of Lecco, sipping a local grappa served by Rossi's wife. Wolf was so tired he felt like he was observing reality from another dimension.

When Maria walked back into the house Wolf threw the tiny bag of white powder from Matthew Rosenwald's apartment on the table in front of Rossi.

Rossi picked it up and thumbed it in the dim light. "It looks just like the one that I found in your brother's apartment. The same size and look of the bag."

"I don't know what to make of the whole cocaine thing," Wolf said. "I'm not sure if this is even cocaine. You'll need to test it. But I don't think my brother did drugs. He may have experimented in the past, but he never really *did* drugs. I know what people act like when they do drugs, and my brother didn't. I need to find this Matthew guy. And something's off about that Cezar guy at the pub, and Vlad at the observatory. They are both holding something back. Something's off about those two."

Rossi took a sip and furrowed his brow. "What if Matthew was supplying your brother with these drugs?"

"I guess it looks that way. But looks can be deceiving. Then there is the belt. That wasn't my brother's belt that was found around his neck. There are only two things that can mean—either he stole a belt and hanged himself with it, or someone strung him up with it ... or more accurately, smacked him on the head and strangled him, then tried to make it look like a suicide, and did a poor job of it, because the chandelier couldn't hold his body weight." Wolf glared into the dark. "That's what happened, and I'm sure of it. And it would take at least two people to string up John from that chandelier. There's no way one person could have done it." He stood and went to the patio railing, gazing at the city below.

Valerio sipped his grappa and kept his seat. "I think there needs to be more evidence. And until then, I don't see what we can do. There is no nametag on that belt. There's no way to find out whose it is, other than finding fingerprints, which we'll check. But it's been handled by more than a few people by now.

"Secondly, we cannot bring in this Vlad character for questioning because he was sweating profusely as you spoke to him. We cannot arrest the bar owner for being rude to the carabinieri and a foreigner coming into his pub to question him." He sighed heavily. "I do think that it is strange that this Matthew fellow left town immediately after your brother's death, though. So, I think we need to find him. Paolo is working on it. He will look at the phone records and find Rosenwald's phone, and who knows what else he can uncover. That boy is marvelously talented."

Wolf yawned uncontrollably once again and nodded his head.

Lia stood up. "You need to get some sleep, David."

"Yes, you need sleep," Rossi declared, standing up. "We will know more tomorrow."

"We need to go over the police report," Wolf said, sitting back down. "And I don't know how the hell to read Italian, so I'm going to need your help." An unstoppable yawn stretched his face again.

Lia stood in front of Wolf and placed her hand gently on his. "You need sleep."

Rossi looked down at Wolf. "David. Please. It doesn't do you any good not to rest. We still have all day tomorrow."

Wolf sat forward. "And if I need your help Saturday? What if I need more time?"

"Then you will have our help on Saturday as well," Rossi answered.

Wolf sat back on the metal chair. They were right. If they went over the police report now, he probably wouldn't remember it in the morning. Every cell in his body screamed for sleep. "Okay. Let's go."

They said goodbye to the Rossis and climbed in the Alfa Romeo.

"Sleep now," she said in a motherly tone. She turned the key and pulled out of the gate with less speed than Wolf was accustomed to in her passenger seat.

"What do you think? Do you really think my brother killed himself?"

"I think ... I think we will find out. I think you need sleep. Go to sleep."

He tilted the seat back and lost consciousness.

CHAPTER 28

A LIGHT BRUSHING on his cheek pulled him from a dreamless sleep.

"Yep?" He popped his eyes wide open.

"We are here." Lia's face filled his view. She was close, tilting her head sideways to the same angle as his, her hair dangling across her face.

Wolf lay still. Without thinking he reached up and brushed her hair behind her ear.

She narrowed her eyes slowly with a short-lived smile that turned to a hard gaze. Her lips parted and she exhaled loudly. Her warm breath caressed his face.

He reached and pulled her head close. There was zero resistance. Zero hesitation.

Lia's mouth gently connected with his, her tongue diving with eager swirls that tasted of sweet saliva and red wine. Her breaths now came hard out of her nose, vividly audible over the soft Italian music that played on the radio. She reached between them and yanked hard on the emergency brake with a loud crank, then groped at his crotch hungrily with the same hand as she moved closer.

He reached his right hand between her thighs and shifted closer to her.

Then she ripped free and pushed his hand away.

"No, sorry. Sorry, I ... we cannot do this," she said, straightening and putting her hands on the steering wheel. "Sorry." She sat, looking forward out the windshield.

Wolf looked at her. "Okay, uh ... okay."

"I'm sorry. I shouldn't have done that. I will pick you up first thing tomorrow, okay?" She looked at him with pleading eyes.

"Yeah, sure." He shifted himself upright, and then struggled with the seat-reclining lever. "See you tomorrow at eight?"

"Okay then."

"Bye."

He got out and stood up, suddenly lightheaded, with absolutely no clue where he was. He looked forward and craned back his neck to see the strange building in front of him. He couldn't remember ever seeing it before. Turning quickly, he reached to knock on the window to stop her, to tell her she'd dropped him off at the wrong place, but she had already peeled off up the road. She turned a corner and the rev of the engine faded into the quiet night. Then he saw his brother's apartment building across the street.

Goodnight.

CHAPTER 29

Wolf's watch showed 10:25 p.m. when he entered his brother's apartment.

He stepped out on the balcony and took a look below at the piazza. It was filled with chatter, billowing smoke, rising food aromas, and clusters of young people. *Thursday night.*

"Hi." A voice startled him from above. Cristina was looking down, exhaling smoke from a cigarette.

"Hi," he said. "Do you mind if I come up and have one of those?" Surprisingly, or *not* surprisingly after the wake-up call he'd just gotten, he felt wide-awake.

"Sure, come on up."

He went upstairs and knocked.

"Come in!"

She was still on the balcony, and she motioned for Wolf to join her outside. Her hair was pulled back in a ponytail and she stood in sweat pants and a T-shirt. Her eyes were swollen with dark circles underneath. "Here you go," she said, handing him a Marlboro.

The cigarette was lighter and a little bit thicker in his fingers than he remembered. He brought it up to his mouth, catching a brief scent of Lia on his hand, and lit it.

The second drag hit him with a harder buzz than he was expecting, so he reached for the balcony railing and looked over the edge. Fighting through the lightheadedness, he enjoyed half of the first cigarette he'd had in years, then had a sudden overwhelming urge to put it out, so he mashed it into her overflowing ashtray.

She leaned on the railing next to him and smiled. "Didn't want a cigarette, after all?"

Wolf laughed. "It's been a long time. It was a little stronger than I expected."

They stood in silence for a moment, observing the bustle of the piazza below.

"So did you find anything out today?" she asked.

"Maybe. We went to the pub my brother was at on Saturday night, the Albastru Pub. You ever been there? It's Romanian."

"Yes, I've been there." She shifted upright. "John used to go there a lot. I went once. I do not like the place."

"Why?"

"The guys that work there. I know their type from home. A few of them have tattoos that are the symbol of gangs from where I come from." She looked at Wolf then took a drag. "Bad gangs."

Wolf thought of the ink on the freakishly tall man's hand. "Yeah, I saw tattoos. What kind of gangs? What do they do?"

"They would go around town, beating people that owned small shops, and make them pay not to be beaten in the future. They would sell drugs. Sometimes they would kill people. I think even policemen were scared of them. I learned to stay away from those types of men. There were many disappearances of girls my age growing up. Not where I lived, but close by, in the city. They were made to be prostitutes and often shipped off to other countries." She took a long drag. "I told John that he needed to be careful there, and not to mess with anyone there. He laughed and said he wouldn't, but I told him I was serious. That they weren't the types of guys you wanted to mess with." She took another drag. "He said he liked the beer."

"Did you ever meet the Romanian guy from the observatory that Matthew works with? His name is Vlad. That's his last name."

She shook her head. "No, I haven't met anyone but Matthew from the observatory."

"Did John ever say anything about the bar? Like he suspected anything else going on there? Like any crime? Drugs?"

She looked at him. "No, not that I can remember. Why? You think they killed him?"

Wolf just shrugged. They stood quietly for another few seconds, then he looked at her. "You holding up all right?"

She exhaled and her bottom lip quivered. A tear ran down her cheek and she wiped it quickly.

He gave her a hug and let his emotions run free for a few seconds, staring out at the orange rooftops with blurring vision.

Somewhere out in those tight streets, a man, or men, were going about their lives, thinking they'd gotten away with framing his brother for suicide. They had something coming to them. They had someone coming for them. He pulled away and wiped his eyes. "Can I use your scooter?"

She laughed. "Well, I kind of need it to get to work. Do you need a ride somewhere tomorrow?"

"No, I mean, right now."

"Oh." She wiped her nose on her sleeve and dried her eyes. "I guess, yes. What are you going to do?"

"I have to go check on something."

CHAPTER 30

THE 50 CC engine Italian scooter screamed underneath him as he rounded a dark corner on the two-lane road. The tiny light bobbed and bounced, illuminating rows of corn on either side of the street and clouds of swirling insects. Thankfully, there was little traffic at this late hour in the countryside near the Merate Observatory.

As Wolf passed the gate they'd entered before, he cut the engine. The sudden silence was deafening after listening to the strain of the tiny engine for more than twenty minutes. He turned and coasted onto a dirt road that lined the south side of the property and pushed the scooter to a dark pocket underneath a tree next to the fence.

The engine ticked and hissed as he propped it on the center kickstand with such ease that it was like manhandling a child's bicycle. He was ridiculously large for the thing, but it had gotten him here.

The observatory hunkered in the dark, with the telescope dome peeking over the top of a pine tree in the near distance. From Wolf's view through the wrought-iron security fence, he saw a bright light from within the back of the property shining up on the damp air and surrounding trees.

There was no movement or sound, save the scooter's cooling engine and the millions of crickets singing in the cornfields behind him.

He reached in the pack and dug out two leather jackets, a heavy hooded sweatshirt, a pair of pants, and a pair of jeans he had borrowed from John's closet. He folded one of the leather jackets like an accordion, then hauled up and draped it length-wise across the spikes on the fence, pulling it down hard on each individual spike to seat it. He repeated the process with each article of clothing.

He pulled, sagging down with extended arms, then propelled himself over with one silent fluid move. A squish pierced the air as he landed on the damp interior lawn on the other side.

Running low and fast, he reached the edge of the southern-most building, crept to the rear, and took refuge behind a broad-leaved bush. He peeked around the corner and saw vivid white light pouring out onto the rear lawn from above two doors that were propped open.

Wolf now clearly heard voices. A heated argument was ensuing between two men, in a language that wasn't Italian. It was more Germanic, harsh sounding.

The first man was tall and lanky, with a spiked hairdo. Cezar. His face was in and out of deep shadow, but the body was unmistakable. The second man was unmistakable as well. Vlad. They were quarreling in Romanian.

Suddenly, a loud slap pierced the silence, and Wolf raised his eyebrows. Vlad was pleading in a crouch, and Cezar was shuffling toward him with a raised hand.

Wolf's pulse accelerated at the unmistakable sight of a pistol in Cezar's hand, pointed straight at Vlad's head. Wolf was unarmed, and he decided at that moment that confrontation was out of the question. Avoiding detection had just become a high priority.

Wolf watched the action unfold. Both men were momentarily frozen in their theatrical poses. Then Cezar shuffled his feet closer, apparently seriously considering the repercussions of shooting Vlad or not shooting Vlad. Vlad hunched down further, apparently hoping the few inches of distance would save him from certain death.

Cezar abruptly relaxed his posture, put the pistol in the back of his pants, and turned and walked away. He stopped a few feet away and stooped over.

Wolf narrowed his eyes. He hadn't noticed until now that a box-shaped moving truck was parked, rear facing and wide open. The interior was pitch black due to the angle of the lights.

Cezar was rummaging through things inside of it, speaking in a nonchalant tone. A few seconds later, they both walked swiftly into the building. Then there were two loud clacks and the doors slowly swung shut.

The lights went off, plunging the property into total darkness. Wolf hunched down with the sudden change. Past experience told him it would be about thirty minutes for his night vision to fully develop after exposing his eyes to that much light. However, waiting was not an option.

There was no noise coming from within the observatory. No conversation. Wolf realized that Vlad and Cezar had entered the building to take care of something—something that would take long enough to justify shutting off the light, but not so long that they would risk leaving the truck open. There wasn't going to be a better opportunity. *Now or never*, he thought.

He sprinted to the side of the truck, stopping with his back pressed to the aluminum exterior, then peeked around the corner. Blood pumped hard in his ears, his breath fast, yet controlled. A fresh taste of the earlier cigarette pumped out of his lungs.

The truck interior was dark. Very dark.

One of the first things he'd learned about night tracking, first from his father, and later in the army, was to use peripheral vision in low-light situations. Looking straight at something utilized the cone cells on the retina, which were rendered worthless if too dark. Scanning with the peripheral used the rod cells, which were distributed more evenly throughout the back of the retina.

He swept his vision, taking in the truck interior with an unfocused gaze, and groped with his hands.

It was filled with computers, laptop computers, of all sizes and colors. They were stacked five or ten deep along the floor of the truck, all along the back and left side. And there was something else. Wolf counted six large cardboard boxes with flipped-open tops, also filled with laptops. None of them were new, Wolf realized, as he reached in and felt a few of them. They were scratched on the corners, and some had stickers on them—A.C. Milan, Vespa, Hello Kitty. *Hello Kitty?* Wolf pressed his face close to the sticker and felt it. It was on a laptop with a soft pink plastic covering.

Wolf remembered the conversation inside the observatory from the day before. Vlad worked for the EAS, overseeing the logistics of moving astronomical equipment between observatories throughout the European Union.

A clear mental picture was forming in Wolf's mind as to the true nature of Vlad's activities. As of now it looked like, along with astronomical equipment, Vlad was trafficking stolen electronics. All of them supplied by a gang of thugs led by Cezar.

Small light-colored boxes caught his attention, stacked underneath the open boxes of electronics. Wolf pushed back one on top, unveiling a stark white cardboard one about a foot cubed in size. A dark-blue logo was faintly visible on the side. He bent closer and ran his finger across it. It was the letters EAS with what looked to be stars or planets. He lifted the box. It was packed dense and heavy, and shaking didn't produce any movement or sound inside.

He straightened and turned an ear toward the doors, stilling his breath. He heard nothing.

The best he had in way of a blade was the tiny scooter key in his pocket. He pushed the small key into the tape, sliced it down the crease, and pulled up the cardboard. Inside was a square plastic bag packed tight, like a clear sack filled with flour. *Cocaine*, he thought. Cocaine was found at his brother's apartment, and a white bag was found at Rosenwald's. There was, of course, no way of knowing for sure, but if the shoe fits ...

A shock jolted through Wolf's body as he heard a jostling inside the two closed doors of the observatory. He shut the flap and replaced the box underneath the larger one in a quick move. He darted around the side of the truck as the outside light went on with a blinding flash. Wolf looked down. His feet were bathed in light. He took one large stride, aligning his feet with the tire, which put them in shadow, and hopefully unseen from the other side.

A door to the observatory swung open and hit the exterior wall with a thud. Vlad and Cezar were in mid-conversation, and one of them walked briskly to the truck.

The truck sagged down with body weight, and rummaging sounds came from the other side of the thin metal sidewall behind Wolf's back. Wolf looked to the front of the truck. He squinted and bore his vision into the darkness to see just where the truck was going to drive. It was parked on grass, with smooth black pavement just in front of the front tires.

His eyes followed the jet-black void cutting through the dark lawn. It went on about ten yards then veered. Wolf swung his body as his eyes traveled down the road, following it all the way to a gate. The road then veered to the right and lowered below the level of the property as it descended downwards along the perimeter.

A secondary punch of adrenaline hit him when he realized that the road was the same perimeter road his scooter was parked on, right out in plain sight, with a stack of coats on the fence directly above it.

He turned back to the rear of the truck again. He tensed as fingers came into view, gripping the back corner of the truck.

Just then, Vlad stepped into view from the back of the truck, illuminated from the floodlight. He turned and looked directly in the direction of Wolf. *Looked right at him.* "Eh?" He turned his head to the back of the truck. Vlad shot an uncomprehending glare to the mumbling voice Wolf heard within the truck and disappeared back out of sight. The truck slumped downwards again. *Further downwards.* They were both in the truck.

Wolf moved to the front of the truck, eyeing the open gate to the perimeter road. If he ran out to the gate, he could do it without detection, but getting the scooter as well? Not unless they stayed inside the truck long enough for him to slip past the fifty-foot section of road that was illuminated through the iron fence.

If they spotted him, would they recognize him? Wolf thought of Cezar's pistol, and then the man wielding it. Was he a shoot-first-and-ask-questions-later kind of guy?

Vlad and Cezar launched into a loud argument, which sounded like it was right next to his ear. They were deep into the back of the truck.

Shaking his head, he clenched his teeth, cursing his options. He shuffled to the rear of the truck and peered around the back corner. Wolf saw the faint flashlight glow and heard them talking, probably eight feet in. It sounded like both men were rummaging through materials.

He eyed the dangling rope above, and the locking latch on the truck's roll-up door.

Wolf sucked in a breath and lunged, gripping it with both extended arms, and pulled down with the full force of his body weight. The door slammed all the way shut faster than he'd expected, bouncing up from the floor a good three feet as he stumbled backwards onto his backside. He landed hard on his tailbone, then rose instantly and pulled down hard again on the handle this time, catching a glimpse of shoes inside. The door began to rise, and Wolf knew that the leverage two men had trying to raise the door from the standing position was much more than he had holding it down with his arm. It inched higher.

The locking latch was right there in front of his face, but the door needed to be completely closed. Putting both of his hands on the exterior handle, he pulled down with the force of his two-hundred-pound body lifted off the ground. It slammed shut, and at the same instant he flipped the latch.

Instinct told him he was already too late. He lay back and rolled just as loud reports from inside pealed open holes next to the door handle. Bullets smacked the asphalt next to him and whirred into the night.

He got up and sprinted back the way he'd come in, more muffled gunshots ringing out behind him. Huffing loudly, he reached the fence and vaulted it in a single bound, barely touching his left hand to the top with the adrenaline coursing through his body.

Wolf was suddenly flying ten feet over the scooter toward the rapidly approaching dirt road. Wind filled his ears as he fell motionless, and then he landed hard on his heels, rolling and smashing his hipbone into the ground. A split instant later, his elbow connected hard with a teeth-clamping jolt. He gasped, stumbled to his feet, and gripped his elbow to contain the pain.

He heard a diesel engine roar to life from within the property fence and he saw the swinging lights of the truck on the trees inside. There was a yell, then the deep gurgling engine accelerating hard.

"*Shit.*" He rammed the scooter key into the ignition and sat on the seat, rolling the scooter off the kickstand. He started it and cranked the throttle, producing more of an ear-splitting whine than any forward movement. He jumped off and pushed, sending a fresh jolt of pain into his hip.

When he couldn't run any faster, he jumped on, and acceleration gently took over as he was propelled down to the main road. To the right was the direction of John's apartment, but it was an uphill climb for a hundred yards or so past the front of the observatory property. The street slanted downhill to the left, which would give him more acceleration from the small engine.

He went left, shooting out onto the black pavement in a deep lean, just keeping his balance as both the front and back wheels skidded sideways.

The tiny vibrating handlebar mirrors showed the bright lights of the truck passing where his scooter had just been parked seconds before.

Wolf looked back toward the front barely in time to see a sharp turn to the right. He handbraked hard and leaned deep again. As he turned, the rear tire slid before grabbing purchase with a jolt, kicking the scooter hard right, leaning him into a sharp involuntary turn to the left. Like a rodeo cowboy, he kept his balance, but the move had caused him to lose all speed.

A straightaway stretched for a hundred yards in front of him. Cornfields lined the right and left, and it ended in a dimly lit township, where there would be small alleys and tight spaces to lose his pursuers. He cranked the throttle wide open and leaned down, the scooter inching forward with maddeningly slow acceleration. He checked the mirrors again. The hairpin turn was illuminated with bouncing light behind him.

They would run him down on the straightaway. There was no doubt. A two-tire dirt road materialized on the right, and he jammed on the brakes and leaned, launching himself toward it. He bounced onto one of the tire troughs, then cranked the handlebars, crashing into the cornfield.

Broad, cool leaves slapped and sliced his face as he rolled and bounced between thick stalks. He ended up lying in a row, staring up at the sky. He quickly crawled to the screaming scooter, which lay on its side, still running with the powerful light pointing to the sky, and turned it off. Then he reached up, steadied two cornstalks, and waited.

Wolf calmed his heaving breaths and listened carefully, hoping to God they hadn't seen any part of his crash, or they weren't looking at a telltale dust cloud on the side of the road in their headlights.

Wolf relaxed a little as he realized they hadn't yet completed the hairpin turn. He heard the diesel slow, and then he saw headlights through the corn as the truck swung out onto the straight portion of road. It coasted slowly and quietly at low RPMs.

Braking to a halt, the truck paused motionless for a few seconds, then turned onto the narrow dirt road Wolf had just crashed into. Light swept across him through the stalks as the truck crunched onto the turnout.

Wolf's heart thumped. Chances were good he could outrun Cezar. Cezar was a smoker, and Wolf would be a hard target in the corn. Of course, Cezar would have quite a stride on him, being so tall, and who knew what kind of shot he was.

The truck squeaked to a stop. It was no more than fifteen

feet and five rows of corn from Wolf. From Wolf and his *white* scooter.

He could see inside the truck clearly. Cezar was in the driver's seat, looking to his left out the glass, but more down the road than into the corn directly in front of him. Wolf stayed frozen, muscles tensed for action.

Cezar lit a cigarette, momentarily lighting the interior of the cab, and rolled down the window.

Wolf narrowed his eyes and kept an eye on the cab for any sign of a pistol. Light-blue writing on the outside of the white truck momentarily distracted him. It was the same light-blue writing as on the wooden Albastru Pub sign. In fact, it said "Albastru" on the side. However, underneath he could make out "International Shipping Co."

Wolf darted his eyes back to the cab as the truck rocked slightly on its wheels. The rear lit up and a continuous beep filled the air. The truck slowly backed up, pulled onto the road, and went back the way it had come.

CHAPTER 31

Drool ran up Wolf's face as he watched Connell, laughing maniacally and sharpening a stick with a camping axe. *Chop-chop-chop-chop.* Wolf dangled by his ankles, which were tied together with a heavy boat rope that had been slung over a tall tree branch.

He pleaded, but couldn't produce any intelligible words. He tried to move, tried to reach his feet, but could only struggle against the pull of gravity, which was way too strong for his beaten body to handle. *Chop-chop-chop-chop.*

Wolf woke with a start.

Knock-knock-knock-knock.

He looked at his watch. It was 8:15. When—p.m.? Had he slept through the whole day? He got out of bed, and stared at his watch again. He looked around the room. He knew where he was; he just couldn't put a name to it.

Knock-knock-knock-knock.

He moved toward the sound of the knocking, wincing at the hot stabbing in his left hip as he walked through the hallway. He turned the knob and pulled. It was Lia, wide-eyed on the other side of the door. Wolf came to the present moment in a sudden instant. He looked down at himself and straightened his twisted boxer shorts.

"Oh shit." Wolf looked again at his watch. "Sorry. I don't know what happened. I forgot to set the alarm last night, I guess. Come in." He stepped aside.

Lia's stiff expression melted to a slight smirk as she walked in.

"They say it takes one day per one-hour time difference to get over jet lag," she said from the hallway as he quickly put his clothes on.

"Yeah, I'm definitely still feeling the effects." Visions from the night before came to him like distant childhood memories.

Lia looked at his bare torso, her eyes stopping at the long scar on the front of his shoulder. "They have all the paperwork done to release your brother from the morgue."

"Okay." Wolf walked to the bedroom and put on some clothes.

"Let's go for coffee in the piazza before we leave," she called.

He felt as if he'd taken a handful of sleeping pills after just running a marathon. "Heck of an idea there."

Wolf freshened up as fast as he could and joined her in the main room.

They went downstairs and outside.

The piazza was warm and bright, bustling once again. Wolf decided that John had been onto something, coming over here for inspiration. Too many people for Wolf's taste. But, had he been here for any other reason than his current situation, he could see himself enjoying the atmosphere. Throngs of people milled around, double the amount he'd seen before, and the space felt more festive than ever. There were large groups of old men arguing, young kids chatting and pushing each other playfully. It was Friday, Wolf realized. No matter where you went, people lived more on Fridays.

They reached a bar, which was bustling no less than the piazza, and stepped inside. People were lined up two-deep against the counter. Baristas yelled and paced behind the bar—clacking, smacking, twisting, and frothing.

"Two," Wolf said holding up his fingers to Lia.

"You want a double?"

"Yes," he said. "It was a difficult night."

Wolf looked in the mirror behind the shuffling baristas and saw Lia's face turn red.

They had a croissant, or a brioche as the Italians call it, and slammed their coffee without eye contact or a word said.

Walking out, Wolf said, "Look, about last night. I didn't mean it was a difficult night because of you ... or because of us."

"I'm sorry about that—"

"No, I don't care. I mean, don't worry about it." He shook his head. "Look, there's more to last night. I went to the observatory, and I found out something big."

As they drove to the morgue, Wolf detailed the night before for Lia. He told her about the load of stolen computers and bags of white substance in the Albastru International Shipping Co. truck, how Cezar had shot at him, and the ensuing chase. He left out the part where he sat motionless in the cornfield for an hour after Cezar had left the scene, only to get hopelessly lost on the way back to his brother's apartment, finally shoving the keys to Cristina's scooter under her door and climbing into bed at two-thirty.

"Okay," she said, "that connects the Romanian bar owner and Vlad to the cocaine. I'm not sure what that means. Was Matthew dealing the drugs for them? Why were the baggies found at your brother's and Matthew's apartments?"

"I don't know. But Cezar was really roughing up Vlad last

night. He was furious about something Vlad had done. I had a little time to think last night." Wolf ran his hand over a scratch on his arm from the cornstalks. "I would bet money that if we found out where these two were from in Romania, the places would be one and the same.

"What did Dr. Wembly at the observatory say about Vlad? He was kind of kissing his ass, like he was surprised that Dr. Vlad had *chosen* to work there. He said something to the effect of, 'He's *gracing us* by working here.' Of all the places in Europe, he chooses that outdated observatory in northern Italy to set up shop. Why? I think it's because he wanted to be close to Cezar. Or maybe he didn't have a choice. Cezar might have something on him, might be forcing him to help. From the little I saw last night, their relationship looked that way—a bully and the bullied.

"Anyway, it's obvious that Cezar is running some sort of electronics fencing and drug operation, and Vlad's complete reign over a respectable European agency's shipping and logistics operation is a perfect means to transport the stuff wherever they want. The Albastru International Shipping Co. and the European Astronomical Society—it's a perfect marriage."

"So how does your brother fit in? And Matthew Rosenwald?"

They saw something they shouldn't have. Wolf stared at the passing cars parked inches from each other on the side of the road. "I think it might be best if I go about this alone from now on."

She laughed, and looked over at Wolf, then turned back to the road. "I will help you."

"I don't want you getting in trouble, Lia. I plan on getting to the truth today. No matter what it takes. I don't have any time left."

. . .

...

John's remains were packed in a heavy-duty plywood box with metal latches and handles. Large gray and black stenciling read "Handle With Extreme Care" diagonally on each side in English.

An air tray. He'd seen plenty in the army. All of them had stabbed his heart, but none like the sight of this one. He gave it a quick shove with his palms to check the quality of construction, an unconscious maneuver that told him nothing.

The agent pointed to where Wolf needed to sign, and he signed. He took his brother's bag of belongings, and the agents wheeled the box to a waiting truck. *Wasting no time.* That was good. John was on his way home. Wolf had accomplished half of what he had come to do.

Wolf and Lia left the morgue and drove to the carabinieri station. The underbelly ground floor was devoid of people, though the odor of sweat hung thick in the stagnant air. Apparently this floor was closed on Fridays.

"What is this place anyway?"

Lia looked over her shoulder as she climbed the stairs. "Immigration office."

Wolf nodded and followed her up.

Lia turned the corner at the top of the stairs and almost slammed into an officer jogging out of Colonnello Marino's office. "Che cazzo!" she said, coming to a stop.

The officer paused, then apologized and moved on.

A silence had fallen over the room, and everyone was stealing glances at them.

"What the hell's happening?" Wolf asked.

"I don't know. Let's go talk to Paolo."

They walked on and everyone resumed talking, looking

toward Wolf and Lia. Lia led the way to the computer genius in the back room.

"What the hell is happening, Paolo?" she demanded.

"Oh, good morning." He didn't smile. "I couldn't trace Dr. Rosenwald's phone. I found that his latest credit-card transactions were normal enough. Local groceries, and then a payment to the Albastru Pub on Friday night at 10:43 p.m. His car is missing at his apartment building. We are looking for it."

Wolf and Lia looked at each other.

Paolo shifted uncomfortably, now speaking at a million miles an hour. "His passport had no activity on it. Rosenwald doesn't seem to spend much time online. Anyway, we don't need to worry about it anymore."

Lia frowned. "And why is that?"

"Because they just found him."

Wolf's eyes widened. "Where?"

"Near the lago by the Osservatorio di Merate. Lying in some weeds."

CHAPTER 32

LAGO DI SARTIRANA was a large lake in Wolf's eyes, even though Lia described it as a retention pond. It was surrounded by dense vegetation and hills on the north side, where a bright-yellow villa reflected the morning sun. A trail circumnavigated the oval lake, the main access point being at a straight outflow canal at one end.

Wolf and Lia parked there and got out. To the left of the straight canal stood a few locals—some curious onlookers, some uncurious fishermen throwing in their fishing lines. To the right, local Police stood smoking cigarettes in front of a couple of portable barriers. Lia and Wolf walked by them without receiving a single glance.

Wolf noted the strange non-interaction. "They didn't say a thing to you."

"That was my ex-boyfriend from high school. He's an asshole, and he knows it."

Wolf resisted a laugh and glanced over his shoulder at the officers, now staring them down as they walked along the lake. One of the officers looked to be sick to his stomach, or love sick, Wolf thought, as the others taunted him with slaps on the back.

"Poor guy," Wolf said. "He still loves you."

Lia scoffed and said nothing.

The path was well worn. Fishermen's trash was strewn about—hooks, weights, old brightly colored lures, brittle knotted line, and lots of cigarette butts.

The lakeshore itself didn't look much cleaner. Plastic and glass bottles bobbed above the water line. A thick film of algae had blown up against the rocks and mud, piling on itself in small folds of bright green. The smell was that of stagnant lake water with frequent whiffs of raw sewage. It wasn't a lake for swimming in.

After a quarter mile, they came around a bend and the trail forked. The main trail went to the right, away from shoreline, and to the left was a narrow trail into wilder, dense marshland. There, the carabinieri were milling about.

Wolf followed Lia onto the path into the thick brush. They stepped on roots and rocks to keep out of the mud and puddles that had accumulated after the recent rain.

Rossi came into view off to the left, bent over a short distance away. He saw them and walked over.

"Ciao."

"Ciao."

Wolf looked behind Rossi. "Hi. What's the situation?"

"We have found our elusive Dr. Rosenwald. A few hours ago, an anonymous tip was called in."

A handful of carabinieri officers stood about smoking cigarettes. Wolf and Lia stepped under the perimeter tape toward an officer in heavy-duty rubber overalls who was bending over and taking pictures of something on the ground.

The body was well hidden. Whoever had found it couldn't have been on the narrow trail into the marsh the officers had just come in on. That person, or persons, would have had to have come all the way into the underbrush to see the body. Maybe chasing a dog. Or looking for a secluded spot to make out. Or maybe a million other reasons.

The first piece of the body Wolf saw was a Converse Chuck Taylor poking out from the dense foliage. It was light gray with mud, the original dark-blue hue of the shoe barely discernible underneath.

From the shoe, Wolf moved his eyes upward. Jeans, button-up white shirt strewn with dried mud and blood. He looked back at the knees. They were darker, with a circular mud pattern similar to how his brother's jeans had been.

Wolf tracked his eyes all the way to the face. He knew he would remember this for the rest of his life, as each dead body he encountered was a new mind-branding image he could never un-see.

The left side of Dr. Rosenwald's head had caved in. It was a blow much at the same angle as his brother's bruise, but delivered with lethal force. He figured Rosenwald had received at least two blows. He narrowed his eyes. Three or more blows were more likely. The first hit had probably opened a wound that gushed with blood. The second, third and other blows had occurred in the same spot, leaving some spattering on the clothing.

The channel in the skull was deep. There was serious aggression behind the blows, pounding the same spot over and over again. Wolf could see gray folds of brain within the wound.

"How many people have been walking in here?"

"Ricardo and I have been taking care of forensics for the last hour. The anonymous caller must have been in here, and who knows how many people he was with. We've had no officers come in here, on my order. But there are footprints everywhere."

Wolf agreed. Surveying the immediate vicinity, he saw little yellow A-framed plastic evidence indicators strewn about in an illogical display—a bent twig here, a footprint there, a cigarette butt too old to be relevant.

But no matter what Wolf thought, he had to admit that this was a difficult, if not impossible, scene to read. The heavy rainstorm they'd encountered yesterday while they ate pizza had hit this area hard as well and had drenched the body. It was sopping wet underfoot. The deluge could have washed away numerous pieces of evidence. Still, a few things caught Wolf's eye—the most definitive being two cattail reeds at Rosenwald's hip.

They'd been bent twice, which was completely unnatural—physically impossible without the help of human intention—once when the body had fallen on them, and again when the killer bent them back up, probably to ensure better concealment of the body.

Which indicated that Rosenwald could have been dumped here after he'd been killed. Which meant maybe he hadn't been killed here. Which told Wolf there may be a crime scene still out there to be looked at.

"Estimated time of death?" he asked.

Rossi looked at Wolf with tired, bloodshot eyes. "Looks like three, maybe four, days. Nothing definite. But Ricardo says most likely over the weekend. Could have been sometime Friday night."

"Underneath? What's it look like?" Wolf pointed and bent down.

Rossi barked to the forensics officer to come over. They rolled the body to the side and looked underneath. Lia put her hand on Wolf's shoulder and got down to look with them. Rossi put on gloves, and pulled the body to the side with the forensic specialist.

Underneath, a mat of leaves, grass, and branches were stuck to the back of Rosenwald's head.

A fresh waft of death and decay filled Wolf's nostrils with the movement of the body.

Dark-brown dried bloodstains covered the back of Rosenwald's neck, shirt, and the underlying vegetation.

"Blood on the vegetation underneath. The blood coagulated around the grass, sticks, and leaves behind his head. Looks like he was dumped soon after he was killed. The blood was still flowing down his neck, not yet coagulated."

"Yes," Rossi said. "That's what I was thinking as well. So we swept the scene, couldn't find a weapon."

Wolf was looking in the distance through the thick brush. Just past the group of officers, now smoking and pantomiming soccer plays, the silver reflection from the observatory dome winked at them through the trees. No more than a few hundred yards away.

"There," Wolf said, pointing. "Is there a path from here to the observatory?"

"Wolf," Rossi said, pulling off a glove and touching his shoulder, "let me finish, my friend. We have been here for over three hours surveying the scene. I have found out much. We couldn't find a murder weapon here but, yes, we followed the trail to the observatory." He walked back toward the narrow trail. "Come."

...

They followed Rossi down the narrow trail, to a small path that joined from the right. An officer stood guard at the narrower-still pathway, staring at the screen of his phone. Rossi grunted an order at the officer, and he looked up from his phone with a red face, then pocketed it quickly.

Pieces of orange ribbon were tied in small bows in various spots on the limbs. Rossi stopped at one and pointed to it, then moved to another and pointed. There were rust-colored bloodstains, not washed off by any recent rainstorms, sheltered by the dense foliage above.

They hiked up a small rise, slapping mosquitoes and pushing aside branches, and broke through to a farm road that led toward the observatory in the distance. Tall cornstalks with fat cobs lined both sides of the road.

Another couple of officers with two German shepherds were fifty yards ahead, talking on the top of the rise.

When they reached them, Rossi stopped and turned to Wolf and Lia.

"The dogs found a weapon here." Rossi gestured toward the side of the dirt road. Both dogs growled; one of them barked with teeth bared, slobber flinging from its lips. The dog yelped as the officer ripped it back, following with a sharp smack on the top of its head.

Rossi yelled at the two men, who pulled the now crouching dogs away to the observatory. He bent down and pointed closely at a tubular groove in the mud.

"The dogs found a copper pipe here on the ground. It had large amounts of blood on it still, on the underside, and fingerprints. I've had it taken for identification. We should know shortly whose they are," he said.

"Good," said Wolf. "About time we come up with some useful evidence. So, otherwise, the dogs didn't pick up any other scent here?"

"No, but they picked up a scent on the grounds of the observatory, even after the rains." Rossi raised his eyebrows and exhaled. "It looks to be where Rosenwald was killed. Then it looks like he was dragged down here, the weapon ditched in the corn here, then the body dropped down where we found him." He pointed back to the lake.

The lawn of the observatory was even more unruly than Wolf remembered, with foot and a half long grasses, weeds, and wildflowers making it difficult for him to walk without lifting his feet high with each step. It was damp, too, squishing with each step, holding moisture from yesterday's downpour or an over-zealous lawn watering, or both.

Other than the unkempt lawn, it was a meticulously manicured yard space. There were rounded bushes of all kinds in all sorts of smooth shapes. Vines clung to the rear of the entire building and the exterior of the rounded dome by design—touches that Wolf hadn't paused to admire the night before.

Rossi led them past a familiar spot. Wolf saw two wide skid marks in the lawn. He looked at Lia and at the marks as they walked by.

She followed his eyes and nodded.

Rossi continued, unaware of Wolf and Lia's exchange, toward a large circle of crime-scene tape. "Here is the spot." Rossi pointed as he came to a stop. "The dogs located a lot of blood in the lawn here. It seems to be where he was killed with the pipe."

Yellow evidence A-frames were everywhere inside the perimeter, numbered all the way to thirty-five.

Wolf grabbed the tape and ducked halfway under. "Can we go in?"

Rossi looked hesitant, then nodded and ducked under the tape. "It's wet. Good choice of shoes you brought to Italy." He looked at Wolf's old leather work boots. "Keep close to me."

Wolf followed, and stole a glance toward the area of the perimeter fence he'd hopped last night. The clothing he'd used to aid his climb over was gone.

Rossi led the way through the soggy lawn, their feet sucking and sloshing with each step. Mud patches were visible at the roots of the lawn. Wolf bent down next to a small yellow plastic A-frame evidence indicator. It was almost impossible to discern any difference between the spot and the surrounding area, all except for a tiny shard of white. Another nearby A-frame tent marked a larger piece, this time with skin and hair on it.

"The dogs were going nuts in this spot. The forensics team found a lot of skull fragments. The largest concentration is there," Rossi said, pointing at the number-one plastic indicator. "That is a large concentration area of blood."

Wolf stepped to the area and crouched down, looking intently. He imagined the A-frame evidence tent to be Dr. Rosenwald's head, then imagined his body lying on the ground. He swept his gaze in a tight spiral around the marker, working his way out.

Five feet from the evidence marker at two o'clock, a pair of indentations captured his eye. Wolf stepped over and felt the ground. There were two holes, just about the size of knees. He could see it clearly in his mind's eye. Dr. Rosenwald had knelt down right here and received the first blow to the side of his head.

He'd probably been hit once, fallen to his side, and was then finished off with numerous blows to the head, right at the number-one evidence marker. Wolf knew there would be chunks of skull, brain matter, and blood strewn everywhere. Probably under the soles of his boots.

He stood up and shuffled to the side, feeling another slight depression under his foot. Massaging the ground with his hands, he found two more depressions a few feet from the others. Realization sent a jolt of electricity up his spine. The mud circles on John's jeans now made perfect sense. His eyes closed slowly as he felt the knee depressions where his brother had taken his last conscious breath.

Rossi's phone beeped in the tone of a police siren from within his pocket. He pulled it out and opened it. "Pronto?"

Rossi held up a finger to them and meandered his way back toward the crime-scene tape.

Lia knelt down next to Wolf. "What are you doing?"

"Remember those circles on the knees of my brother's jeans?"

"Yes?"

"There were similar circles on Rosenwald's jeans, but less noticeable. Probably from being out in the rain." Wolf lifted his hands and pointed down. "There are four indentations right here on the ground. Two for each man who knelt down."

Lia let out a gasp and bent down to see for herself. "*Madonna*."

"Have you spoken to anyone at the observatory yet?" Wolf stood up, turning to Rossi.

Rossi was twenty yards away with his phone to the ear, looking at Wolf with wide eyes and propping an index finger. He looked to the trees and asked some sharp questions, then closed the phone, keeping his head bowed for a few seconds. He pocketed the phone and looked to Wolf with a pained expression.

"What?"

"That was forensics at the station. They have the fingerprints match on the pipe."

"Let me guess. A Romanian national."

"No, Sergeant Wolf," he said with a deep breath. "They are your brother's fingerprints."

CHAPTER 33

"WHAT?" Wolf's head spun as a splash of molten lead hit his stomach.

"They are your brother's fingerprints." Rossi folded his arms and looked to his feet.

Lia put her hand on Wolf's shoulder.

Wolf and Lia walked to Rossi, looked back at the evidence tents strewn about, then ducked underneath the crime tape.

Wolf walked slowly away to the observatory gate, turning his head to look at the skid marks as he passed. He continued on through the gate and out onto the dirt road, turning back toward the lake, toward the way they'd just come.

Rossi and Lia followed in silence, keeping their distance from Wolf.

Wolf continued until he reached the groove in the mud where the pipe was found and swiveled around. "This is too perfect."

Rossi and Lia stopped and looked at him with neutral expressions. Silence enveloped them as Wolf bent to study the impression in the mud.

Finally, Wolf stood and faced them. "My brother's being framed for the murder."

Rossi blinked and looked to the ground at his feet. Lia shifted uncomfortably and lowered her gaze, too.

As Wolf watched them avert their eyes, his impatience mounted. "So let me get this straight. He beats his friend to death, then drags him down here along the road, leaving the copper pipe right here for anyone to find. Why not throw it out in the cornfield at least? Or a better idea ... toss it in the lake a few feet away from where he supposedly dumped the body."

Lia pointed toward the lake. "David—"

"No, I'm not buying it," he said, shaking his head. "There are just too many questions that don't add up to anything. You just felt those indents in the ground, Lia. And you saw the marks on his jeans. My brother was kneeling down next to Rosenwald and got hit by this same pipe." Wolf pointed to the ground and glared at them.

"Okay, let's completely ignore that fact, and say my brother beat Rosenwald to death. Why lug the body all the way down there to the lake when he's just going to go kill himself at home?" Wolf looked up to the sky. "Here's a good question ... *How* did my brother get home? There's no way he walked. His girlfriend said she heard the crash at one fifteen that morning. There's no way he went home on foot; he wouldn't have made it in time. I'll tell you how he got home. His body was removed from this lawn, by someone else, and taken to his apartment to be strung up from a chandelier, that's how."

"He could have taken Rosenwald's car," Lia offered.

Rossi stared at Wolf.

Wolf turned his back and kicked a small rock into the cornstalks. "Okay, yeah. We need to account for the car." He closed his eyes and tilted his head into the warm sun, listening to the insects hiss all around them.

Wolf turned. "We need to go talk to Vlad in the observatory. He said the reason he wasn't at the bar with them that night was because he was at work. So, let's ask him what he saw. If he was here, then he can tell us what happened. You don't just miss a blowout argument between two guys that ends in a murder in the back yard, do you? It's beyond suspicious."

Rossi raised an eyebrow and nodded his head, looking to Lia.

"And you don't know everything yet, Rossi," Wolf said, pushing past him. "This guy, Vlad, is involved in cocaine and electronics smuggling with the owner of a Romanian pub in Lecco named Cezar. His pub is called the Albastru Pub. You heard of it?"

Rossi looked stunned. "Well, yeah. I have. Wait—"

"I was here last night. I saw the truck they were packing with stolen computers and drugs. A truck that said Albastru International Shipping Co. on it. I actually looked in the back of the truck and saw what had to be a hundred or more stolen computers. I ripped open a white cardboard box and saw what looked to be cocaine. There were at least ten of those boxes. It was dark. There could have been many more."

"When were you going to tell me all of this?" Rossi held out his hands.

Wolf blinked and shrugged. "There hasn't exactly been a good time this morning."

Rossi shot Lia a questioning look.

She shrugged her shoulders. "What?"

"Last night, I was shot at and chased by this guy, Cezar. The way I see it happening that night is, my brother and Rosenwald have a few drinks at the Albastru Pub and head here to the observatory, to take a look in the telescope. At Jupiter, apparently. We have proof of that on Twitter. Things go sour at some point, sour because of Cezar and Vlad. Maybe my brother and

Rosenwald saw exactly what I saw last night—them packing drugs and stolen computers in a truck. Whatever the exact situation, they somehow see something they shouldn't have, and Vlad and Cezar know they can't *un-see* it. Now that my brother and Matthew are a liability, Cezar deals with them the only way he knows how.

"They take them out back, force them to kneel down. But gunshots could raise some alarm from the neighbors, so they get a pipe. Some words are said, and Cezar flies off the handle, beating Rosenwald's head in.

"Maybe Vlad injects some calm, scientific reasoning into the situation. They know that getting rid of the two bodies is going to be hard, so they leverage a little deception. They decide to frame my brother for the murder. My brother is hit on the head with the same pipe, and then strangled with one of their belts. It wouldn't have been Cezar's belt—he's too skinny. Vlad," he said pointing toward the dome with a steely expression. "Ferka Vlad is a man with an ample belly."

"Okay. Then they take your brother back to his apartment and string him up?" Rossi asked with a tilted head. "How do they bring the dead body into the apartment building?"

"On a Friday night? They carry him in," Wolf said, shrugging. "Anyone watching thinks John's drunk and his buddies are bringing him in. They could have pulled right up to the gate in a car, brought him in, and strung him up. Then they make sure Rosenwald's body can be found in due time, and the weapon is left here in plain sight, with my brother's fingerprints on it. They probably figured my brother would be out of the country in a box before too long anyway, making the case even more complicated to figure out for you guys."

"How did they get your brother back to his apartment?" asked Lia. "That would have been a tough situation. How do they know where he lives?"

Wolf continued walking in front of them. "Maybe Vlad knew my brother better than we thought. Maybe he'd been there before." Wolf thought of Cristina, John's girlfriend. A Romanian too. *Was there a connection?*

"It seems to fit, but there is still no evidence. We just have your word of what you saw last night, and ..." Rossi shrugged with an apologetic smile. "We have to have something solid, David."

"Well, then let's go talk to Vlad and get something solid."

CHAPTER 34

VLAD SAGGED in the desk chair, sipping on a Coke Lite, when he saw them approach the office doorway. A puzzled, startled expression briefly contorted his face, and he coughed a mist of Coke into the air.

"Vlad, how are you doing today?" Wolf said as he entered Vlad's office.

"David, please." Rossi grabbed Wolf's shoulder from behind and eased past him. "Let me handle this. We need to keep this official."

Rossi reached out and took the Coke can from Vlad's quivering hand, clanked it on the desk, and swiveled Vlad's chair so the two men were face to face.

Vlad looked into Rossi's eyes with horrid fascination as Rossi placed his hand on Vlad's chest. Vlad looked at Wolf and then at Lia with a pleading expression.

With a violent movement and the sound of ripping fabric, Rossi twisted Vlad's shirt, pulled him out of the chair, and pushed him against the window. The aluminum blinds clanged and bent, letting in haphazard rays of sun.

"You were here on Friday night. And yet you told these two that you did not see anything at all."

Vlad looked confused, then nodded his head quickly. "Y-yes, sir. I didn't see anything! I was working all night Friday in my office—"

"I don't believe you!" He wadded the shirt underneath Vlad's chin, exposing his jiggling belly.

"You didn't hear anyone come into the building? They didn't simply come down the hall and see you working here with the light on? They didn't say hi to you? What is that, twenty feet away?" He jerked his head toward the observatory room down the hall.

"No, they didn't. I-I-I ... I heard them down the hall, and I shut my door to block out the sound. I had a lot of work to do. I was talking on the phone and had important conversations. They didn't speak to me. Then they just left. I didn't see them at all. It was only a couple minutes!"

"Why did you lie to us earlier?" Wolf asked. "You said you didn't see my brother or Dr. Rosenwald Friday night."

"You asked if I went out to have beers with them! I did not."

Wolf said nothing.

"I did not ever see them," Vlad continued. "When they showed up here on Friday night, I heard them from here. I was on the phone, and I could hear ... *someone*. But I never saw them," Vlad's expression hardened. "I'm sorry. I was in here working. I saw no one."

Rossi let him go and stepped back with wild eyes.

Vlad pulled his shirt down and heaved with labored breaths.

"What were you doing last night, Vlad?" Wolf asked.

Vlad paused. "Last night? I was home last night. Why do you ask?"

Rossi held up an index finger. "I'd like to see a list of shipments you have been overseeing for the past twenty-four hours."

Vlad looked at Rossi with an imploring expression. "Why would you want to see that?"

"Let me see them. Now. Pull them up on your computer screen there."

Vlad pushed a few buttons. A jumbled mass of numbers filled the screen in different-colored columns.

Vlad held his hands toward the screen and pushed his chair back.

Rossi gripped the back of the chair and slammed him into the desk with a crash. Papers dropped to the floor and the can of Coke Lite tipped on its side, spilling its remaining ounce onto the desk. "Show us the shipments for the past twenty-four hours. Now."

Vlad pulled his hand from below the desk and grabbed the mouse while Lia and Wolf approached to look.

Wolf pointed at the screen. "Click on that shipment there."

The shipment had an address from Merate, Italy, to Cluj, Romania. There were blue links lined up underneath the shipment title and description.

"Click on the commercial invoice and bill of lading," Wolf said.

Vlad clicked and an official-looking invoice sheet displayed on the screen. The list of contents included technical components with numbers, dashes, and letters.

"And the Bill of lading."

The document took a while to build from top to bottom on the screen—a scanned copy of an original document. As it appeared slowly in front of them, Wolf tried to read the pertinent information, written in Italian. Two words materialized on the screen.

"Albastru Shipping," Wolf said. "The same name as the Albastru Pub."

"Yes," Vlad looked at Wolf. "The owner of the shipping company also owns that pub."

"You guys have some serious ties to the Albastru brand, it looks like," Wolf said. "Beers after work and now the shipping company?"

"Well, that's how I learned about the pub. The owner of the shipping company approached me, and he told me about his pub. We are both Romanian ..." Vlad finished his sentence with a shrug.

"You Romanians all stick together, huh?" Rossi glared.

Vlad stayed silent.

"All right. I'm going to need the truck information for this shipment here." Rossi tapped the screen.

Vlad looked at Rossi with another strange expression, as if it were an impossibly unreasonable request.

"Now!"

"All right, all right." Vlad pressed some buttons and a printer whirred in the corner.

A piece of paper shot out of the laser printer into the collection tray. Rossi picked it up and studied the page, pulling it close to his face with a squint.

"Ah," he said, pointing to the piece of paper. "Thank you, Mr. Vlad. We will find this truck en route and search its contents. We have come across some anonymous information that you may be helping with the smuggling of stolen electronics. And drugs. If we find anything suspicious in any truck you are involved with, you'll be spending some hard time in San Vittore."

Vlad sat still without any expression.

Rossi turned. "Have a nice day." He looked to Wolf and nodded. "Anything else?"

Wolf stared at Vlad for a few seconds. "I guess that will do for now."

. . .

...

Wolf and Lia followed Rossi out to the rear of the building.

"I'll call this in right now. It shouldn't be any trouble to find this truck and search its contents at any of the few eastern borders. There are only three or so routes it could have taken, and only one reasonable one." Rossi tapped the sheet of paper. "According to this manifest, shipment delivery date is Monday in Cluj. They would leave for that delivery date today. There are truck restrictions on Saturdays in Italy. So with two days' travel time, they would have to leave today." Rossi looked seriously at Wolf. "But if it left last night, well, then it could be out of the country by now. Wolf, you are sure about what you saw last night? I'm putting myself on the line here, making this call."

"I swear on my life. There were stolen computers and boxes packed with kilos of cocaine in the truck that made these marks," he said, pointing at the lawn. "The owner of the Albastru Pub was driving the truck. The side of the truck said 'Albastru International Shipping Co.' and Vlad was with him."

"And you just happened to be on a night-time walk last night, seeing all this?" Rossi smirked, sweeping his arm out toward the surrounding land.

"Yeah, I took a wrong turn on a scooter ride."

"Madonna. You looked like a zombie after last night's dinner. You are crazy."

"I got a second wind," Wolf said.

"A second ... wind?" Rossi looked puzzled.

"Never mind. Just make the calls. I swear I saw what I saw."

Rossi pulled out his phone and began dialing.

They walked down the country road back to the lake.

Dr. Rosenwald's body had been removed by the time they returned. They continued past the taped scene to the wider pathway surrounding the lake.

Rossi put his phone back in his pocket. "Okay, I have every border crossing into Slovenia and Austria looking for the truck. It will be stopped, I will be notified, and it will be searched thoroughly. I've also sent out a, how do you say in English, notification for all law enforcement agencies for the entire northeast of Italy to look out for this truck."

"We call that an APB in the United States. All-points bulletin."

"Yes, now I remember that from the television shows," he said. "I just hope our friend Vlad doesn't decide to call the driver and turn him around before he gets to the border. If that happens, the truck is going to be difficult to find."

Wolf nodded. "I get it. Don't get my hopes up."

CHAPTER 35

WOLF'S STOMACH growled as they approached the car. So loud that Lia heard it.

She looked up at him and leaned back. "I guess you are hungry?"

"I thought you'd never ask. I would kill for another pizza."

She looked at her watch. "It's a little early, but I know just the place." She turned to Rossi. "You coming?"

Rossi was concentrating on something, eyes glued to the dirt path. "What?"

"Do you want to go have pizza with us for lunch?"

"Uh, no thanks. I have to go take care of some things at the station. I'll catch up with you guys afterwards."

"See you then. Keep Marino happy for me, please. I'm supposed to talk to him this afternoon."

"I promise nothing!" Rossi called out as he climbed into his car.

...

. . .

The uncut pizza spilled off the edges of the plate. Steam moistened Wolf's face as the waiter pushed the food under his nose, edging aside two cans of Coca-Cola.

Half a pizza and a full Coke later, Wolf asked, "What does Colonnello Marino need to talk to you about this afternoon?"

Lia shifted in her chair and wiped her mouth. "I have a ... deadline."

"A deadline?"

She looked at her plate. "To wrap up this case. To make you happy that all of your questions have been answered."

"I have a plane ticket for Sunday," he said, "and John is already on the way home."

"I know."

They ate in silence for a few bites.

"It's my job to make sure you are on that plane on Sunday."

"Believe me, it's in my best interest to be on that plane. It's in a lot of people's best interests for me to be on that plane," he said.

"I know. I'm just telling you what he is telling me." She forked a piece of pizza. "I think you have convinced Valerio about your brother's death, about him being murdered."

"Yeah? And what about you?"

"*I* believe the evidence is clear your brother was murdered. But you don't need me to be convinced." She leaned forward. "I'm just saying, if you have to go home without this situation being resolved, it would be good to have Valerio on your side. There are a lot of unseen forces at work here. Your brother's situation has come at an interesting time in our station."

Wolf frowned. "What does that mean?"

She leaned forward. "Colonnello Marino is looking to be promoted out of the current position he is in. The generali above him are choosing their next ... successors, and he is well known to be on the top of that list. Only the top colonnelli will be considered, and those top colonnelli won't have Americans coming in to question their investigations. If this gets out that you are here and somehow contributing to change the outcome of an already closed investigation, then that wouldn't be good for him."

"This case was going to be complicated anyway with the discovery of Rosenwald's body."

She nodded and took another bite.

"I know, I know. I'm just saying that everything is even more complicated now. The evidence points directly to your brother being responsible for the death of Dr. Rosenwald, and him committing suicide. The fact that Valerio has just stuck his neck out for you, as you Americans say, is very big. He is risking a lot by searching for this truck you saw last night." She raised her eyebrows. "Because he is next in line for the position of colonnello."

"And right now it's all tied up in a nice bow."

"Exactly. Everything makes perfect sense. Your brother's fingerprints are on the pipe, and it will look like a perfect explanation to Marino." She swiped her hands against each other, another done-and-dusted gesture.

"I don't care about Marino's career if it's at the expense of my brother's memory."

"Yes, I know. I am on your side. I am just telling you what I know he is going to talk to me about this afternoon. Marino has been angry and uptight the last month, and it gets worse every day." She forked another piece of pizza. "I know he'll not like the way we are reading the evidence presented to us."

They ate in silence for a minute.

"What is it, election time or something for you guys?"

"Something like that, yes. Everyone is trying to keep their positions, or move up in the coming weeks and months. I do not know the exact time everything will happen, but change is in the air and everyone is well aware of it. It happens like this every year or two. Men and their power struggles ..."

"Yeah," he said. "And how about you?"

"How about me what?"

"How's this big shake-up going to play out for you?"

She scoffed and put her head down, forking another chunk of pizza into her mouth.

"What? You aren't expecting to be moved up?" he asked. "You don't have your sights set higher?"

She rolled her eyes and shrugged. "I do. We'll see how things play out."

"What position does Valerio hold?"

She pointed her fork at Wolf, then touched her nose with her index finger. "He is a maggiore. A major. If Valerio moves up to colonnello, it will likely shift a lot of others up in rank, opening a spot for an officer. But I am young, and I am a woman. I don't think I have a realistic chance." She looked at the table, her eyes unfocused. "But I am by far the best candidate in the entire station."

"Good luck," he said. "I hope you can beat out Tito."

She paused mid fork and glared at Wolf.

Wolf smiled and held up his hands.

They ate in silence for the rest of the meal, and he thought of home. He had to get Sheriff Burton on the phone. Not being there in the days following the fight with Connell, and Connell spreading lies, was proving to be a PR nightmare.

Entrusting his future to the Derek-Connell-influenced minds of others was killing Wolf inside, especially since he'd lived his entire life not caring what others thought. Now, his whole future hinged on what others thought.

"Thinking about home? Seems like you have much the same situation going on," Lia said.

He sat back in the chair and wiped his mouth. "Yeah, it's a bit more complicated, but essentially the same thing."

"More complicated?" She scoffed. "I don't believe it. Nothing is more complicated than Italian bureaucracy. Nothing."

He set his napkin on the plate and sat forward, putting his elbows on the table. She matched the move, leaning forward conspiratorially.

"Let's say you and Tito were up for the same job promotion."

She shrugged. "That's not a stretch. He probably is up for the same promotion. His father is a very powerful man."

"Okay, okay. But how about if you knew a secret about him."

"A secret?" She scrunched her face. "Like, what?"

"A secret only you knew about him. One you couldn't prove but you knew to be true. One that would quash his promotion if it were known."

"I do know a secret about Tito. He is an idiot. It would be very bad for him to be promoted."

He leaned back and squiggled his right hand in the air to the waiter.

"Okay, okay. Sorry. What do you mean? A secret? I don't get it."

He leaned forward onto his elbows again. "What if you knew he was a murderer?"

"A murderer?" She leaned back and laughed out loud at the ceiling, a high-pitched natural lilt that drew the longing eye of every single man in the room. She looked again at Wolf.

Wolf hadn't moved.

"Okay," she said. "And how would I know that?"

"What if he'd tried to kill you? What if he'd attacked you, and tried with all his might to kill you, but you'd got away?"

"Then, yes, that would be very bad," she said, confused.

She looked at the plate in front of her, then started with realization. "Oh my God. This man you got in a fight with, he tried to kill you?"

Wolf took a sip of his second Coke and nodded.

"And you haven't told anyone?"

Wolf shrugged. "The opportunity never presented itself."

"Madonna," she whispered.

"Why is everything about Madonna with you Italians? You guys don't like taking the Lord's name in vain?"

She looked straight at Wolf. "You have to tell someone. It must be eating you up inside."

"Can we have a look at that police report now?" Wolf leaned back, letting the waiter clear the plates and drop the check.

Lia pulled it from her bag. It was a thick red paper folder with a half inch of neatly stacked papers inside. She exhaled, swiped a smattering of crumbs on the floor and opened it up. The top of the first page had an ornate swords-and-shield letter head. Underneath the logo was a series of cells with boxes, some checked.

The police report was foreign in every aspect to Wolf. He recognized his brother's name, Johnathan Dennis Wolf. Apart from that, he may as well have been looking at a schematic for a nuclear bomb.

She turned the first page over and looked at the second, then turned back to the first page again. "I will translate."

"Who wrote this? Was this Rossi?"

"No, a different officer."

They spent the next twenty minutes going through the written report sentence by sentence. It was mundane, and it was biased. Biased, Wolf thought, because it was written from the point of view of a group of cops called in to investigate a suicide of an unknown foreigner.

The report was written with conviction and little skepticism about the cause of death. An American had been found on the ground, strangled by hanging. The superintendent had called it in on Sunday on the advice of the woman who lived above, who was a troubled young woman.

She was self-described as dating the man, and was concerned that he hadn't return her calls or shown up for a date on Saturday night. She reported hearing a crash on early Saturday morning, which was most likely the chandelier dropping to the floor. She then knocked and tried to enter the apartment; there was no answer and it was locked from the inside. This, coupled with observations by the coroner on scene, determined the time of death to be early Saturday morning, just after one o'clock. The woman reported neither hearing nor seeing anyone else in the apartment with John that early morning, or leaving the apartment. Drugs were found on the scene, and close examination of the nostrils indicated the victim had used drugs.

And that was that.

Nothing jumped out at Wolf as any different from what he had heard from Rossi, Lia, the superintendent, or Cristina.

Wolf spent another ten minutes clarifying the wording Lia used, not wanting anything lost in translation. The clarification process didn't tell him anything. Nonetheless, something was nagging him. A subliminal whisper was telling him something he couldn't yet understand.

Lia looked at her watch and got up.

"We have to go. Marino awaits."

They went out to the street and got in the Alfa Romeo.

"I'll need to be in on that conversation," he said as he looked at his watch. *Two o'clock.* "I'm at the end of my rope."

CHAPTER 36

MARINO SAT on his leather throne inside his office, shouting loudly into the phone. There was a roiling stream of cigarette smoke rising from the ashtray, adding to the choking haze in the hot and bright room. As his skin and throat itched from the humid stench of sweat and tobacco, Wolf wondered once again why the window was closed.

Marino twisted, raised an eyebrow and a finger, motioned to the two chairs against the wall, then finished his conversation. He gently lowered the phone and then rocked back.

"Mr. Wolf, Officer Parente," he said, extinguishing his cigarette. Almost. It sat smoldering. "I am sorry to hear about all of the developments of your brother's case, Mr. Wolf."

He tented his fingers against the bottom of his nose. "I was shocked, to say the least," he said. "I ... I do not know how to, uh ... what to say? I know it must be difficult to hear these things about your brother. Especially being a police officer." He gestured to Wolf.

Wolf shifted forward, tilting his head, and took a breath to speak.

"But I don't like what you did this morning, Mr. Wolf."

Marino's voice raised in volume. "You put one of my best in a bad situation. He trusted you." He stood up and walked halfway around his desk, sitting one buttock on top.

"I don't know what you are talking about, sir," Wolf said.

"You don't?" Marino folded his hands on his leg and stared motionless.

Wolf waited.

Marino glanced at Lia, then back to Wolf.

"We've had some interesting developments in the last couple hours. We almost had all of north Italia going on a wild turkey chase looking for this white truck of yours. A hunch from an American ... consulente."

"That wasn't a hunch, I saw—"

"We found the truck." Marino spoke loudly, holding up his index finger again. "Without having to call a national search, Mr. Wolf. National search orders have to come from me." He pecked his chest with his finger. "So Officer Rossi took every action he could to keep me out of this cowboy show. I am in debt to him for that. And do you know why that is, Mr. Wolf?"

Sergeant. "No."

"They stopped the truck in question at the Trieste border within the last hour." He held up a piece of paper between his thumb and index finger. "The truck was searched thoroughly, by human and by dog, just like many of the shipments that go through that border. There was nothing but the parts listed on the manifest prepared by the employee my officers harassed this morning at the Osservatorio di Merate!"

"It was the wrong truck then, or they moved the goods off the truck." Wolf said. "I know what I saw, and I saw a truck loaded with cocaine and stolen electronics."

Marino chuckled, yanked a cigarette from the pack sitting on the desk, lit it, and dismounted in a highhanded pirouette.

"Ah, yes! The brilliant piece of detective work you did last night. I hear you broke into the osservatorio and saw some interesting things."

"Yes," Wolf said. "I did see some interesting things."

"Did you? Well, let me tell you a few interesting things. You were trespassing. Trespassing illegally in a foreign country. As my guest in this country," he gestured wide with his arms, "you cannot come strutting into Italy, and doing as you please. If you would have been caught, you would be in jail right now and there would be nothing I could do to get you out."

"If I would have been caught I'd be dead like my brother right now. Because I was shot at. How can you turn a blind eye to this? You've got a pub fronting as a legitimate business, going around murdering people, smuggling stolen electronics and drugs! If you don't care about that, then what the hell *do* you care about?"

Marino snapped his head toward Wolf and gave him a dangerous smile.

"Don't test me, Mr. Wolf. I am warning you."

Wolf took a deep breath. "I know what I did was ... unorthodox, and I could have put you in a compromising position." Wolf clenched his teeth. "I apologize. I was acting on a hunch. A hunch I should have talked to you guys about first, I admit. But I swear I saw what I saw."

"And I will take your observations under consideration and proceed accordingly, Mr. Wolf. But just because you have a flight to catch back home doesn't mean we can cut corners and ignore laws in this country. So, you are going to have to make a decision right now, Mr. Wolf. You have to trust me, and trust Detective Rossi, and trust Officer Parente and the rest of the carabinieri to follow up with this case. The proper way."

Wolf exhaled and put his elbows on his knees.

Marino's expression melted to sympathy, and he flopped down in the chair with a grunt. "Look at this from-a my point of view. I have hard evidence that a man used a pipe to beat another man's head, killing him with much anger. I have fingerprints, in *blood,* on the weapon. I have evidence that both men were taking drugs. We all know what drugs can do to men. It can bring out otherwise hidden rages in a person.

"I have evidence that a man hanged himself from his ceiling. I have evidence he died of strangulation. Putting those two pieces of evidence together tells me that I have evidence this man killed himself. There was no one else in the apartment at the time. We have a testimony from the upstairs neighbor that she did not hear anything at all. If there were men inside, she would have heard, would she not? The door to your brother's apartment was locked from the inside, keys still in the door. All of the evidence points to no one being in the apartment that night.

"And then," he gestured to Wolf, "we have a brother who doesn't want to believe the evidence that is staring him in the face."

Wolf didn't move. "You guys dismissed this case from the beginning. You haven't given it enough attention. There's more to it. You didn't even perform an autopsy, which probably would have told you that the bruise on his head was not after death, but before death. You would have found out that my brother doesn't take drugs. There wouldn't have been any drugs in his system."

A tinge of doubt crept into Wolf's mind with the last statement—doubt that had stuck him like a barbed thorn, burrowing deeper with time—but he kept his poker face. "If you had followed up on the receipt in my brother's pocket, you would have seen that he was at a pub the night he died. A pub owned by some shady individuals who are either current or former gang members. The kind of guys you want to look into further. Guys that I now know are smuggling drugs. It's not a stretch to figure out where the cocaine found at John's and at Dr. Rosenwald's came from.

"There wasn't even an investigation into the night of his death. Who was he with? What exactly was he doing? Where were the people he was with? These questions didn't come up for your investigators?"

Marino inhaled deeply on his cigarette, and let the question hang.

"Mr. Wolf, it looked like a suicide." He swiped his hands together and held them up, a gesture Wolf was becoming intimately familiar with.

"Not to me."

Marino took another drag and swiveled in his chair. Smoke seeped from his nostrils as he sat for a few seconds, and then he stood up. "I will have my men look into it further. Parente will help," he said. "You have my word. Now, I need you to go home and let us do our job."

Wolf shook his head and looked to the dirty tile floor.

Marino sat on the edge of his desk. "You will let us do our job. I do not want to have to take you into custody, Mr. Wolf. But I will not have you going around breaking into property and conducting an investigation by yourself. How would you like it if this happened in your town? How would you deal with it?"

Wolf looked at Lia, who gave him a sympathetic sideways glance. He narrowed his eyes and stared back at the floor, coming to a lucid conclusion. "All right. I have your word you will look further into the pub owner and the observatory employee?" He stood up.

Marino put his cigarette in his mouth and stood, hands out to his sides.

"You have my word."

Wolf exhaled, looking to the ceiling, a resigned look on his face. "Okay. I'll take the next day and get my brother's things in order. Then I'll be leaving on Sunday morning." He looked back down to Lia, who sat obediently. "Is it possible to get a ride to the airport on Sunday morning from Officer Parente? Rather than take the train again?"

"If it is her day off. You will have to arrange that with her."

"I'm on duty Sunday, sir," she said.

"Then Lia will take you to the airport in the morning. You two can arrange it. Now if you will excuse Officer Parente and myself, we need to speak about something."

Wolf shook Marino's hand and opened the door.

"Deputy Wolf," Marino called.

"Yes?"

"I'm so sorry. Good luck to you and your family."

Wolf nodded and closed the door.

In the room outside a few officers pecked at their cream-colored keyboards. The air was stagnant, hot and damp, and all the windows were shut for reasons Wolf could not fathom.

Rossi looked up from his desk and hurried over. "David, I'm so sorry. Did you hear about the truck?"

"Hi, Rossi. Yes, I did. They must have been spooked and changed their plans."

Rossi shook his head. "I'm sorry. I was going to let you guys know about it, but I was just inside Marino's office myself. I didn't have a chance to call. Then I saw you enter his office just now."

"No problem. Don't worry about it."

Lia came out of Marino's office, almost running into Wolf.

"Why didn't you tell us about the truck, Valerio?" she hissed, closing the door.

"I was just telling David, I didn't know about it until just now, then I had to talk to Marino. I didn't get a chance to talk to you when you came in here."

She shook her head in disgust, looking back at Marino's office.

"Anyway, thank you, Valerio, for everything." Wolf held out his hand and stood tall.

Rossi straightened and shook it. "You are welcome, Sergeant Wolf. I wish you and your family the best of luck."

"I would really appreciate it if you looked into this further after I leave."

"David, I am going to look into this personally. I've already spoken to Marino about it. If they are running a smuggling operation, I will get the evidence needed to bring them in. Then we can find out if they are behind your brother's murder, once and for all."

Wolf fetched his brother's computer from Paolo, said his goodbyes, and made his way to the stairs, giving one final wave to Valerio, who was dialing his desk phone. Valerio stopped and put the receiver to his chest. "Goodbye, David. Do not worry." Rossi narrowed his eyes.

Wolf nodded. He wasn't worried at all.

...

Lia glanced at Wolf for the twentieth time of the car ride. "What are you thinking?" she asked.

"I'm thinking I let my brother down." He looked at the hordes of Friday-afternoon lakeshore walkers whizzing by.

"We will ..." She let her sentence die.

Wolf glanced in the side mirror as they swept around a traffic circle. Another carabinieri Alfa Romeo cruiser trailed them.

He looked at her and nodded. "I appreciate it. I really do."

They pulled up to the courtyard of his brother's apartment building. He unbuckled his belt and climbed out.

"What are you going to do for the next couple of days?" She leaned over the seat, looking up at him with those vivid eyes.

"I'll probably get some rest tonight and just pack up my brother's things. Then, I have no clue," he said. "How about tomorrow night you pick me up and I take you out for a pizza?"

She smiled wide and laughed. "There's more to Italian cuisine than pizza! I will take you for Risotto alla Milanese."

He shrugged. "I have no clue what you just said. Sounds good to me." He closed the door and slapped the roof.

"Eight o'clock!" She rolled up the window and peeled away.

CHAPTER 37

THE ROOM WAS dark as a cave, the only light coming from the screen of his cell phone, which was chiming incessantly on the floor next to him. He shut off the alarm he'd set, ripped off the sheets, and stood with forced enthusiasm.

A bright flash flickered through the shutter slats and the building rumbled. He walked to the bedroom balcony and opened up the shutters, revealing a bright-orange sunset sky with jet-black storm clouds stacked up against the mountains. A long ground strike of lightning flickered for a two count halfway up the mountain, followed by a deafening boom that shook the windows near to the point of breaking. The thunder rolled for what seemed like a minute, the sound waves sloshing back and forth between the mountains of the lake valley.

It jolted him into action. He put on his pants, socks, and shoes and ran up the stairs to Cristina's.

He knocked and she cracked the door, showing her milk-chocolate eyes. She smiled pleasantly and pulled it open. The apartment was filled with the sounds of modern electric jazz and an aroma that made his mouth water.

"How are you?"

The three-hour nap had energized him. "I'm doing well. How are you?"

"One second. Come in!" she said shuffling to the stereo. She wore a pair of black tights without shoes, a long gray sweater and black leather belt that cinched to show her slender waist. Her sandy blonde hair was pulled up in a quick ponytail, which draped over her face as she bent to turn down the volume.

"Please," she beckoned again. "Come in."

He realized he was just staring dumbly. She looked a lot better than he remembered, and she didn't seem to be trying too hard. Maybe it was her chipper mood and the spring in her step. Or the perfect body, face, hair, and eyes.

"Who was that?" He pointed to the stereo and shut the door behind him.

"Oh, it's a group from New York. Incognito."

"Okay. Yeah, I know them."

She looked skeptical. "Really? You? Country boy from the Colorado mountains?"

He smiled. "I swear. I like them, actually. I've got some of their stuff, but I've never heard this CD."

"It's their newest. It's great," she said. She turned it a little louder. "I would think you listened to country music."

"I do," he said, shrugging.

She laughed, walking to the kitchen. "So what's happening?" She lifted a pan lid revealing a simmering tomato sauce.

"I was hoping you could give me a ride somewhere tonight."

"Right now? I'm about to eat. Are you hungry? I have plenty of food. Besides, it's about to pour!"

He looked out the window at the black skies, then at the spread of bread, cheeses, meats, and olives, and was suddenly not in such a hurry. "Yes, I am hungry now that I think of it. Thank you."

. . .

...

They ate pasta and listened to jazz while the rain outside drummed the dining-room window in sheets.

Swapping stories about John put them in a good mood, and it was a much-needed respite from the sorrow of the last few days for both of them.

"Cristina." He looked at her with a serious expression.

"Yes?"

"I need to know about these guys who own this pub. The Albastru Pub that John was always going to."

"Okay."

"Do you know the guys from home? From before you came here?"

"No, I don't. Why? Because we are both Romanian?"

Wolf wiped his mouth and looked out the window. The rain was letting up gradually. "Yeah. That's what I was thinking. How about this guy, Ferka Vlad, from the observatory? Did you know him from before?"

"I've met him before, that one time I went to the pub. But it was just the one time. There really are a lot of people from Romania in Italy. But I don't know many. I know that they are often looked at as criminals here, though. There is a lot of crime in northern Italy. There is more money in northern Italy than the south, so there's a lot of theft and people's houses getting robbed. The finger is often pointed at the Romanian." She shook her head. "There are bad Italians just like there are bad Romanians. But I do know that those guys at the Albastru Pub look bad. I would bet a lot of money they are criminals."

"So would I." Wolf looked out the window. There was nothing in her voice or mannerisms that said she was lying.

"Why? What's going on? What have you found out?"

"I'm pretty sure that the owner of that pub and this guy, Vlad, killed my brother. But they've covered all their bases, and I can't prove it. They're smart. Or one of them is smart." He set down his fork. "Or, they're getting lucky."

He looked around the kitchen, then got up and walked over to the knife set on the counter. He pulled four smaller knives from the bottom row, then checked the larger blades on the top. "You know my brother doesn't have a single knife in his apartment other than four butter knives? Didn't he ever cook?"

She laughed, then stopped, watching him put back all but two blades. He picked them up in one hand and brought them back to the table.

"What are you doing?"

"I need these."

"What are you going to do?" she asked. "You have to be careful with those guys from the pub. I'm serious. They are probably killers."

"Yeah, I know."

She shook her head with glistening eyes. "What are you going to do?"

"It will come to me." He picked up the plates and put them in the sink. "They beat my brother over the head and strangled him to death. And they beat Matthew Rosenwald's head in. Making it look like my brother did the whole thing."

He fetched the blades from the table, walked back to the counter, and put them back in the wooden housing.

"I'm just going to bring this down to my brother's apartment, okay? I'm sorry, you're going to have to get another set. If anything happens, I don't want anything tied to you. And, come to think of it, it really would be better if I could borrow the scooter tonight."

CHAPTER 38

FAINT AMBIENT LIGHT from the city beyond the piazza streamed into his brother's otherwise pitch-dark bedroom. Wolf was certain he was being watched, so he'd made a show of walking around in his underwear, turning off the lights in the entire apartment, as if he'd been going to sleep early.

Now he dressed quickly, putting on the darkest clothes he had, without overtly looking like a cat burglar. The two most important things he wore were tucked into his socks—two kitchen knives, the blades loosely covered with folded paper towel sheathes to protect his skin.

He patted the knives, twisting his ankles to test the tuck-job, adjusted his socks, and went to the balcony. The piazza was ninety degrees to his right and out of sight, on the other side of the A-ridged roof. The roof extended straight out at least fifty yards. He could hear the murmur of a bustling Friday-night crowd and see bright lights streaming upward against the humid air, thick with swarming insects.

There was no moonlight shining on the ceramic roof. It was dark, difficult to get a sense of the exact angle of pitch. He knew it wasn't too steep to navigate, no more than thirty degrees, but steep enough to keep his heart rate racing, and wet enough to quicken his pulse even more. If it was a ski slope, it would have certainly been labeled black diamond, he knew that.

The roof butted right up against the balcony to his lower right. Ceramic tiles could be brittle, and he had no idea how old and brittle these were. He also knew that old ceramic tiles that were wet after a rainstorm were probably slick with a thin film of clay.

He looked over the edge to his left, away from the roof to the narrow walking alleyway below. It was far—three vaulted-ceilinged floors up from the hard cobblestone ground. He stared for a full minute, not seeing a single soul.

He gritted his teeth, gave a sharp exhale, and stepped over the railing. He put his left foot on the roof and gradually placed more and more weight on it while still straddling the balcony. There was a creak. He placed more weight still and tested the traction of his left foot.

Satisfied, he stepped his other foot over, and made the entire transition to the roof, lying forward in a low push-up position, on his hands and tiptoes.

Wolf thought briefly of slipping over the edge, hearing the gradual rush of air become so loud as to be deafening right before he hit the ground with unfathomable pain. He shook his head with a humorless chuckle and began climbing up.

Small scrapes and creaks accompanied every movement up the kiln-hardened tiles, though none moved more than a fraction of an inch under his weight. He shuffled quickly up toward the ridge of the roof that was a straight line of shadow against the bright light of the piazza beyond. He stopped just before the top, not wanting to risk being seen from the other side. He got to the soles of his feet, stooping, his right hand in contact with the tiles, and made his way parallel to the ridge line.

Step by step, foot by foot, the tiles held up beneath him as he carefully crept along.

Impatience overwhelmed him, so he stood up with bent knees, arms out for balance. He looked to his right, unable to see the other side of the roof, so he knew no one could see him from below. He began walking faster toward the dark void that was still twenty yards ahead.

No more than three paces into his light-footed trot, his left foot gave way, sweeping violently down to the left with a ceramic crack. His right foot shuffled forward in mid-stride and caught on a tile as his body weight plummeted toward the roof. His right knee bent, smashed into his chest, bounced him up to the left and into an uncontrollable fall.

He hit the roof with a hollow thud on his left side. For a moment, he stalled, planking parallel to the roof ridge line, shifting slowly, unstoppably into a roll toward the roof edge. He extended his right leg out and up to stop it, but it was no use.

Without thinking, he kicked up with his left leg, extended his right arm straight above his head, and twisted hard to his right, toward the drop. A two-hundred-and-seventy-degree turn later, he split his legs and arms into a wide X, toes and hands digging for purchase, belly against the wet roof. He landed in a cacophony of cleaving tiles, which tumbled like the sound of plates sliding off a waiter tray into the darkness, now just a foot to his left.

Panting now, every muscle in his body straining, he forced himself to take a deep breath, then heard a few distant splatters of tiles hitting the cobblestones below, giving him yet another shot of adrenaline.

Ten seconds later, he managed to get back to a position perpendicular to the crest of the roof. This time, he went all the way to the peak, willing to trade being seen from within the piazza for living to see another day. Straddling the crest, he walked, low and quick, the remainder of the distance to the end of the roof.

As he approached the black void, growing discouragement gave way to instant relief as his eyes adjusted, revealing a one-meter drop onto a flat-topped black roof below. He could see puddles reflecting the city-lit clouds. The roof extended twenty feet, and then there was a steel rectangular structure at the edge.

He slunk over the edge and made his way there.

It was a fire escape. Steps zigzagged all the way down to the ground, or so he assumed. He wasn't about to test the strength of the railing by leaning over to see.

It wobbled and creaked with each step, but he was on the ground safely within moments.

His body tingled with adrenaline as his feet hit the ground. Turning to look back up at the stairway, he shook his head with wide eyes, cold-blooded conviction pounding in his veins. Now he knew. *This is exactly how the murderers got out of John's apartment that night.*

The piazza was just around the corner. He walked the opposite way, through a narrow gap, and to where Cristina had told him to go earlier. The familiar white scooter was parked right where she said it would be. He cranked the key, fired up the kazoo-sounding engine, and took off down the side street.

CHAPTER 39

He rode the scooter as fast as it could take him to the Merate Observatory. The gate in the rear of the property was wide open, just like every other time he'd seen it, so he planted the scooter in the corn and walked in. Checking the back door with a tug, he was surprised as bright light poured out, opening without any resistance.

Walking in like a stalker would have drawn unwanted attention. So he walked into the building like he belonged.

Opening the door, he strode across the brightly lit telescope-room floor while looking down at his hooded sweatshirt zipper, making a mild show of struggling to unzip it. A man at a computer terminal looked to him over a pushed-down set of reading glasses.

Wolf nodded and gave a quick wave as the man looked toward him. Wolf didn't break stride, walking through the big room and into the hallway beyond.

"Ciao," the man said distractedly, already turning his head back to the computer screen.

Wolf veered to the right, down the hallway toward Vlad's office, and allowed himself a quick look over his shoulder. No one was in sight along the hall that extended in the opposite direction, but a few lights were on. He glanced at his watch. 8:44 p.m. For a Friday night, it seemed positively bustling. But, then again, it was an observatory, where work was done at night.

He walked past an occupied office on the left. Inside, a man sat with his face to a computer screen. There was an Asian man looking over his shoulder—Dr. Chang. Wolf passed unobserved and continued down the hallway. Blinds were drawn tight over Vlad's hall windows, lights on inside, and his door was shut. Wembly's office was dark, looking locked for the night.

Wolf stopped, swiveled another look down the hall, and pressed his ear lightly against Vlad's office door. There was no sound.

He twisted the handle and entered fast.

Before he'd finished shutting the door, he already knew he was in big trouble.

CHAPTER 40

Nothing inside the office moved but the swirling digital lines on the computer screen. Nothing. Including Vlad.

Vlad sprawled motionless, directly face down. His head was tilted back, face balanced on his nose and gaping jaw, which was mashed into the terrazzo floor.

What bothered Wolf was not Vlad's lifeless body, but what was wrapped around his neck—a shiny black leather belt. A shiny black belt of a design he *might have* remembered seeing in his brother's closet earlier in the week.

His mind raced.

He looked at the computer screen. The lines had just disappeared, blanking out to a black sleep-mode screen. He snapped his head to Vlad and bent down, feeling his cheek with the back of his hand. The body was still warm.

Wolf stood up with a jolt and turned toward the door. He pulled it open with his sweatshirt-pocket-covered hand and scrubbed clean the exterior knob. Suddenly, he heard a faint two-tone siren somewhere in the distance. Turning to the exterior window, his breath quickened when the flicker of red and blue flashed through the closed blinds, and the siren became louder.

Wolf sprinted down the hall, past the Asian scientist, who was now taking a long swill of soda in his office doorway.

"Hey!" Chang's voice called as Wolf blew past him.

Wolf ran hard through the telescope room and out the door. He stopped outside with a skid and lunged back to the handle, wiping both inside and outside knobs quickly with his sweatshirt before turning and sprinting as fast as he could out the gate.

Red and blue pulses lit the cornrows in front of him as he ran. They were shining from behind him, on top of a quickly accelerating vehicle. He dove straight left into the cornfield, this time not touching a single stalk as he plunged onto the ground.

The siren was now muted, but he heard the fast crunch of tires, and the brightening strobe of red and blue told him the vehicle was getting closer by the second.

Wolf inched to the edge of the corn and stole a glance just in time to see a carabinieri Alfa Romeo Gazelle whipping into the rear property of the observatory. He waited for the next car, which never came. He held his breath and listened. A faintly familiar clack of the observatory door told him the officer had entered the building.

The body wasn't even cold yet, not even discovered by his fellow employees milling about, and the carabinieri were racing to the scene? Wolf instinctually twisted and looked behind him, half expecting to see whoever had killed Vlad sneaking up on him, but there was nothing but corn.

He stepped out and craned his neck to look over the corn at the building, seeing only flashing blue and red against the trees. Static and beeps, clipped Italian conversations, the sound of radio noise echoed in the still air.

He ran down the road to the scooter and pulled it out of the corn. Then he paused, looking and listening again. Nothing had changed. He pushed it up the dirt road, away from the observatory grounds, until he reached the crest of the rise where the pipe had been found. With a quick look back, he jumped on and coasted toward the lake—toward the narrow trail they'd navigated earlier in the day. *Toward the crime scene.*

That thought made him jam the brakes, skidding to a stop. Whether or not the crime scene would be manned was a toss-up. He knew there was a farm road to the left and to the right at the bottom of the small hill ahead, right where the narrow trail began. He had no choice but to risk it.

The narrow path at the bottom had yellow tape across the entrance, but no officer in sight. He fired up the scooter and gave it a small rev, sounding like a handful of pebbles in a tin can. He chose the road to the left, toward the road he'd taken here. It was also the road the carabinieri had just screamed in on, but it was the only way he knew to get back to Lecco.

CHAPTER 41

WOLF GOT off the ticking scooter and eyed the Albastru Pub across the piazza. It was lively, chock-full of patrons, with laughter gushing from the pub doorway as it opened and closed with coming and going patrons.

He walked to the front of the pub and studied inside the large windows. A thick and solid bartender worked behind the counter. His huge arms were heavily inked, pulling taps and pushing mugs to people crowded around the bar. A young waitress with a face that sparkled with piercings weaved in and out of standing customers, expertly balancing an impossible number of drinks on a tray.

A group of young men wearing soccer jerseys charged out with cigarettes in their mouths and sloshing mugs of beer in their hands. They were raucously arguing, probably about the soccer match on the televisions inside.

He dug in his pocket and pulled out a cigarette from the pack he'd borrowed from Cristina. In his experience, a box of cigarettes was a prop with many uses. Never mind the toll his lungs would pay. "Excuse me, do you have a light?" He flicked his thumb, ignoring the lighter in his pocket, which he'd borrowed as well.

Two of the bigger guys turned toughly, eyeing him up and down. "Yes, I have one!" Another guy stepped forward with a friendly smile and extended a lighter. "Where are you from?"

Through the window Wolf saw Cezar's tall head bobbing behind the bar, high above the other patrons. Wolf took the lighter and turned his back to the building.

"Tijuana." Wolf lit his cigarette, tossed the lighter back without looking, and walked away.

"Che cazzo?" the man asked.

Wolf hung a left, walked thirty yards and took another left onto a cobblestone road, and then took the next left into a dark rain-soaked alley that looked like it led to the rear of the pub.

He made his way through a slot canyon of thousand-year-old buildings. They were seamlessly connected, each with unique, and dark, arching stone doorways.

Ahead was a blind curve. Beyond it, a bright glow that reflected off the wet ground. He tossed the cigarette in a puddle and walked ahead, stopping when he saw two men standing in a brightly lit garage doorway, sucking on cigarettes of their own.

The two men were wiry, much like Cezar, as if they didn't eat much or had the metabolism of ferrets. They didn't look particularly dangerous, being neither tall nor muscular, but they'd likely been raised on the streets of a country he had no knowledge of. Whether from Italy or Romania, he didn't know the skills these guys brought to the table. They were heavily tattooed, and his gut told him they weren't just a couple of dishwashers out for a smoke break.

The shorter of the two guys was telling an animated story while the other one stood still, chuckling silently, looking self-consciously at the cigarette in his hand. Neither looked to have weapons.

They finished their cigarettes, tossed them onto the wet street, and stayed there, like they were going to wait for something. Then, after a minute, they walked inside the garage.

Wolf put another cigarette in his mouth and walked toward the bright garage.

As he got closer, he heard two men jabbering in Romanian.

He walked into the light blazing out of the door and squinted a look inside. The bright interior of the garage was large enough for one American SUV, or two Italian cars. Boxes were stacked along the walls of either side. It looked to be used as a loading dock for food and supplies. Here they would be offloaded from a truck, stacked, and brought into the restaurant, through a door on the back-left corner wall that probably went to a kitchen, judging from the clanking sounds that came from within.

The two men were hard at work, pulling full boxes from a haphazard area in the middle of the garage, taping them shut, and stacking them along the walls.

The boxes were brown, of the same dimension he'd seen in the back of Cezar's truck the night before, and, just like the night before, they were filled to the brim with what looked to be stolen electronics.

One of the guys did a double take when he saw Wolf, who was now standing in the garage doorway with a cigarette in his mouth, digging in his pocket with a frustrated look.

They both stood with wide eyes and walked to Wolf, chests out, heads leaned way back and to the side.

"Excuse me," Wolf said. "Do you have a lighter?" He flicked his thumb.

The shorter guy on the right took the lead, skipping in front of the other guy. "No, no, no, no." He wagged his finger as he approached Wolf.

Wolf took his left hand out of his pocket and pulled the

cigarette out of his mouth with his right. Then he splayed both hands out in a defenseless gesture. "No, sorry, I'm just looking for a lighter!" He pointed wildly to his cigarette.

The small guy put his right hand on Wolf's chest and pushed gently.

Wolf kept his hands up and shuffled backwards out into the center of the alley, a look of horror now displayed on his face.

The short guy laughed and patted Wolf's chest a few times, pushing him back further with each smack. The guy looked him up and down, like he was creepily sizing up a woman, then launched into an amused conversation, looking over his shoulder to speak to the man behind him.

Wolf snapped his left hand forward in a blur, landing a knuckle punch to the man's temple, and followed with a right elbow to the middle of the man's face a fraction of a second later. The first punch had been enough, knocking the man out instantly. The elbow was just to make sure the man wouldn't be getting back up, and to serve as a lifelong reminder to be warier of men bigger than he was.

The taller guy spat out his cigarette with wide eyes, ripping his hands from his pockets.

Wolf stepped over the crumpling body , watching the other man weigh fight against flight. Flight won out, but not nearly fast enough.

Wolf, in full stride, easily closed the distance between them, put his shoulder down, and tackled him from behind, just underneath the waist, landing on him hard, driving the man's chest and face into the smooth concrete floor with a slap. He bounced up onto his knees, grabbed two fistfuls of the man's greasy hair, and slammed his head down. The man went limp beneath him.

Turning back to the alley, the first man lay motionless with twisted legs.

Wolf got up and pulled the man he was on top of out into the dark, leaving a long red smear on the smooth concrete floor. He flipped him over onto his back to remedy the situation, feeling a slight twinge of pity for the man as Wolf studied the damage he'd done to his face.

Within a minute, he had both guys stowed up against a dark doorway in the alley.

He hurried back into the open garage and began rummaging. Boxes—some open, some shut—were filled with electronics. A stack of the white EAS logoed boxes was piled along the right wall. He lifted one. They felt the same as the night before, heavy and densely packed.

Clipboards hung on the wall. He pulled down the first board and studied the papers clipped to it. It was an original bill of lading from an Italian shipping company. The dark print was all in Italian, making it illegible to Wolf, except one line that said *Genoa, Liguria, Italia*. Wolf recognized it as the port city of Genova on the west coast of Italy. The line before it read *Tenes, Algeria*.

A shipment from Algeria? North Africa?

Sheet after sheet was the same. *Genoa, Liguria, Italia and Tenes, Algeria*. Another line item on the paper stood out, being that it was the same on each and every sheet. *Fratelli Importatori*.

A loud clang of a pot or pan from inside the door jolted him into quick action. He set the clipboards back on their hooks and ran out of the garage, careful to step over the darkening blood streak on his way out.

As he turned the corner, he heard the door inside the garage open with a squeak.

He ran quietly down the road and around the bend.

CHAPTER 42

Wolf ran down the alley, to the right, to the right again, and up to the front of the pub. He walked inside, nodding to the man he had bummed a light from earlier.

The man nodded with a resentful eye as he sucked on his cigarette.

The pub thumped with dance music, too loud for anyone to speak over. The televisions were all on the same channel, playing a soccer match that drew the eye of every male in the room. It was hot and steamy and smelled like he was wading in a soup of cologne and sweat.

Wolf looked for Cezar, but didn't see his head towering above the crowd anywhere.

Wolf weaved his way to the counter and found the stocky guy with the tattoos alone behind the bar.

He nodded and leaned an ear to Wolf, looking with beady pollution-brown eyes.

"Stella Artois!" Wolf screamed over the music.

The man twisted to the glasses and swiftly poured him a beer from the tap.

Wolf took a sip, paid the behemoth, and sauntered behind a

line of standing patrons to the right side of the bar, which gave him the best view into the back hallway.

The hallway ended in a kitchen where two employees were pacing back and forth. Beyond them was a brightly lit doorway, wide open to the rear garage.

Wolf watched as Cezar appeared in the open doorway and then stepped into the kitchen. He slammed the door and leaned against it, then turned and marched through the kitchen toward the bar. He was gritting his teeth and flexing both fists as he glided forward on his long legs.

Wolf grabbed his beer and threaded through the standing patrons, wincing at the various cheap colognes and bodily emissions as he made his way through the room. There was an open small table next to the front window, so he took it.

The waitress was quick to arrive. She had a half-circle piercing dangling from the center of her nose, a couple lip rings, and three neck tattoos. Her blue spiky hair was shaved on the sides with stripes exposing the white scalp underneath, much like a 1980s NFL football player, Wolf thought.

She asked something he didn't understand, then looked at the dumb expression on his face and smiled. "Would you like a menu?"

"Yeah, that would be great," he said.

She looked him all the way down and up, then left with a mischievous smile.

He watched her shapely body go for a second, and then took a sip of his beer. Tipping the mug back, he watched Cezar, who was now behind the bar and bending in toward the thick-necked guy's ear. He was yelling over the music, snapping his head sharply as he did so.

The bartender nodded toward the front window, just to Wolf's left. Cezar stood up straight and looked, eyes hardening. Wolf froze, the beer pouring down his throat slowly. He stopped drinking, letting the beer rest up against his closed mouth, and breathed through his nose, hoping the mug of beer was concealing his face from recognition. Then he realized they were looking at the front door as a warm, smoky breeze hit his face and a fully clad carabiniere walked in.

Wolf set the beer down on the table and bent down to his boot. He fondled his laces as if tying them and looked sidelong toward the red stripe of the carabinieri uniform pants. The officer was poised right inside the door for a few seconds, then turned and stepped away from him.

Wolf straightened in his seat and strained to see through the throng of people. He spied Cezar, who was wide-eyed and looked to be turning pale. His Adam's apple was bobbing up and down fast as he swallowed, like he desperately needed a drink of water.

Cezar seemed to be shitting himself, and he should have been, Wolf thought, with the stuff he had sitting a few feet away in his garage.

Wolf stood and shuffled through the crowd to get a better look, his curiosity piqued. Had the carabinieri begun their investigation into the shady dealings of the Albastru Pub?

The waitress with the piercings cut him off. "You not going to eat after all?" Her bottom lip was out with a pouty look.

"Uh, yeah, sorry. I think I'm just going to go up to the bar." He pointed past her, and then stopped abruptly, accidentally juking the waitress into bumping straight into him.

She laughed excitedly, placing her tiny hand on the small of his back. "Oh, sorry!" she giggled, pressing into him a little too hard.

He ignored her, because he was still looking at Cezar, who had made a subtle move that didn't make sense. Cezar had just nodded his head toward the far end of the bar.

Wolf looked to the carabinieri officer, who changed the direction of his approach, following the nod.

It was an odd interaction. It was like Cezar was calling the location of the conversation, which he was, or else he wouldn't have nodded his head. It was too familiar a gesture, as if they were friends.

The officer reached the end of the bar, plopped his hat down and leaned over onto his elbows.

Cezar reached him and leaned down, launching into a conversation in the officer's left ear. The carabinieri officer turned his head to his right, revealing the unmistakable profile of Detective Valerio Rossi. Cezar gestured behind himself with a thumb, and then also sat his elbows on the counter.

Cezar was looking at Rossi with raised eyebrows, looking like he was waiting for some kind of an answer from the carabiniere.

Rossi stood slowly and stared at his hat on the counter, contemplating something. Then he looked around, down the length of the bar, then at the mass of people.

Wolf's heart skipped. Something wasn't right.

He looked down at the waitress, who was pulling her hand back and moving on with her life. As she shuffled past, Wolf twisted away from the bar to follow her, then gently pulled on her arm.

She turned back with a puppy-dog look of curiosity.

He bent and kissed her, and she returned the gesture eagerly, clicking her tongue piercing against his teeth. Wolf opened his eyes and searched the reflection in the front window while they kissed. Rossi was walking straight toward him.

He stopped kissing her and breathed in her ear. "Sorry, no. I won't be eating tonight after all."

"That's too bad." Her breath was hot, her lips flicking his earlobe. "Well, we could always eat together later."

"What's that?" he said, pointing at his ear, keeping his head down. She repeated herself as Rossi pushed past Wolf's right shoulder, *brushing right up against him*, and out the front door.

Wolf stood and watched Rossi leave. Rossi walked out in a fast march, took a left down the road, and went out of sight.

Looking in the window reflection again, Wolf saw Cezar turn the corner back into the rear of the pub.

Wolf pushed past the waitress and walked to the door.

"Fucking American piece of sh—" the waitress's voice was snuffed out by the door as it shut.

"Goodbye, asshole." The soccer fan with a lighter raised his beer to Wolf as he walked past.

CHAPTER 43

Wolf drove the scooter back to Cristina's parking spot and headed into the piazza. He threaded his way into the crowd, all the while keeping an eye on his brother's apartment three floors up. The lights were blazing inside, and a plain-clothes officer stood on the balcony looking into the thrumming Friday night crowd below.

Wolf stopped and watched. The officer looked to the northwest corner of the piazza, then, raising a radio to his mouth, turned to look directly at him.

Wolf flinched as static erupted just a few feet away, and a tinny voice spoke through a radio.

Without looking at who it was carrying the radio, he slalomed through the crowd and made his way to the side shops, then ducked into a narrow street. He lit a cigarette and puffed, surveying the piazza from behind the thin smokescreen.

Scanning the crowd, he shuffled the events of the past week in his mind.

Rossi was everything. And Wolf needed to be careful, or surely he'd be spending the rest of his life in an Italian prison for the murder of Ferka Vlad. Either that, or going home in a box right behind his brother.

Wolf dropped the cigarette and walked downhill along a side street, working his way right, then right again, into a pulsing artery of people that flowed back into the light of the piazza.

Wolf centered himself within the flow of people and shuffled forward, surveying ahead. He saw the familiar face of Tito, just inside the entrance to the piazza along the left side, talking conspiratorially on his cell phone. Wolf made his way toward him.

A few moments later he made his way to the edge of the river of humanity and stood near a wall watching Tito. Waiting.

As the young officer finally ended his phone call and was pulling out a cigarette, Wolf approached him. "Can I get one of those, Officer?"

Tito's eyes widened as he froze.

Wolf nodded and stepped close. "How's it going? You looking for me?"

Tito's mouth sagged open, dropping the unlit cigarette from his mouth. "What are you ..." Tito stopped talking when Wolf walked around him and applied pressure sharply to the small of his back. Wolf waited patiently for Tito to fumble with his empty holster, look down, and finally realize that his own Beretta was being held on him.

"Don't you dare make a move or a sound," Wolf said in Tito's ear. "I've got nothing to lose here. If I have to kill you to get away, that's no problem with me."

People streamed by, each person pushed forward by the current of humans behind them, none seeing the situation for what it was.

Wolf jabbed the barrel up into the back of his ribs. "Give me your phone."

Tito pulled it out, and Wolf took it. *Capitano Rossi* was displayed on the screen as the last call made.

"What was Rossi telling you?"

Tito arched his back at the gun's pressure and winced.

"Relax, Tito." Wolf stepped in front of him and removed the radio from Tito's chest clip. "Just relax. You stay right here as if all is fine." Wolf put the radio and phone in one of his sweatshirt pockets, and pointed the gun at Tito's belly through the fabric of the other. "Otherwise, I'm going to shoot you."

Tito's face paled and his arms went limp by his sides.

"Good. Now tell me. What did Rossi just say?"

"He wanted to know if I had seen you yet."

"Yeah? And what did you tell him?"

"I said I had not."

"Okay, and what did he say?"

"He was angry, and said to call him when I saw you."

"Why?"

"What do you mean, why? He did not say why, just to call him."

Wolf eyed him. "Remember what I said. I'll be watching you, so stay here." Wolf smiled. "We'll have a laugh about this someday, I promise."

CHAPTER 44

Wolf walked briskly away from the piazza against the flow of traffic, sure that Tito was already running for help. Wolf took one random turn after another, making his way downhill.

He searched the phone contacts and dialed a number. The long tone rang against his ear as he walked.

"Pronto?" Paolo's voice was distant sounding.

"You in front of a computer?"

"Tito? What? Who ees thees?"

Wolf stopped walking. "It's David Wolf. I'm here with Lia and Tito. But, listen, we have a few favors to ask, well, *Lia* has a couple favors."

He proceeded with one of the best acting jobs of his life, and hung up with a spark of hope.

Wolf continued walking and scrolled through the phone contacts, and finally found Lia's phone number under *Tenente Parente.*

The phone rang unanswered, and then cut out with a rapid beeping noise.

Wolf cursed and looked at the phone. The reception bars were gone, a dashed line in their place.

"Shit." He backtracked his route, keeping his eyes on the reception bars and the people around him. As he turned a corner, the reception came back.

He dialed again, and pressed the phone to his ear, listening to it ring for a full thirty seconds. His stomach sank. He hadn't thought of the simple fact that Lia would probably screen Tito's calls at all costs.

Wolf ended the call and exhaled. He stared up, pleading to a higher power for another idea. A swarm of huge insects clouded around the lights along the tall walls of the surrounding buildings.

Shit. There was no other plan.

The phone vibrated in his hand. Wolf looked at the phone, the illuminated screen displayed *Tenente Parente*. "Hello?"

There was silence on the other end.

"Lia? Is that you?"

"Yes, who is this?"

"It's David. I'm on Tito's phone."

There was silence on the other end, then a group of 50 cc motorcycles revving loudly into the phone. A split second later, Wolf heard the same sound in his free ear, though much fainter, coming from the direction of the piazza.

"How's the surveillance coming?" Wolf asked.

There was silence for a second. Wolf looked back at the phone reception. "Where are you, David?" she asked.

"I'm near."

She stayed silent.

"I didn't do it," he said.

"Didn't do what?"

"You know what I'm talking about. Vlad. I didn't kill him."

She exhaled into the receiver.

"Look, I need to meet with you," he said. "I've figured everything out. I need to meet with you and Rossi. Get hold of him, and you two meet me at John's apartment in one hour. Okay?"

She paused a beat. "What's going on, David?"

"I'll tell you when you show up, all right? All I ask is that you make sure you answer each and every phone call you get tonight. All right? It's important."

He hung up and headed back down the street and around the corner. There he stood and smoked another cigarette in a dark alleyway, for no other reason than he was getting used to the vile things once again, and he needed to kill time.

After watching the thin stream of people walk by for ten minutes, he walked out of the alley and headed downhill again. He went a block and took a right at the next corner, and straight into a pistol pointed in his face.

CHAPTER 45

BEHIND THE SOUND-SUPPRESSED pistol was the now familiar tiny smiling mouth of Cezar. "Don't move."

Wolf didn't move.

The pistol didn't waver, and Cezar's knuckle was white with tension on the trigger. He wondered just how fast Cezar was. If there would be any hesitation in shooting him. The sound-suppresser said no.

"I said, don't move," Cezar repeated, reading Wolf's thoughts.

Wolf slowly raised his hands out to his sides. Just then a shuffling came up behind him, and hands dug into his waistband, pulling out the Beretta tucked into the back of his jeans.

"Ciao," Rossi's husky voice said behind him. "Let's go." He shoved Wolf on the back.

They walked for three or four minutes to the soundtrack of Cezar's long stride and his energetic throat clearing, and Rossi's shorter stride and heavy mouth-breathing.

Down and down they continued along twisting and turning narrow streets, through pockets of open-sewage smell. Of the few people they saw this far from the piazza, only a few noticed what was happening as they passed. Those that did let out hushed whispers and turned with interest to watch the strange procession.

They came around a slight bend to Rossi's parked carabinieri Alfa Romeo.

They reached the door and Rossi turned to Wolf. "Put your hands behind your back."

Wolf stopped and looked around, putting his hands on his hips.

Rossi raised his hand in a fluid motion, pointing his own suppressed Beretta at the side of Wolf's face. "I said, put your hands behind your back."

Wolf narrowed his eyes. "It was you who killed my brother."

Two gargantuan hands gripped his wrists and shoved him up against the side of the car. Steel handcuffs clamped hard and tight.

Wolf lashed his right heel up and back with as much strength as he could muster, connecting hard with the tall man behind him. Wolf looked over his shoulder to check the damage.

Cezar was doubled over on the ground, grabbing at his crotch with both hands.

Wolf smiled, and then all went black.

CHAPTER 46

Cold water slammed into Wolf's face, forced itself underneath his eyelids. He sat up straight, sucking in a hard breath, blinking and wincing in pain.

"Ancora!"

Another cold explosion hit his face, knocking his head back and shocking him into a wide-mouthed inhale. He shook the water away and opened his eyes, then shut them against the blinding onslaught of light.

A bright halogen light on a pole stood in front of him, shining directly in his face. He tilted his head down and squinted. The first thing he saw was a man sitting cross-legged against a wall to his right.

The guy had a bloody towel pressed against his nose. He lowered it, revealing a rueful grin.

Wolf nodded a greeting. It was the guy he had tackled in the garage earlier.

Next to the man were clipboards hanging on the wall, and a door. Wolf realized he was back in the Albastru Pub's garage.

The light shifted upwards toward the ceiling, and Wolf turned to look straight ahead.

Rossi was lounging in a chair with his foot on his knee, smoking a cigarette.

Wolf coughed lightly, lungs itching from the smoke. "Everyone's always smoking in this country."

Rossi took a long drag and smiled, but it was a different smile than Wolf was accustomed to seeing on the man. His face had changed. His eyes had changed. A cold stare replaced his usual friendly squint.

"You should have stayed home, Officer Wolf." He didn't blink.

Wolf did a double take to his left. A dead body, a man, lay on a sprawled-out piece of clear plastic. Nose to chest, he was caked with dark maroon blood. There was a neat hole in his head, and he lay in a large pool of brighter red blood. A pool that, upon closer study, was still spreading slowly. Wolf recognized the man, but couldn't recall from where.

Wolf's head ached. He looked back at Rossi, a movement that sent a pulse of pain bouncing through his skull. "It's *Sergeant* Wolf, dickhead."

Rossi's eyes widened with amusement. "Oh, I am sorry." He pointed to the body on the floor. "The man you murdered tonight."

Wolf looked again at the body, then back to Rossi.

"The man who also murdered you, I'm sorry to say." He took another drag of his cigarette. "You two shot each other."

Wolf leaned forward to sit up, to shake the cobwebs. He went dizzy and fell forward. Subconsciously, Wolf had assumed he was somehow fastened to the chair, but there was just a pair of steel cuffs on his wrists behind his back, so he kept plummeting forward.

Rossi caught him and pushed him upright again. "Whoa, attento, Deputy Wolf! I guess I should not have hit you so hard. You are not doing so well."

Wolf remembered the pistol in his face. The side street. Being escorted out at gunpoint by Cezar. The walk. Kicking Cezar in the balls. *The phone calls.* Wolf smiled at the memory of Cezar buckled over on his side on the damp alley street.

Rossi sat back and returned the smile with a tilt of his head. "What is it ... Sergeant Wolf?"

Wolf's smile vanished and he glared into Rossi's eyes. "I'm going to kill you, Rossi. You were the one who killed my brother, and I'm going to kill you for that."

Rossi inhaled sharply and sat back, launching into a lazy overhead stretch with his arms. "I don't think so, Mr. Wolf. Just a few more minutes now, and you'll be dead." He smacked his lips and crossed his arms.

Bouncing light filled the space beyond Rossi, and Wolf realized that the door to the garage was wide open behind him.

Rossi got up slowly, turned around and poked his head out the garage. "Ah, here is your ride right now."

A white truck emblazoned with a blue Albastru International Shipping Co. logo slowed at the door then rumbled past. Reverse lights lit the rear of the truck and a loud continuous beep split the air.

Rossi slapped the back of the truck. It stopped, and he lifted the rear door.

Wolf noticed the metal patchwork on the door of the truck, covering the bullet holes from the night before.

Cezar stepped into view from the driver's side of the truck, and the thick-necked rhino of a guy stepped into view from the other side.

Wolf watched as Rossi launched into a speech, gesturing to the guy on the floor, Wolf, and the other man sitting against the wall. Cezar and Thick-Neck-Tattooed-Bartender nodded their heads, and then sprang into action. They set down a fresh sheet of plastic, moved the dead guy onto it, and then wrapped him up like a burrito. Then they carefully picked up the old blood-soaked sheet of plastic from each corner and folded it without spilling a drop.

Cezar and the bartender moved the body and plastic into the back of the open truck, and then unfurled a fresh piece. Rossi leaned against the wall and lit another cigarette, watching with a hint of a smile on his lips.

Wolf flexed his feet up and down. Blood was circulating poorly in his legs. Through the numb tingling, he could still feel the pressure of the knives tucked into his socks.

Wolf eyed the plastic sheet with indifference. "So, do you want to know why you're killing me too late, Rossi?"

Rossi took the cigarette out of his mouth and narrowed his eyes at Wolf.

Wolf had his attention. "I know about your dad."

Rossi rolled his eyes and tilted his head back. "Please, Mr. Wolf. Die with dignity, why don't you? Your brother did, you know. He died with dignity. Of course, he was unconscious when I strangled him, but—"

"In fact, I've already told other people about your dad," Wolf said. "People in the carabinieri. Your days are numbered. Hell, your hours are numbered."

Panic flickered for a tiny moment in Rossi's face, and Wolf knew he'd hit home.

Cezar saw it too, because the tall man paused in the middle of cutting the sheet of plastic and stared imploringly at Rossi.

Rossi gave him a sideways glance and glared at Wolf. "What exactly are you talking about, Mr. Wolf? What do you *think* you know?"

"It's over, Rossi. It's just a matter of time before they tie you and your brother with the activities going on here. A good forensic accountant will find you out in no time."

Rossi stared hard and then shook his head, laughing. "You don't know what you are talking about, Mr. Wolf."

"You're laughing, but you're going down, and you know it. It's over. Your life is over. I know that your father didn't leave you an inheritance three years ago. And now other people, your fellow carabinieri officers, do too. Tomorrow your job won't be waiting for you, Rossi. But a jail cell will be."

Rossi nodded. "And a coffin is waiting for you, Mr. Wolf. Goodbye." And with that, Detective Rossi turned and walked out of the garage.

CHAPTER 47

CEZAR and the bartender followed Rossi out the door and out of sight into the alley.

Wolf looked to his right. The guy whose face Wolf had smashed into the floor earlier was just a few feet away, still slumped against the wall. He sat looking eagerly toward the garage door, gently patting the bloodied towel against his face.

Wolf leaned forward, slid off the chair, twisted one hundred and eighty degrees, and rolled along his back to his shoulders, all the while wondering what was happening to that man leaning against the wall. Was he not in any better position than Wolf right now? Was he going to be shot in the head like his buddy in the plastic wrapping?

Wolf brought the handcuffs over his feet in a swift soundless move.

The man stared as Wolf rolled back to his feet, twisted, and stood.

The guy dropped his towel and stared at the three-inch kitchen blades Wolf held in each hand. Then he looked up at Wolf and closed his gaping mouth.

Wolf nodded, then kicked the man in the temple with a steel-toed boot.

The guy slumped over, out cold.

Wolf snuck to the open garage door, sticking to the wall to minimize his shadow outside. He listened as two men spoke in the guttural tones of Eastern Europe, not the staccato of Italian. Rossi had apparently left.

He wanted Rossi. That was the only objective he cared about. There was no sense flicking the ear of fate with two very big guys. The carabinieri, the real ones, could bust this place wide open later.

But fate had other plans.

Just as he began making his way to the door to the kitchen, it swung inward. The nose-ringed waitress stuck her head out, asking a loud question in her native tongue. She was looking straight ahead to a blank spot on the garage wall, as if consciously averting her eyes to any goings-on outside.

Wolf froze.

When no one answered her, she turned and saw him. She looked at the unconscious figure on the floor, then back to Wolf, who stood with his two knives pointing at her.

He raised his eyebrows. "Ciao."

"Cezar?" She panicked. "Cezar!"

Wolf turned away from her, rushed to the edge of the garage and put his back to the wall. He tensed and listened for footsteps.

The bartender came into the garage first, flying past Wolf with animal athleticism. Wolf jumped out an instant later with arms chest high, blades sticking out from the pinky side of his fists, thumbs hooked on each knife handle. Cezar didn't have time to stop or put his hands up as Wolf planted his feet and drove his arms forward. Both blades pierced Cezar's chest plate with a thump, and Wolf knew the right blade had hit the heart directly.

Two hundred pounds of dead weight smashed into Wolf, along with a warm spray of blood, pushing him back into an uncontrolled fall. Wolf pulled the blades out and twisted, bracing for impact. As he fell, he caught a glimpse of the bartender pulling a pistol from his waistband. Wolf hit the floor hard and frantically tried to get under the falling body for protection. A warm gush from Cezar's chest relentlessly pulsed on his face. The last thing he saw was the bartender bending toward him with his pistol extended. There were three pops of gunfire, and then he went still.

...

There was no pain, just the warm flow of blood soaking his neck and face. Suddenly, the weight of Cezar's body was lifted off him. He sat up as fast as he could, shaking his head and blowing air out his nose to expel the blood that had flowed into it. He wiped his face with his arm and held the knives in front of him, trying to see through the red liquid.

"David, it's me!" It was a female voice. "It's me!"

"Lia?"

"Yes, it's me! Put down the knives!"

He dropped the knives and wiped his face with his hands properly. He pointed at the door in the back of the garage.

"Be careful—that girl in the door. Where did she go?"

Lia stood and turned. As his eyes finally refocused, he saw she wasn't in her carabinieri uniform. She was in civilian clothes —jeans and a sweatshirt. Her gun was still smoking and the bartender was motionless on the ground, a pool of blood growing underneath him.

She walked low with her pistol aimed at the door.

"Wait a second," he said. "Unlock me here."

Lia took out her handcuffs key and unlocked him.

Wolf pulled the pistol from the bartender's stubby hands. It was an Eastern European-manufactured CZ-99 ready to go, safety off and round in the chamber.

He went to the door and turned the knob, opened it a fraction, then gently let go, careful not to let it slide closed. Then he kicked and aimed his gun.

The door opened, banging against the inner wall and revealing a vacant hallway.

He pushed aside the rebounding door and Lia followed right on his heels. The lights inside the kitchen were turned low, the space shut down for the night.

Commotion and mayhem resonated from down the hallway. The bar was going nuts—people screaming, glasses breaking, wood chairs bouncing off hard floors.

Wolf continued onward, cautiously looked around the corner, and then lowered his gun and walked out.

There were no employees, only customers now clumped at the door, pushing hard against one another to get out. A woman looked at Wolf and screamed. The sudden appearance of a man with a gun, drenched in blood, with a gun-toting woman behind him, sent the crowd into a heightened frenzy, desperately groping for escape.

Wolf went to the stereo on the wall and turned down the music.

The pub door slammed shut, and they were now in relative silence. Wolf watched the commotion retreat outside, then took a look at himself in the mirror behind the bar. His face and chest below were bathed in bright red.

He put his gun down, grabbed a wet bleach towel from the back bar sink and wiped his face, digging into the crevices of his eyes, blowing his nose. He threw the towel in the sink and got another one, repeating the process.

"Gettala!" a voice boomed from a few feet away.

Wolf turned just as a pistol clanked on the floor next to his foot.

Lia stood frozen, staring at a Beretta pointed at her from the other side of the bar. She had her hands up in a simultaneous defenseless and what-the-hell gesture.

"What are you two doing here?" Rossi said, shifting the Beretta to Wolf. "You're wanted for murder, Mr. Wolf. Tenente Parente, what are you doing? Are you helping him right now? What is going on?"

Wolf shook his head. "You going to play that angle, Rossi?"

"Get your hands in the air and come out here!" Rossi waved the gun at Wolf. "Now!"

"I know the truth about your father," Lia said quietly.

Rossi gave a quick dismissive look to Lia. "Come out, Sergeant Wolf. Now."

Wolf looked over at Lia. Her eyes were wet and her lower lip was quivering.

Rossi thrust his gun at her and shouted in Italian.

She shook her head. "He never left you an inheritance," she continued in English for Wolf's benefit. "Paolo just told me your dad was killed twenty-five years ago in Sicily. He checked thoroughly. You've been lying this whole time?"

Rossi shouted in Italian again; this time, spittle flew out his mouth.

"Rossi, you don't want to do this," Wolf said quietly. "It's over. We know about you and your brother smuggling drugs in from Africa. We know your brother didn't get a big inheritance either. You and your brother are in business together. You two have been leveraging his position in the Guardia di Finanza—in Genoa. Lia told me your brother works there, and how the Guardia di Finanza ultimately oversees port activity."

Rossi shifted his aim toward Wolf. His whole body twitched while he stared through Wolf. He was thinking—calculating. He seemed to come to a conclusion, and looked at Lia.

Wolf watched Rossi's gun, trained loosely in Wolf's direction, waver for the first time.

"Killing us both won't change anything," Wolf said quickly. "Paolo knows everything. I told him everything I know on the phone earlier. He checked out your father, and now it's just a simple task of looking into you and your brother's finances to prove what you've been up to." Wolf shook his head. "It's all over. It's all out in the open. There's nothing you can do to cover it up now. Killing us both won't help."

Rossi looked at Wolf with hatred, and then tracked his gun to Lia. His face shook, and sweat dripped from his hairline. He was pale as milk. With a suddenness that made Lia gasp, he stepped back, dropped his arm to his side, and looked down at the floor.

Wolf and Lia glanced at each other briefly, and then Wolf took the brief opportunity to search the back counter of the bar.

The CZ-99 lay too far away to grab, hopelessly beyond his arm's reach. Wolf stepped forward, narrowing the distance some, and then stopped as Rossi's head jerked up.

"Is that what you were doing with these guys here in the pub, Valerio?" Lia asked, seeing what Wolf was trying to do. "Did you kill John Wolf? Did you kill David's brother?"

Rossi sniffed hard and went perfectly still as he looked at Lia. A quick smile quivered across his face, then disappeared.

"Did you?" She was pleading.

"Yes, he did," Wolf said. "He was there that night at the

observatory. With Vlad. He killed Matthew Rosenwald and John."

Rossi turned his unblinking eyes to Wolf. He stood motionless, arms still hanging at his side, finger still tense on the pistol's trigger.

"They saw something they shouldn't have. And you killed them. You killed them both. Isn't that right?"

Rossi's lip curled into a snarl.

"Then you couldn't trust Vlad anymore," Wolf said. "After I saw you in the pub here, I realized some things about the past few days. Like, you weren't roughing up Vlad the other day for my benefit. You were warning him, goading him into saying what you wanted him to in front of Lia and me. You were telling him to cover up the shipment. But you must not have liked the way he was acting." Wolf turned his head to Lia, keeping his eyes trained on Rossi. "So he killed Vlad, earlier tonight in a way that would implicate me. But even that wasn't enough. I was getting too close. After he and Cezar found me, they knew I knew too much and must be killed."

Rossi looked at Lia with dead eyes.

Wolf stole a glance back to the CZ-99. With a full stretch, it was now in reach of his left arm. But it lay on its left side, pointing forward. It would be an awkward move, picking it up, repositioning it, pointing it, and firing. Even if he'd been left-handed. Which he wasn't.

Rossi's face twisted in agony, his mouth moving silently and rapidly as if saying a well-practiced prayer. Then he slowly, steadily lifted his gun.

Wolf reached out to Lia with his right hand, gripped her sweatshirt, and flung her behind him to the floor. At the same time, he reached for the CZ-99 with his other hand.

Rossi's eyes were shut tight. "Non avevo scelta! Prenditi cura di loro per me!"

Wolf transferred the gun to his right hand, slapped it into his palm, and threaded his finger through the trigger guard. He aimed true with as much speed as he could muster.

One deafening pop reverberated as two muzzle flashes lit the barroom, Rossi's and Wolf's rounds discharging simultaneously. Rossi's head exploded into a red twist of expanding skull and hair. For a moment, what was left flopped sideways, dangling from his still standing body, and then he teetered and crumpled to the hard barroom floor.

Wolf set the smoking CZ-99 down and looked to a wide-eyed Lia sprawled on her back. He raised his eyebrows, and she nodded. Satisfied she was okay, he walked through the open bar gap to Rossi's lifeless body. He stepped directly into the expanding crimson, bent close, and spat.

CHAPTER 48

THE SATURDAY LUNCH crowd in the piazza was the largest he'd seen yet. Day-trippers from Milan, Lia had told him, flocked to the lake when it was good weather. And it was great weather. The air was warm, and the gentle breeze carrying the scent of pizza and espresso kept the humidity at bay.

Wolf took a bite of one of said pizzas and shook his head in disbelief. "How the heck were you there last night at the pub?"

"The whole thing was lucky," Lia said, taking a bite of her own. "I saw Cezar in the piazza just a few minutes before we talked on the phone, and thought it odd to spot him there, so I was watching him the whole time. He kept stopping and looking around, like he was searching for someone. Then he got a phone call and left the piazza in a flash, and I watched him go out of sight down an alley."

"And you followed him?"

"No. After he left I got the call from you, then I got a call from Paolo no more than a minute later. He told me Valerio's dad wasn't buried in Lecco, so I couldn't send flowers. And that I had the time of his death completely wrong. I was puzzled, to say the least. I didn't even know what he was talking about.

Then he said that Valerio's dad had been killed twenty-five years ago in Sicily, something to do with the mafiosi.

"I asked him what the hell he was talking about, and he said that you called saying that I was the one requesting the information. I hung up, and remembered what you'd said on the phone, and figured you were trying to tell me something about Valerio.

"From that second on, all I could think about was Cezar in the piazza. And I realized he had been looking up at your apartment also. I wondered if maybe he was looking for you. Since he ran off, and I realized you must have been near the piazza, I decided to follow his trail."

"They caught me shortly after our phone call," Wolf said with creased brow. "I was pretty far away from the piazza. How did you find us?"

She shrugged. "I went down and down, and wound my way toward the lake. Then I saw Valerio and Cezar loading you in the back of Valerio's Gazzella. You were out cold, which was shocking to see. Then, of course, there was no call on the radio from Valerio that he'd caught you, so I was suspicious. So I ran to my car and went to the only place I could think they'd be taking you, the Albastru Pub." She gave another shrug and dove back into her pizza.

He stared at her.

She smiled and took a sip of Coke.

"Thanks. Have I thanked you yet for saving my life?"

"Yes," she said laughing. "You have. Last night." She took another sip. "So my question for you. How did you get the idea to have Paolo look into Valerio's father's death?"

"Everything came to a head when I saw Vlad's dead body. I knew someone was trying to set me up, and doing a damn good job of it. And there were only a few people who could have been doing it—you, Rossi, or Cezar." He shrugged. "That's basically everyone I know in this country. Well, there's Cristina, the girl who was dating my brother, but I was *with* her just before Vlad had been killed. And Colonnello Marino or Tito?" Wolf shook his head. "No. Those guys have issues, but they aren't murderers.

"Then I saw a few things, and then I saw Rossi inside the pub," he continued, "and, well, I realized it had to have been Rossi. I saw some shipping documents last night, and couldn't read anything but the ports. The destination port was Genoa, Liguria, Italy, and the source port Tenes, Algeria. The only other thing I could gather from them was the shipping company name, which was Fratello Importing, or something like that.

"What caught my eye was Liguria. I remembered that as the place Valerio said his brother lives, and you said his brother worked for the Guardia di Finanza. Just like your brother. Remember he said that *his* brother bought a nice house in Liguria with the inheritance money their father had left?"

"Yes," she said, nodding. "That's where he lives. Liguria is the region. Genoa is the capital, where the port is. In fact, his brother lives minutes from Genoa." She shook her head. "And it was called *Fratelli* Importers?"

"Yeah. I think so."

She looked at him expectantly.

"What?"

"Fratelli means *brothers* in Italian."

"Huh. That would have been nice to know at the time." He stared for a beat at the ground, then snapped out of it. "But it was seeing Rossi talking to Cezar in the pub that clicked everything into place.

"And, I thought, that could be a great cover story for a pair of brothers who were involved in smuggling drugs and actually wanted to enjoy spending the money they earned. 'Our father died. It was an inheritance.' Who's going to call them out on such a sensitive subject? Nobody.

"Then I remembered Rossi saying that his father was never around, but suddenly gave him and his brother an inheritance. So I started wondering what their father's true history was. I suspected Rossi and his brother had to have been exploiting that, and I was hoping they'd made up the whole dying three years ago thing." Wolf shrugged. "And I was right."

Lia stared through her pizza. "Our family always assumed that the parents were divorced that their father just *lived* in Sicily, and that's why he was never around. It never came up that he was dead. They *never* talked about their father. It was like a taboo subject."

"It probably was. Maybe he died in a disgraceful way back then, and, growing up, no one liked to talk about it." Wolf took a few more bites and stopped. "Rossi's wife," he said.

"What?"

"You'll have to check on her. See if she was in on all this, or if she was duped into thinking Rossi's father had left the inheritance."

Lia took a deep breath and shook her head. "I think they don't know. He was ashamed at being exposed so much that he shot himself. I don't think his wife would have known. She's not the criminal type." She looked at Wolf. "I hope for the kids' sake she wasn't in on it."

They ate silently for a while, meditating on that sober thought.

After a few minutes she looked at him with a wry smile. "How did you get Paolo to do that for you?"

"Simple. He didn't do it for me. I just pretended like I was calling in the favor for you, like you were too busy to talk at the moment, and we didn't want to bring it up to Valerio. You know, because it was a touchy subject. He seemed pretty reluctant, or suspicious, but I sealed the deal when I told him to just call you directly with where to send the flowers."

She blushed and forked her pizza.

Wolf gave a shrug. "Any excuse to talk to you works for Paolo. The guy is smitten." Wolf turned serious. "I wish I could say I'm sorry Rossi's dead. I know he was a lifelong friend. A friend of the family ..." He let his sentence trail off.

"No. It's okay. I know now he was just a shell of a person. A phony. It's strange to say, but the person I was a friend with probably died a few years ago and maybe a long time before that. He was just using me for reasons I can't even imagine."

"Yeah, you're probably right," he said.

As they finished eating, Wolf thought of Rossi's death again. The images replayed in his mind like a GIF file. He would never know which bullet had arrived first, Wolf's or Rossi's. Which had penetrated that part of Rossi's brain that ultimately ended his life. In the end, all that mattered was that John's honor was restored, and those responsible for his death were dead. All of them.

CHAPTER 49

Wolf and Lia spent the rest of their Saturday in Marino's office, recounting the week's events leading up to the harrowing demise of Detective Rossi.

Relief flooded Wolf that evening in a crashing wave, allowing him a much-needed release of grievous emotion. He called his mother, told her the real story of her son's death, and joined in her emotional outpouring as well.

To his surprise, his later date with Lia was the most enjoyable night with a woman he'd had in years.

They both slept at John's, and Wolf found out that Lia Parente was a liar. She *was* vicious. And he told her so facetiously as they lay in bed next to each other, completely spent.

The next morning, she took him to the airport, and they hugged, and gave each other a soft kiss, knowing it was a long shot that they would ever see each other again.

"Goodbye Sergeant Wolf."

"Goodbye."

"Will you think of me?" she asked.

He smiled, and then he nodded. "Eating pizza will never be the same."

With a back of the hand wave, she rolled up her window, the wheels of her Alfa Romeo chirping as she drove away at Italian speed.

...

Wolf's back pressed deep into his coach window seat as the 777 Lufthansa flight lifted from the Tarmac of the runway. He stared at the receding clay-tile buildings below, looking forward to seeing the mountains of Colorado once again.

The plane climbed to cruising altitude, and Wolf requested a coffee from the flight attendant pushing the drink cart. As he sat back sipping the watery confection, the thought of home raised his pulse. The past six days had colluded to mercilessly change his life, bringing him to a wholly foreign land, and now back home with a dead brother.

He had the sense that he'd missed so much at home, and at such a critical time. Connell and his lies, slandering Wolf while he was a half-world away, undoubtedly hurting his chances for an appointment.

Then there was Sarah and her new sober life, with a new man to share it with. A suspicious death in Rocky Points on Wolf's watch, one that he wasn't around for to help the other deputies investigate.

Though he was going home, he felt control slipping away with the ground underneath him.

"Sir." A flight attendant with a bored expression and a thick accent snapped him out of his thoughts. She held out a steaming tray of food. "Would you like some breakfast?"

Wolf nodded. "Yes, thank you."

"And for you, sir?"

"No!" The man next to Wolf blurted, lifting up his glass of liquid. "I have my ginger ale. That will be enough."

The man leaned back into his seat and closed his eyes tight as the flight attendant moved away. Then he dug into his shirt pocket and pulled out a pill without looking at it, put it in his mouth, and swallowed it down with a sip of ginger ale.

Wolf peeled the cellophane off his steaming food tray.

"Dramamine," the man said with a deep breath.

Wolf turned to see that the man was looking at him through the corner of his eyes.

"Ah," Wolf said.

"Yeah. I get terrible airsickness. Same with boats, cars, you name it. Any sort of motion. I'll be fine, though. Just as long as I don't try eating one of those ham-and-cheese omelets, that is. Otherwise, we'll be sopping up ham-and-egg chunks in less than an hour."

Wolf closed the lid on his meal and pushed it forward. He could eat when he reached Denver. He sat back and closed his eyes, trying to keep his mind off the gag reflex of the man next to him.

A few moments later, he snapped his eyes open and stared at the food in front of him. Then he looked at the man next to him. And then he smiled.

The man apparently sensed someone staring at him, because he cracked an eye and turned to Wolf. "What?"

Wolf shook his head, still smiling. "Nothing. You just gave me an idea, that's all."

The man peered at Wolf suspiciously for a few seconds and then faced forward and shut his eyes.

Wolf sat back and looked out the window. He was suddenly more anxious than ever to get home.

CHAPTER 50

It was mid-afternoon Sunday by the time Wolf and Rachette drove into Rocky Points.

The weather was dry and warm, but they had driven through rain on the way up from Denver, and there was a thunderstorm looming behind the peaks.

At Wolf's insistence, they didn't drive directly to HQ, where Wolf's truck had been parked for the past week. Instead, they passed by, continued a few blocks, and pulled into the Sunnyside Café parking lot.

"Okay." Rachette put the truck in park and looked at Wolf. "You going to tell me what you're thinking?"

Wolf unbuckled his seatbelt. "I'm going in to ask a question. I'll be right back."

Wolf only needed five minutes inside the Sunnyside to get what he needed. He came outside with a sliver of white paper in his hand and sat back in the SUV.

Rachette eyed it as Wolf settled in. "So?"

"Do you remember when we were talking to Vicky Mulroy on her porch the other day, and she got all angry when we talked about how the Wheatmans were worried about their son, and she took it as us implying she didn't care about her daughter?"

Rachette frowned and looked out the windshield. "Yeah, I guess."

"She said something about how Julie had been spending a lot of time there."

Rachette shook his head. "Yeah, okay. So what?"

"Then she said, *That family of fairies turned my daughter vegetarian*. Remember that?"

Rachette looked at Wolf. "Yeah. I do. I didn't really think anything of it."

"Me neither. Not until the plane ride over. Let's go to the mayor's."

Rachette didn't move. "The mayor's? To talk to Chris Wakefield? Why?"

Wolf sighed and sat back in the seat. "You take the car ride up there to figure it out. I don't feel like explaining this twice today." Wolf yawned. "I'm too jet-lagged."

Rachette headed out of the parking lot and east on Highway 8, where they passed the small residences and businesses backed by narrow dirt alleys, headed out of town through a cattle field, and finally up into the forest.

Soon they were passing large homes with thick log trusses, natural wood siding, copper trim, horse barns, vast tracts of land, and other amenities a lot of money could buy. Before long, they came upon their destination—Greg Wakefield's residence, the mayor of Rocky Points, Colorado.

"Are you sure you want to do this?" Rachette asked, slowing the SUV to a stop without driving into the property. "You know, with the sheriff appointment vote tomorrow? We could postpone ..." Rachette looked at Wolf and let his sentence die.

"If there's one thing I've learned the past week, it's that hesitation kills."

Rachette eyed him, then sighed and looked out the window at the big house. It was a large and modern home with a magnificent view of the valley behind it.

Wolf opened the door and got out.

Rachette turned off the truck and followed him down the dirt driveway.

The front door, a stained-glass mountain scene framed with dark wood, stood open. Inside was the mayor with a puzzled look on his face.

"Sergeant Wolf," the mayor said. "What can I do for you?"

"Hello, sir," Wolf said, walking toward him. "How are you doing today?"

"I'm fine. I ... I hear you've been in Italy."

"Yes, sir. In fact, I just got back into town."

"And you came here?"

Mayor Greg Wakefield was dressed in his Sunday casual attire—jeans and a T-shirt with a mountaineering equipment logo on it. The latter was tight-fitting, accentuating his athletic build. At fifty-two years of age, the mayor was a perfect specimen of health. His skin was tanned from spending time outdoors, his hair sandy-brown without a speck of gray, and his face was handsome with an engaging smile.

Good looks aside, Wolf had always considered Greg Wakefield a good man. And when he'd become mayor of Rocky Points a year ago, as far as Wolf could tell, he'd stayed the same man, not letting whatever power he'd acquired cloud his judgment in any way.

All this factored into coming to his house to question his son. Wolf saw Wakefield as a man of principle, a man who did the right thing. Wolf knew that if Wakefield's son had done something unlawful, he'd want to know about it. Wakefield wasn't the type who would surround his kid with a bunch of lawyers to shield him from consequences of his actions.

At least, that was the idea.

The mayor stepped out the door and shook Wolf's hand. "I heard about John. I'm so sorry."

Wolf nodded. "Thank you, sir."

The mayor shrugged and put his hands in his pockets. "So, what's going on?"

"I need to talk to your son, sir. It's about the death of Jerry Wheatman."

The mayor's face fell. "Again? Haven't you guys already gotten what you need from my son? There's no sense upsetting him anymore. Look, he made a mistake not telling you guys about it right away, but he was just protecting that girl, Julie." He looked at Rachette, then back to Wolf. "But they came in. They did the right thing. Come on, guys. Seriously. Let's let these kids grieve."

Wolf stared a beat at the mayor. "Greg, you know I wouldn't be doing this without a good reason. I need to ask your son one question. Just one. Then we'll be on our way. I promise."

The mayor stared at Wolf for a long time. He was probably wondering what could have possibly been so important, at the final hour before the sheriff appointment, which was set to happen the next morning. He was probably thinking there was no way Wolf would harass his son with so much on the line. After all, the mayor's vote would be counted tomorrow, too.

Mayor Wakefield sighed and waved his hand. "Come in. I'll get him."

They followed the mayor into the vaulted entrance of his house.

"Just a second," Mayor Wakefield said, and he disappeared around the corner.

Rachette whistled softly. "Wow."

Ahead of them was a tall room filled with leather couches and wood furniture. Windows dominated the far wall, framing the valley below and a perfect view of the ski resort in the far distance. It was a million-dollar view, and with it, the house probably cost five times as much.

"Chris!" the mayor belted from somewhere inside the house. "Chris!"

"What?" A distant reply sounded deep in the house.

After a minute of silence, they both came around the corner

Chris Wakefield was dressed in sweat pants and a T-shirt, and looked like he had not showered all weekend, which probably was normal for a sixteen-year-old. But he looked tired. His eyes were bloodshot, with half-moons under his eyes so dark it looked like he'd been punched a couple times.

Wolf stepped forward. "Chris. How are you? I'm Sergeant Deputy Wolf. This is Deputy Rachette."

Chris nodded and pulled his shirt down, like he needed something to do with his hands. "Yeah, I know you guys."

"We'd like to ask you a few questions," Wolf said.

"You said *one* question," the mayor warned. Then he rolled his eyes and led everyone into the great room. He pointed at them to sit on the thick couches, sat down next to his son, and leaned forward with an expectant look.

"Chris," Wolf said, "I need to know why you're covering for Julie Mulroy."

Chris's chest heaved as he sucked in a breath. Wolf watched as panic flashed and disappeared within an instant on the boy's face.

He glared at Wolf. "What? What the hell are you talking about?"

"Chris," The mayor frowned at his son. "You're talking to a sheriff's deputy right now."

There was a tense moment of silence as father and son stared icily at one another.

"Show some respect, please," the mayor said.

Chris stared at his hands and picked at a fingernail.

"Where's Julie now?" Wolf asked.

"I thought you said one question," Wakefield said, turning his scathing look to Wolf.

They stared at one another for a few seconds, and then Wakefield gave a resigned sigh.

"Where's Julie?" Wolf asked again.

"Home." Chris shrugged. "I don't know."

"Chris," Wolf continued, "I know Julie Mulroy killed Jerry Wheatman."

Chris kept his eyes on his busy hands.

The mayor shook his head and sat straight. "What?"

Wolf kept his eyes on Chris, who sat unmoving, still fiddling with his fingers.

"You said Julie called you that morning, the morning Jerry died, and you went to help her down the mountain." Wolf's voice was quiet. "You said she was catatonic. You even said that she was vomiting on top of the mountain. She was frozen, and you had to help her down."

Chris looked up at Wolf. "Yeah. That's what I said."

Wolf stared at him for a few quiet seconds. "If Julie killed Jerry Wheatman, and you're helping her cover it up, you know that makes you an accessory to murder, right? You've probably seen enough cop shows to know that."

The mayor put up a hand between them. "Okay, Wolf. My son says he did what he did, and that's that. Do I need to call my lawyer and—"

The mayor went quiet when he saw Wolf holding up a slip of paper.

Wolf thumbed the receipt he'd gotten from the Sunnyside Café and made a show of studying it.

"Okay, what's that?" the mayor said.

"This is a credit-card statement from the Sunnyside Café, signed by you, Chris, on the morning of last Friday. The morning that Jerry Wheatman was found forensically to have died."

Chris clamped his eyes together and shook his head. "So?"

The mayor stared expectantly at Wolf.

"It's an itemized receipt, showing you paid for a ham-and-egg omelet, some toast, and orange juice. I also checked who you were eating with. They said you ate alone that morning." Wolf paused for effect. "When we went up to the top of the cliff where Jerry fell off, we found some vomit. It contained, ham, eggs, orange juice, and toast."

Wolf watched Chris's chest heave up and down again. His blood pressure was clearly skyrocketing.

"That was Julie's vomit," Chris said, still staring at his hands.

Wolf didn't blink. "That's what you told us when you and Julie came to the station, yes. But I checked, and Julie and Jerry didn't eat there that morning. They ate somewhere else."

Wolf cleared his throat. "Did you know that Julie Mulroy has recently become a vegetarian? Her mom told us the Wheatmans converted her. Did you know that Julie had had breakfast at the Wheatmans' that morning?"

Wolf kept his eyes on Chris and watched the question sink in.

The leather of the couch squeaked as Rachette squirmed next to Wolf.

A tear slid down Chris's cheek. "No, I didn't know she was a vegetarian," he whispered.

The mayor smothered his face with his hands and then looked at his son. "Did you two kill Jerry Wheatman, son?"

Chris looked wide-eyed at his father. "No, dad. I swear. I didn't do anything. I just ..."

"You just what? Tell us!" The mayor's voice echoed through the house.

Chris's tears flowed freely now, but he stayed silent.

"You went up there because she asked you to," Wolf said, "and when you got there, you freaked out. Right? You were the one who vomited, not her. Because you couldn't believe what you were looking at, and you had just found out that Julie had pushed him."

Chris wiped his nose and glared out the window with wet eyes. After a few seconds, he started speaking as if he were watching the events unfold in front of him. "I didn't know she pushed him, I swear. I got the call from her right after I was at the Sunnyside. She said that Jerry had fallen. I didn't know what she was talking about. I told her to call 911, didn't know why the hell she was calling me. Then she freaked out and said she couldn't do that. She said you guys would think it was her who did it. She asked if I would come up and help her down. She said she was totally freaked—"

"I still don't see why you did that, Chris. That was so irresponsible. A boy had died."

Chris broke down crying. "I told her to call 911!"

Wolf held his hand up to the mayor and leaned forward. "Just tell us what happened, Chris. The truth is the only way out of this thing."

Chris nodded his head and sniffed. "Like I said, she called me, so I went up. I hiked up as fast as I could. When I got up there, she was hysterical. She was blabbering about how Jerry was messing around near the edge of the cliff, and just fell off." He shook his head and stared at Wolf. "That's when I looked over the edge and ... then I puked."

Wolf nodded to keep him going.

"That was the story she told me. I believed her, and I told her everyone would totally believe her, and we needed to talk to the police. But then she started talking about how we needed to hike all the way down and hide his body. Then I was kind of like, what the hell? You know? Like, why was she wanting to hide the body if it was an accident?"

"Did you ask her that?" Rachette asked.

Chris hung his head. "No. I just tried to calm her down and told her we needed to leave. I was going to bring her to you guys. To the Sheriff's Department. I figured she was just hysterical or something, like she didn't know what she was saying and she would snap out of it sooner or later. But she kind of, like, went crazy. She was begging me, and begging me." His voice lowered to a whisper. "And kissing me, and begging me not to go to the police. To the sheriff."

Wolf took a deep breath and put his elbows on his knees. "You like Julie Mulroy, right? You've always kind of had a crush on her?"

Chris huffed. "Yeah. I guess. But I still was like, *no, we have to go to the cops*. So we hiked down, and I said I would take her to the sheriff, but she wanted to drive her car, so I said I would follow her there. But she drove straight here, to this house." Chris shook his head. "So I just followed her, and then ... I just wanted to keep her happy until we went to talk to you, until she got the guts to tell you guys."

"Why didn't you just leave her and come to us?" Wolf asked.

Chris looked down with a blush. "She was being ... nice." He looked at Wolf and flicked a glance at his father. "She and I ..."

Wolf and the mayor gave each other knowing looks.

"She kept you occupied? As in, sexually?" Wolf offered.

Chris nodded. "Yeah."

"So then what?" Wolf asked.

"My dad came home and said it was okay for her to stay

here for the weekend. I lied and said she was having trouble at home. Everyone knows about her parents."

Mayor Wakefield shook his head in disgust.

"All weekend, I was telling her we needed to go to the cops, and it was, like, getting worse with every day. Told her the more she didn't go, the more it looked like she had pushed him off. Like she was hiding something. Finally, on Monday we heard about the search going on, and I told her I was going to the cops whether she liked it or not. So she finally agreed to come with."

Wolf frowned. "Okay, then what? Why did you lie about the vomit?"

"I don't know. I guess I was trying to like, make her look more ... vulnerable or something. Like I was trying to help out her story. I just wanted you guys to believe her, and let her get on with her life." Chris took a deep breath and his lip started quivering. "I'm sorry. I don't know why I did that. But I think I really screwed up doing that, though."

Wolf nodded. "Yes. You—"

"No, you don't understand." Chris's eyes were wild. "I screwed up because she did it. I know she did it. She told me."

Wolf blinked. "When?"

Chris stared at the coffee table in front of him. "Right after we left the sheriff's office. I followed her home. I was hugging her goodbye in front of her house, and she called me 'her hero.' She whispered it in my ear, then said, 'You were great in there. You made it all sound so believable.' I was like, what? And she just, like, smiled at me, and walked off. So I grabbed her and asked her, made her tell me. She said, 'Yeah, I pushed him. And now he's gone.' She had this, like, really evil look in her eyes."

Wolf took a deep breath and peered out the window. The pines were swaying back and forth now, the room darkening as the clouds rolled in.

"I swear. I didn't know she did it until after I talked to you guys."

Wolf looked back at him with disappointment. "And then you didn't come back to us to correct yourself, or to let us know what she said."

Chris sat back and stared again at his hands.

"Chris. We'll need you to come down and do that right now. We need an amended official statement from you as soon as possible."

The mayor turned to Wolf and nodded. "I'll bring him in, is that okay?"

Wolf nodded. "Yes."

CHAPTER 51

Rachette eyed Wolf as he drove them back into town. "You had no clue about what Jerry and Julie ate that morning."

Wolf shrugged. "I knew that was Chris's vomit. No doubt after I went and checked in the Sunnyside. Frankly, I'm a little disappointed you didn't put that together while I was gone."

"Yeah, yeah." Rachette drove in silence for a minute. "Risky."

Wolf stared out the window at the approaching storm.

"So, how we going to get Julie to confess?" Rachette asked.

"She's not going to confess. I have a feeling that family is poisoned. No consciences. She probably already convinced herself she didn't do it. We'll try, but in the end, it's not going to be up to us now. It's he-said-she-said, and it'll be figured out in court."

Wolf closed his eyes and leaned back to dismiss further conversation. Wolf was dead tired, dead tired of shitty people doing shitty things, and dead tired of thinking about it.

Rachette apparently got the hint and kept silent for the rest of the drive back to HQ.

Wolf stepped out of the SUV into the headquarters' dirt lot

and swiveled on his heels. He looked at the peaks and sucked in the scent of pine and approaching rain. It was good to be home.

The air shook with a continuous rumble, and Wolf could feel the hair on his arms rising as the sky darkened above.

Rachette pulled Wolf's backpack out of the SUV and set it at Wolf's feet. "It's been raining every day since you left. That looks like a mean one, though."

Wolf nodded and slung the backpack over his shoulder. "Thanks for the ride again. I'm going home."

"You aren't going to stick around for Wakefield's statement? And what about Julie Mulroy?"

"You guys can handle it. I have a lot of sleep to catch up on. Kind of a big day tomorrow." Wolf started walking to the open garage where he'd left his SUV.

"Hey, Sarge?" Rachette hadn't moved from the side of the truck.

Wolf stopped and turned. "Yeah."

Rachette looked over both shoulders and toward the garage, then stepped close. "You going to stick around if you don't get the sheriff's appointment?"

Wolf gave a half smile as the air around them lit up with a bright flash. Thunder crashed almost immediately, and a large dollop of rain smacked the bill of Wolf's hat, but they both stood unmoved.

There was a funeral for his brother to be arranged, his mother to comfort, and, yes, either he or Deputy Sergeant Derek Connell was going to be appointed to sheriff within the next twenty-four hours—something Wolf couldn't stop thinking about, especially hanging around this second-year deputy.

Rachette stared unblinking, shifting his weight from side to side.

Wolf turned and walked to the garage as the sky opened in a downpour. "I'll see you tomorrow."

CHAPTER 52

Monday Morning—9:08 a.m.

Wolf sat motionless in the stiff wooden chair as a trickle of sweat rolled from his armpit, down his torso, and against his tucked uniform shirt. The council meeting was progressing at a no-nonsense pace, and what started out for Wolf as a case of sweaty palms had quickly escalated to an all-out body drenching.

The smell of glazed doughnuts and burnt coffee filled the air, and a bright beam of sunlight shone through the distorted window, illuminating a swimming cloud of dust particles.

The deafening collective murmur faded as a wave of hushes swept across the packed, standing-room-only town hall.

Wolf kept still as the county council members and the mayor passed their votes toward the chairman at the end of the table on stage.

Gary Connell collected all eight votes, seven for the council sitting at the front of the room, representing the collective political clout and wisdom of the entirety of Sluice County, and one for the mayor of Rocky Points, and stacked them in a neat pile.

Five votes. That's what Wolf needed; the majority vote of the eight people on stage to become the next sheriff of Sluice County. One of them had a son Wolf had beaten to a pulp seven days ago, and another had a son they'd been questioning all night about Jerry Wheatman's death.

Wolf knew these two men alone had influence over the other five votes on that stage. Margaret Hitchens was unflappable, and would undoubtedly vote for Wolf. But the other five? Their votes were easily persuaded, and now their votes were etched in pen on those tiny sheets of paper.

Wolf flinched as hot breath moistened his left ear. "You got this. You got this." Rachette patted his shoulder from behind with one loud slap, which attracted a few glances their way, then sat back in his chair a row behind.

"Yeah, you got this." Nate Watson, his long-time teammate on the football field growing up, and now lifelong friend, sat next to him. The veins were bulging from his forearms, and he bent the Styrofoam cup in his hand to the point just before breaking.

Nate used to be his hard-nosed running back, always there to block even the largest of guys for Wolf in the backfield. Now he had that same intense look Wolf had seen a million times, like he needed to protect Wolf, but he couldn't find who to bash his shoulder pads into.

Wolf gave him a quick slap on the knee.

Nate flicked him an annoyed glance and glared forward again.

Wolf's mother was to his right, leaning forward and bouncing her leg, with eyes glued to the front of the room as well.

They were sitting in the middle rows of the large room with a lot of bodies between him and the small stage in front, but

Wolf had a clear enough view of the back of Derek Connell's head.

When they had entered the building twenty minutes earlier, Connell had already been sitting there. Since then, his head hadn't turned more than ten degrees.

A good-looking man Wolf had never seen was sitting to Connell's immediate right. He wore a denim shirt, jeans, and cowboy boots, and he lounged back with his cowboy hat on his chest. His facial hair was just past a five o'clock shadow by design, shaved neatly around his neck. His medium-length surfer-blond hair was deeply grooved and shiny, like he'd dunked his head in a bucket of gel and then combed it.

Wolf didn't understand the man's presence, so he didn't like it one bit.

Gary palmed the microphone and it squealed, and then he leaned back to speak to the mayor in a hushed whisper. They nodded their heads, and then the chairman leaned forward. "Okay, all the votes are in. Derek Connell. Eight votes to none."

Wolf blinked and his face flushed as the room's collective gasp echoed off the hundred-year-old walls.

"Awwwwww!" Rachette's voice was loud in Wolf's ear, snapping him out of his stunned state.

"Mr. Connell, do you accept this appointment by the convened county council as the new sheriff of Sluice County, Colorado?" Gary continued.

Derek Connell stood up. "I do, Chairman."

"Mr. Connell. This job is to not be taken lightly. Please stand before the council and raise your right hand. Do you swear to ..."

"Sssssssscrew this." Rachette shoved his head in between Wolf and Nate. His pupils were pinpoints, eyes fixated on the muscle-bound frame of Derek Connell, *Sheriff* Derek Connell, who was now speaking with his right arm raised at the front of the room.

"Are you kidding me?" Nate Watson looked around the room, and then stood up. "Are you kidding me?"

The room went silent for a moment at Nate's outburst, and then Gary continued swearing in his only son as the new sheriff of Sluice County.

Wolf looked down the line of council members. They were all, including Margaret Hitchens and the mayor, reading memos or shuffling papers, or whispering to their neighbor behind a hand—anything but making eye contact with anyone in the rest of the room.

The mystery man that Connell had been sitting next to was turned sideways in his chair, staring at the townspeople with a glimmer of amusement in his eye. The man caught Wolf's gaze and held it for a second before turning forward.

Standing with clenched fists, Wolf's mom stomped down the row of chairs and pushed her way to the back of the room.

In mid-sentence of the official swearing-in ceremony, Gary locked eyes with Wolf and flicked his head to the back doors.

"This guy is our boss now?" Rachette shook his head and walked away.

Wolf put his hat on and stood up.

At the front of the room the father spouted his lines, his voice loud and unwavering. Before the father, his son stood tall and rigid, his hand raised, nodding as though he'd rehearsed this moment long before.

Wolf narrowed his eyes, disgusted at the sight. "This guy is our boss now."

THE END

ACKNOWLEDGMENTS

Thank you for reading Foreign Deceit, and I hope you enjoyed David Wolf's first adventure. It was my goal to bring together the two worlds I've been frequenting over the last several years with my beautiful wife: Italy and Colorado. My wife is from Merate, which is the town south of Lecco with the observatory featured in the book.

THANK YOU FOR YOUR SUPPORT

If you enjoyed the story, please spread the word about this novel on Facebook or other social media, or good old-fashioned word of mouth, and thank you so much for following the link below and leaving a review on Amazon. Exposure is everything for an indie author, and reviews help so much.

PLEASE LEAVE AN AMAZON REVIEW HERE

I would like to thank my wife for putting up with me during this process of learning how to write, writing, failing, fixing, and the other six-hundred steps it took to finally publish this first novel in the state you have just finished reading it now. She's an infinitely patient and supportive human being, and I'm lucky to have her. I'd also like to thank my two sons, without your unconditional love at the end of the day, I'm not sure I would have ever followed through to the end.

Thanks to Matt, Nate, and Heather, for being my first fans and my first wave of encouragement. Thanks to Angela and Vittorio, and Dennis and Kathy for all the support, and Louise Harnby for the terrific editing.

Would you like to be the first to know about new David Wolf book releases?

You can CLICK HERE to sign up for the New Release Newsletter, and you'll receive a complimentary copy of Gut Decision, an action-packed short story about Wolf's tumultuous first weeks in the department, as a gift.

If you'd like to contact me, my email address is Jeff@JeffCarson.co (no "m"). I love communicating with readers and if you take the time to email me, I'll take the time to respond. Otherwise, you can visit my blog at http://jeffcarson.co .

ALSO BY JEFF CARSON

Gut Decision: A David Wolf Short Story
Foreign Deceit (Wolf Book 1)
The Silversmith (David Wolf Book 2)
Alive and Killing (David Wolf Book 3)
Deadly Conditions (David Wolf Book 4)
Cold Lake (David Wolf Book 5)
Smoked Out (David Wolf Book 6)
To the Bone (David Wolf Book 7)
Dire (David Wolf Book 8)
Signature (David Wolf Book 9)
Dark Mountain (David Wolf Book 10)
Rain (David Wolf Book 11)
Drifted (David Wolf Book 12)
Divided Sky (David Wolf Book 13)
In the Ground (David Wolf Book 14)

PREVIEW OF THE SILVERSMITH (DAVID WOLF BOOK 2) CHAPTER 1

Sergeant David Wolf leaned against the bumper of his Sluice County Sheriff's Department-issue Ford Explorer and watched a few angry people stream out of the town hall building.

It was warm already for a September morning and getting hotter by the second, and Wolf was sweating under his khaki uniform shirt.

"Oh my God," Deputy Tom Rachette pleaded to the cloudless sky. His hands gripped his head and his mouth was wide in horror. "This isn't happening."

"Something's going on." Nate Watson, Wolf's long-time teammate on the football field growing up and lifelong friend ever since, stood shaking his head. "Eight votes to none? For that guy? This is BS."

"This is unacceptable." Wolf's mother was shaking, tears in her eyes. "What are you going to do?"

Wolf stood still, eyeing his mother.

"Your father would be horrified. I don't understand. After all our family has given to this county over the years ... after all we've just been through—"

"Don't worry, Mom," Wolf said, because that's all he could

think to say. Because since Derek Connell had been announced as the new appointed sheriff of Sluice County, Wolf had been speechless.

A steady stream of citizens of Rocky Points and other far-flung regions of Sluice County were pouring out of the town hall building now, and many of them looked at Wolf with shakes of their heads and shrugs of their shoulders.

Wolf put on his poker face and waited. Gary Connell, the county council chairman and Derek Connell's father, had signaled Wolf to wait and talk to him, and Wolf intended to do just that. The meeting had left a foul taste in Wolf's mouth.

A few seconds later, Derek Connell came out of the building. His thumbs were hooked on his belt, his pectorals were out, and he moved with a heel–toe sheriff's strut.

Wolf hadn't seen Derek Connell's ugly face since a week ago today—not since their *altercation* on top of the cliff, when Derek had tried to push him and Wolf had gotten lucky and seen it coming.

Wolf still hadn't told a single soul about what had happened that day, but now it was apparent that Connell had been filling the ears of the council with a story of his own. One that Wolf hadn't been around to defend himself against. By the looks of Connell, he probably didn't have to work very hard to garner any sympathy.

Connell's face was a mess. Both eye sockets were deeply bruised; a mix of blue, purple, yellow, and green puffy flesh. His nose was larger than normal, split on the bridge with a red horizontal slice, and a large bump in the middle that hadn't been there a week ago. His lips looked like they were in the middle of a particularly nasty herpes outbreak, and a line of stitches above his right eyebrow gave the illusion of one brow longer than the other.

Wolf marveled at the damage, vaguely remembering the

repeated elbows he'd given Connell once he'd finally gotten him on the ground. He honestly couldn't begin to guess how many times he'd hit Connell in the face. Apparently it was more than just a few.

Connell's beady blue eyes found Wolf and narrowed. He wiped his nose gingerly and walked over.

"Mrs. Wolf, so nice to see you. Glad you could make it today." Connell opened his muscular arms for a hug.

She turned around and got into Wolf's SUV without saying a word.

"Huh. Okay." He held out a hand to Wolf. "Sorry, man. Better luck next time."

Wolf didn't move.

"Aren't you going to congratulate me?" Connell shrugged and thrust his hand towards Rachette.

Rachette hesitated and then shook it. "Congratulations, Derek." He winced as his skin went white under Connell's grip.

Connell shook for a few seconds too many, his blue eyes boring into Rachette's. He finally let go and walked towards his own SUV.

"Aren't you going to shake my hand there, tough guy?" Nate flexed his chest and squared off to Connell's back.

Connell kept walking and held up his index finger. "Meeting in the sit room at ten. Be there or be sorry."

The SUV rocked as he jumped in and slammed the door. The mystery blond man that had been sitting next to Derek in the town hall meeting was in the passenger seat, staring at them with no particular expression.

The SUV backed up fast, skidding to a halt, then spit rocks at them as it left.

Rachette shook his hand as the SUV turned onto Main Street with a squeal. "Oh good." He squinted and coughed on the dust. "This is going to be good."

Wolf walked back toward the hall building.

"Wolf!" Nate ran up next to him. "I'm heading up to Laramie for the week."

Nate's tenacity on the football field had never been enough to make up for his lack of size, so he never did play college ball after high school. Instead, he steered his determination toward academia, double majoring in geology and business at the Colorado School of Mines. Now he owned Watson Geological Services, a thriving enterprise that employed forty-one geologists in Wyoming, Colorado, and Utah. Wolf knew he'd be going up to Laramie to help some big oil and gas company for a substantial amount of money.

"All right. Have a good week."

"I will." Nate pulled Wolf to a stop, and then patted him on the shoulder. "I know how much this meant to you. I'm sorry. You going to talk to Gary?"

Wolf nodded.

"Give him hell. I'll see you on Saturday."

"Hey. I'll take Brian fishing with me and Jack this week," Wolf said.

Nate nodded. "Thanks. I owe ya."

PREVIEW OF THE SILVERSMITH (DAVID WOLF BOOK 2) CHAPTER 2

Margaret Hitchens stood just inside the door speaking to Gary Connell in a hushed voice.

Turning to leave, she almost ran into Wolf and looked up with a start. "Oh, hi, David."

He grasped and shook her outstretched hand.

Margaret's family had always been close to Wolf's growing up, and she had known his father personally. As far as Wolf had been able to figure out, there had been a love affair that hadn't lasted between Margaret and his father. Maybe when they were ten years old. He didn't know. All he knew is it was before his mother was in the picture.

Despite Margaret's obvious past longing for Wolf's dad, she had always been a good friend to the entire family, Wolf's mother included. Wolf thought her a good person with a sharp wit. She was fun to talk to, and everyone in town considered her *the* real-estate expert.

"Hi, Margaret." He nodded and moved to step past her.

To his surprise, she held on to his hand and squeezed. "Good luck with everything, David. The job sounds great." Then she let go and left the room.

He paused, and then twisted on his heel, but he didn't have a chance to ask her what she meant. She was already out the door.

Gary stood speaking softly, cupping an old man's hands with both of his own.

The old man stood with the reverence of a devout Catholic praising a beloved priest after mass. Three people waited in line behind.

Mayor Wakefield was scooping up his leather bag from a chair and putting it over his shoulder. He noticed Wolf and walked towards him with an exhausted expression.

"We didn't see you last night at the station," Wakefield said.

Wolf nodded. "I needed to get home and take care of some things."

"I hear Julie Mulroy is denying everything Chris told you."

Wolf nodded. Yesterday the mayor's son had shed some light on the suspicious death of a teenaged boy named Jerry Wheatman, implicating a girl in town, Julie Mulroy, as the killer.

"I'm not sure justice will come for what happened. But Chris will be okay. He did the right thing in the end."

Mayor Wakefield gave Wolf an unreadable look, then nodded. "I hope you enjoy your new job. You're going to be missed. I hope you know that."

"New job?" Wolf asked.

The mayor paused, stared at Wolf, then laughed and shook his head as he walked out the door.

More than a little confused, Wolf walked to the now vacant wood seats in the room and sat down.

Five minutes later the doors closed, muffling the outside crackle of tires on gravel.

The old boarded floor squeaked as Gary walked up behind Wolf.

He cleared his throat. "How you doing, David?"

Wolf stood up and walked to the window without saying anything.

People were still milling about in the parking lot, talking in pairs or small groups. Arms were flailing, pointing to the hall, anger creasing their foreheads.

Gary joined him and sighed. "They'll get over it." He folded his muscular arms and leaned against the window.

Wolf gave him a sideways glance. Gary stood looking out with a mischievous half smile.

"Eight votes to none?" Wolf asked.

Gary rubbed his face and looked over his shoulder to the closed door. "I convinced everyone on the council to vote for Derek."

The floor seemed to drop an inch under Wolf's feet. He looked at Gary and felt his face warm.

Gary had just admitted to sabotaging a moment that Wolf had been working towards for years. A moment that Gary Connell knew the full weight of.

Wolf forced himself to look back outside. He could hardly contain the anger.

Gary seemed to read Wolf's expression and shut his eyes. Holding up both hands he said, "Just listen. I know you wanted to be sheriff. But I convinced everyone because I've got something much better for you. Please, don't fret about it." Gary glared at Wolf and put a gentle hand on his arm. "Just keep your cool and come over tonight to my place for dinner. Have I ever let you down in the past?"

Wolf looked at Gary but said nothing.

"I'll explain everything tonight. Seven o'clock. Don't be late." Gary patted his shoulder and walked out.

—> Click here to continue reading The Silversmith now!

Made in United States
Orlando, FL
04 May 2022